MONEY BEAR

CATHERINE — A LOT
OF YEARS, A LOT OF
LIFE. YOU'RE ALWAYS
IN MY HEART.

MONEY BEAR

A NICK TANNER CRIME THRILLER

BY
KERRY K. COX

To my wife Leah, who somehow saw potential despite precious little evidence.

The greatness of a nation can be judged by the way its animals are treated.

—MAHATMA GHANDI

Praise for MONEY BEAR

"Vivid characters, a compelling storyline in a unique setting, and razor-sharp writing. What more could you ask for? I'm already looking forward to the next Nick Tanner novel." – Robert Cochran, Two-time Emmy award-winner as Co-creator, Executive Producer, and writer of *24*.

"*Money Bear* snaps you up like a bear trap, and holds you in its steely jaw until the last page. A fast-paced story that delights with authenticity and wit, even as it exposes the evils of wildlife trafficking. A brilliant first novel in what promises to be a must-read series." – Kay Foster, Writer/Executive Producer on *Heroes*, *The Following*, and *American Odyssey*.

"Kerry K. Cox's stunning debut is a rollicking thriller that brims with subversive humor and white-knuckle plot twists. The stakes are as high as the redwoods, the pace arrow-quick, and the hero as unforgettable as his sidekick, a blind bobcat named Ray Charles. Don't miss it!" – Peter W. J. Hayes, Silver Falchion and Derringer-nominated author of the Vic Lenoski mysteries.

"Absolutely one of the most entertaining thrillers I have read in years! Nick Tanner is a fresh new hero that delights with a wit and toughness comparable to any Elmore Leonard character. *Money Bear* is a fast-paced, tightly written page-turner that gets this series off to a roaring start. Looking forward to more!" – Lance H. Robbins, Executive Producer, *Hallmark Murders* and Mysteries Network *Matchmaker Mysteries*

"An impressively complex, eco-conscious crime story with plenty of action and intrigue. Cox shows an uncanny talent for characterization…and effectively keeps up the story's momentum as it speeds to a rousing conclusion." – *Kirkus Reviews*

Chapter One

Redwoods State and National Parks

Orick, California

The body was within a hundred yards of a relatively well-used trail, yet no effort had been made to hide it. It lay on its side, a dark mound bulging through the ground cover of leafy ferns, five or six yards from moss-slick rocks that lined a small creek.

The smell was what compelled a pair of hikers to go off the trail and look. Once they hurried back into cell phone range, they called 9-1-1. The operator routed them to the Orick Ranger station, and Enforcement Ranger Kathleen Shepherd.

* * *

An hour later, Shepherd stood over the body. Her eyes watered from the Vick's under her nose. Or, maybe, from frustration and anger. She couldn't be sure.

Like the others, a single surgical stroke had opened the belly. Decomposition gases belched organs onto the grass. Thick-bodied, blue-bottomed flies and ravenous yellow jackets jostled for their share of the blackened entrails. Shepherd didn't bother to wave them away.

The quadruple amputation had been clean and quick. Maybe a large axe? Could be done with one swing from someone really strong. Maybe a chainsaw. The noise would be a risk, though.

Cause of death was easy enough to see. The shot was centered, far behind the shoulder—a through and through lung-shot. From the size of the wound, a broadhead, just like the others.

Shepherd retreated a couple of steps up a path of flattened ferns that led to the body and took a few deep breaths to clear her head. In a minute she'd walk the whole area to see if she could find anything.

Maybe this time.

She came back to the body and knelt beside it, fanning her hat without any noticeable effect on the cloud of insects. She stroked the fur, smoothing a ruffled patch behind the ears. Heat swelled behind her eyes.

The victim was male.

Shepherd checked the teeth—some slight browning at the base, nothing cracked. Canines intact. Appeared to have been in good health. A trail of dried blood ran down the slack tongue and crusted the fur into a black mass under the chin.

Number three.

From what Shepherd could tell, the youngest so far.

Two, maybe three years old.

Chapter Two

Inglewood, California

Nick Capretta and Angel Santos sat on hard wooden chairs. Both were drenched in sweat. Even though he wore only cargo shorts and a white t-shirt cut off at the shoulders, Capretta's thick black pony tail glistened with moisture. A small athletic bag stuffed with cash nestled in his lap, adding to his discomfort. Not to the point where he would put it down, however. No way.

"You got no air conditioning?" he asked. "Fuckin' stifling in here."

Sammy Prado shrugged from the other side of a battered desk. "It's a warehouse. You don't air condition a warehouse. Too expensive."

The puffy Filipino sat on an old swivel chair that squeaked with every motion. Dressed in baggy shorts and a wildly patterned Hawaiian shirt inexplicably buttoned right to the top, he seemed unaffected by the oppressive heat in the cramped, glass-enclosed office.

"Fuckin' stifling," Capretta said, shifting in the chair. "Maybe you oughta get a/c just for your office, y'know, like the kind that sits in the window or you build into the wall or something."

"I'm not uncomfortable. Are you uncomfortable?" Sammy turned to the man seated beside Capretta. "Angel, are you uncomfortable?"

At three hundred and fifteen pounds of sloppy blubber, it was unlikely there were three consecutive seconds that Angel wasn't uncomfortable to one degree or another. Still, he shook his head. "I'm good, Mr. Prado."

"See? Angel is comfortable. I'm comfortable. Maybe it's you, Mr. Capretta. Maybe you're too much muscle, not enough fat. You need to get some padding, like him and me." His laugh erupted like a yelping dog, ending as abruptly as it began. His eyes narrowed even more, if that were possible. "Maybe you're nervous about something?"

"Not nervous. What I am is pissed off." Capretta checked his watch. "Now you're almost an hour late."

"Customs works on a timetable all its own. I'm sure Angel told you this." He didn't wait for a response. "If you're going to be in this business, Mr. Capretta, you need to develop patience. Am I right, Angel?" This time he looked at the fat man.

Angel nodded and mopped rivulets from his forehead with a sodden handkerchief.

Sammy checked his computer screen. "There, you see? Nothing. We have received no indication that the shipment is being held up for inspection, or unduly delayed in any way. Sometimes the process takes a little longer."

Capretta checked his watch again.

For a minute or so, no one said a word. Finally, Sammy broke the silence.

"So, Mr. Capretta, Angel told me a little about you. He vouches for you, and as a longtime business associate I place great trust in him. I know this is your initial foray into our line of work, but I understand you have a solid background in a related industry. I've never dealt in firearms. I would be very interested in learning a little more about it. And you."

Capretta sat back in his chair. Took his time pulling a cigarette from a pack in his shirt pocket. Lit it, took a long drag, blew it out. "Try to imagine how little I care about what you're interested in."

Angel's head snapped around, first to Capretta, then to Sammy. Sammy's expression froze for a moment before he willed a suggestion of a smile.

"Mr. Capretta, I am trying to pass the time. I did not mean to intrude in any way. Just making small talk until the truck arrives."

"And I got no fuckin' desire to pass time. I came here to receive goods, make payment, and get the fuck outta Dodge. I don't want to chat. I don't want to tell you about my hobbies or where I went to school or what I did

4

last fucking summer. I want to get the deal done, that's it. That's all I care about. That's all you should care about. So, where the hell is that fucking truck? I've had mine sitting in a parking lot for over an hour now, which is not only costing me money, it's a big fuckin' risk that I can't control. The kind of risk that one day fucks you in the ass. I don't want today to be that day, Sammy. This is not the way I'm used to doing business."

He took a quick sideways glance at Angel, who was breathing audibly, face flushed, veins popping on his forehead. The fat man dragged the saturated handkerchief over his face again, a futile effort with no effect.

Sammy held up his hands. "Please, I meant no offense. Truly. I understand your concern, and I apologize for the lateness." His phone's text alert chimed, and he checked the screen. "Ah. As I suspected, Customs simply took longer than we anticipated. But it has cleared, and the shipment is en route. In fact, ETA is under a half-hour."

Capretta leaned forward and crushed out his cigarette on the desk. "Okay. Okay, good. That's more like it." He looked at his watch and tapped it. "All right. Once I have a look at everything, I'll call my truck and we'll switch over the load."

He sat back again. "Look, Sammy, I'm sorry I got a little hot. You seem like a straight guy and Angel spoke highly of you. But goddamn it. You gotta get a fuckin' air conditioner."

Sammy barked out another laugh, and Capretta joined him. All Angel could manage was a nervous smile.

* * *

Three miles away and a little over two hours earlier, a Boeing 747 Large Cargo Freighter touched down at LAX and disgorged its contents for Customs inspection. Among the goods were a number of crates originating from Nigeria, each packed with handcrafted furniture: wildly colorful deck chairs, coffee tables, dining sets, and barstools.

A team comprised of two CBP officials and two Fish and Wildlife Service Special Agents redirected all the Nigerian crates to a special Customs

Inspection Station for an initial pass through the Vehicle and Cargo Inspection System, a first stage examination using x-rays. Although standard operating procedure would require a notification to the Customs Broker or the Consignee on Record that this shipment was flagged for inspection, no such notification was sent.

Once the VACIS was completed, the Customs men—officially the Contraband Enforcement Team—moved into the next phase, an Intensive Exam. The first crate was opened, and several of the multi-hued deck chairs removed. Each chair was subjected to gamma ray visualization, which—assuming the chairs were constructed of ordinary materials—would reveal nothing of interest.

In this instance, that was definitely not the case.

After thorough, yet accelerated, documentation, the items were replaced and the crates resealed. They were then released, but not before one of the Special Agents took care of a last piece of business.

* * *

The three men walked to the loading dock at the back of the warehouse. Capretta carried his bag of cash. Angel trailed behind, wheezing and wet.

When they reached the dock, Sammy flipped a switch, and a corrugated metal door slid noisily up its track. Outside, a twenty-foot unmarked box truck backed down a loading ramp towards the opening, its warning beeper echoing off the cement walls.

"Want to call your truck now?" Sammy asked.

"I'll take a look inside first."

"Sure, why not."

The truck came to a stop. Two burly Hispanic men climbed down from the cab. One unlocked and opened the truck's back doors, revealing a full load of crates. The other moved several paces away from the truck, his eyes on Capretta.

"There they are, Mr. Capretta," Sammy said. "From Nigeria, to you. And now...the final payment, please."

Capretta walked to the edge of the loading dock and looked at the crates. Saw what he was looking for, turned and tossed the bag at Sammy's feet. "I'll call the truck. I want to be on the road pronto."

He pulled out his cell phone and punched a speed dial number. "You ready?" he asked. There was no answer.

Instead, sirens erupted from half-a-dozen squad cars and three utility vehicles that roared into the loading area. Two slid to a skidding stop in front of the truck, an unnecessary precaution as the Hispanic men showed no inclination to drive away. They were off and running at the first squeal of tires. Two LAPD cars swung around to give chase.

"God damn it!" Capretta yelled and launched himself at Sammy. The chubby little man threw a flailing punch before he was tackled to the ground. "Where's the wire, you fuck? Where's the wire?" Capretta screamed in rage as he tore at Sammy's shirt.

LAPD and Fish and Wildlife agents swarmed in with guns drawn. "On the ground! On the ground!" Two LAPD officers ran toward Capretta. "You! Get off him and lie flat on the ground, now!"

"You're gonna fucking burn for this!" Capretta yelled, and slammed his fist into Sammy's nose. The officers levelled their guns a few feet from Capretta's head.

"Down on the ground, now!"

With Sammy wilting and half-conscious, Capretta slid off him and went prone on the ground, hands and legs spread. He was familiar with the drill. "All right, all right, I'm down, I'm down." Then he lashed out a final kick that connected solidly with Sammy's ribcage. "Fuck you!" Sammy moaned and curled up like a sowbug.

One of the cops sat on Capretta's legs while the other cuffed his wrists. Capretta lifted his head and spotted Angel. The fat bastard was sitting on the warehouse floor, hands cuffed, sobbing. His pants were soaked. "You're a dead man!" Capretta yelled. "You hear me Angel? A dead man!"

* * *

Two hours later, U.S. Fish and Wildlife Service Resident Agent in Charge Steven Moore strode out of his corner office, carrying a file folder and munching on an oatmeal-raisin energy bar as he passed the cube farm.

Still chewing, he stopped at a door marked *Conference Room*, and opened it without knocking. The room was an unremarkable space, barely containing an oblong, wood veneer table ringed with stains, ten well-worn chairs of various fabrics, and one occupant: U.S. Fish and Wildlife Service Special Agent Nick Tanner.

Moore settled into a squeaking leather chair at the head of the table. "You're gonna burn for this?"

Tanner shrugged. "Not my best line."

"Uh-huh. And the kick at the end?"

"I strive for authenticity."

"Yeah, well. You busted two of his ribs. It was totally unnecessary."

"Fuck him."

"Nick, we already had him, it was over. There was no reason for it."

"He's an asshole."

"You better hope one of the LAPD boys doesn't pipe up."

Tanner shrugged again. "You're dropping crumbs."

Moore flicked at his tie, clearing some remnants. "Tasteless shit. This goddamn diet. I'd kill for a cheeseburger."

"Think how handsome you'll be when you finally look more like me."

"It's my dream." Moore leaned back and sighed. "Ah, hell, Nick. Seriously, you gotta get a handle on it. I don't need every suspect to start the booking process in the hospital."

Tanner said nothing.

"Say yes, sir, I hear you, sir."

"Yes, sir, I hear you, sir."

"God damn you're a pain in the ass." Moore popped the last of his bar in his mouth, brushed his hands together, then folded them behind his head. "So. You hear how much was in the shipment?"

"I heard it was big."

"Set a record," Moore said, allowing himself a smile. "Eighteen untouched tusks, most of 'em probably male. Could be twenty-five hundred pounds of ivory, built right into the chair and table legs."

"Sweet. Think Prado will lead anywhere?"

Moore shrugged. "We'll cut him a deal if he gives us anything worthwhile."

"The guys from the truck?"

"LAPD grabbed both of 'em. Right now, they're *no habla Inglis*, they know nothing, they were never even near the truck, it's all a big mystery to them."

"They moved like pros. Pretty sure both were armed."

"Not when we caught 'em. But we'll squeeze them, and of course their docs are bullshit, so we'll bring in *la Migra* at some point and send them back from whence they came. So, all looks good."

"Great. Oh, and going forward, tell whoever's at the Customs intercept not to make the go-mark so obvious. I was worried the truck guys would spot it and ventilate me. It was a big black mark on the facing side of the crate, I don't know how the one guy missed it."

"Okay."

"One other thing. Angel Santos is the absolute worst CI I've ever worked with. We're lucky Sammy has the brains of a turnip, or he'd have made me in a heartbeat. Angel looked like he was gonna have a stroke. Don't put him out there again. He'll either croak or blow the play."

"Duly noted. Now, some news. Once you finish the paperwork on this, I need you to head upstate."

Tanner shook his head. Enough was enough. "Come on, boss. I need a couple weeks at least, I'm whacked. This thing was six months solid, and before that I was down at the border for what, three? You said I'd get some PTO, and I'm taking it."

"I said that?" Moore shook his head. "I'm such a liar. I've got to work on that." He tossed the file folder in front of Tanner. "Anyway, this came in from Sacramento, by way of the Arcata office. Someone's poaching bears in Redwoods."

Tanner rubbed his eyes. "So let the Rangers handle it."

"It's not just poaching. They're taking the gallbladders."

"Oh, shit." Tanner leaned forward, resting his forehead in his hands. "How many?"

"Up until today, three. That they've found, anyway. Last one only a couple years old. All done with an arrow."

"Keeping the noise down."

"No doubt."

"God...dammit," Tanner said, drawing it out. He stood. "Anyone with me?"

"At this stage of the fiscal year? What do you think?"

"So, it's just me and Ray Charles."

Moore stood and pushed in his chair. "Finish up your paperwork, hit the road, and say hi to Ray for me."

Chapter Three

Orick, California

"For thousands of years, humans and the vast Northern California redwood forests shared a peaceful, symbiotic relationship. The various independent Native American tribes that dotted the forests and coastline enjoyed the plentiful bounty—fishing, hunting and gathering—to their heart's content. Fallen redwoods provided planks for crude but adequate housing."

Ranger Kathleen Shepherd ushered the tour group a little further down the trail and continued the speech she could now recite while drunk, asleep, or both.

"The majestic redwood itself was regarded as a Spirit Being, part of a deific race that pre-dated humans in the region. The trees were, in essence, divine gifts to humans, teaching them the proper way to live in harmony with the forest. With each redwood living an average of five hundred to seven hundred years—some as much as two thousand years—the forests have been linked to fossil records that date back millions of years. Prior to 1850, about two million acres of verdant land was blanketed by these magnificent, towering giants."

She stopped and delivered her next line with practiced severity.

"Starting in 1850, it took gold-crazed Euro-Americans less than sixty years to reduce the redwoods range by more than half. While they were at it, they did a pretty good number on the Native Americans, too."

As always, the crowd tsked-tsked, groaned, sighed, and emitted all the politically correct noises. Also, as always, Shepherd knew it was inevitable that some of these nature lovers would leave plastic water bottles and other trash scattered around the woods, abandon a smoldering campfire, smoke cigarettes as they hiked, leave food scraps out when they tucked themselves into their sleeping bags at night. All the routine knucklehead moves made by park visitors on a daily basis.

Shepherd motioned for the group to follow her to a small ridge that overlooked a canyon. There, she treated them to a stunning view, thousands of hillside acres carpeted by old-growth redwood.

"By the early nineteen-hundreds concerned citizen groups like Save the Redwoods worked in tandem with the State of California to purchase and protect old-growth redwoods from extinction, but it wasn't until nineteen sixty-eight—when an estimated *ninety percent* of the old-growth forests had been logged—that the feds also took action. Redwood National Park protected an additional fifty-eight thousand acres, merging with the hundred-thousand already under State protection."

Shepherd smiled at a cluster of three women in the group, one of whom was quite attractive.

"Today, the Redwood National and State Parks—or Redwoods, for short—is cooperatively run by the National Park Service and the California Department of Parks and Recreation, bordered and bisected by reservation land for various tribes. The Visitor Center here in Orick is our operational headquarters. If you haven't visited yet, I definitely recommend it."

What she definitely would not recommend was living here for four years. She didn't say it, but she felt it.

Shepherd was thirty-three years old and single. She considered herself to be in decent shape and reasonably good looking, yet hadn't been laid in a year. The pickings in Orick were slim to none, assuming one's standards included nominal dental hygiene. She'd had a little thing going with an RN down in Arcata, so intense and incendiary it seemed certain to flame out. Oddly, it didn't. It kind of fizzled. Shepherd figured it was mostly her own fault things went south. She found it hard to commit to someone when all she really wanted was to leave the area as soon as possible.

As the Park Enforcement Ranger, Shepherd was the law in Redwoods. In the course of her duties she'd been spit on, shot at, cursed out, run from, disobeyed, willfully ignored, burned, fish-hooked, and generally disrespected. It was her observation that there was a good reason city folk should stay in the city. In general, they tended to approach the wilderness with the same mindset as a trip to Disneyland, and most were disappointed as a result.

"Are we gonna see any bears?" asked a pimply teenaged boy.

Someone always asked. Shepherd plastered on her patented Friendly Ranger Smile. "In fact, the highest density of black bears in California live right here in Redwoods, so it's always a possibility."

"But we ain't seen any yet."

The boy's mother, a graceless, heavyset woman sucking from a straw in a gigantic cup, spoke up. "We come a long way, we thought there was bears here to see."

"Yeah!" the boy yelled.

"Well, they don't come when you call, heh, heh," Shepherd said. "But if you're lucky enough to see one, please remember it's strictly forbidden and very dangerous to feed the bears or approach them in any way. And if one happens to approach you, stand up, wave your arms, you can even throw small rocks. That'll usually discourage it from coming closer."

Now it was the father's turn, a guy with a Humpty Dumpty build and pants a little tight around the armpits. "You said 'lucky enough.' You mean it ain't likely? You mean all we're likely to see is more of these trees?"

Ah, fuck me, thought Shepherd. She briefly fantasized about this annoying family being devoured by rampaging bears and comforted herself with the thought of the transfer request she'd put through. There was an immediate opening available at Liberty National Park in New York City, and right now, that was Shepherd's dream job.

No more city dwellers becoming instantly "bored" with nature. No more dealing with roaming meth labs, outlaw marijuana farms, drunken campers, or, most disturbingly, the recent appearance of murdered, butchered bears.

Instead, an endless stream of sleek, beautiful, exotic women from all over the world, their eyes moist with emotion, lips quivering as she delivered her inspiring Statue of Liberty tour speech and infused them with patriotic fervor.

She walked the group to a large relief map mounted on a stand overlooking the canyon. "Okay folks, you can see here on the map where the Yurok, Tolowa, Hupa, and Karuk Native American tribes still live in this area today. The yellow areas indicate reservation land. For instance, this land here, the Yurok reservation, is the largest and runs all along Redwoods Creek, right through the middle of the parkland."

"Woo-woo-woo-woo, woo-woo-woo-woo," trilled the boy, patting his mouth with his hand.

* * *

Later, Shepherd sat in her cramped office. She started to check her email yet again, something she'd been doing obsessively of late. But this time she stopped, and stared a moment at her screen saver. It was a photo of a moon-faced rookie Ranger posing by the Orick station sign, a lop-sided grin showing perfect white teeth. Shoulder-length blonde hair worn loose and easy. An open, eager face still ruddy from the Georgia sun. Exciting times; the first posting after the six-month training course at FLETC in Brunswick.

Shepherd sighed. Could that really have been her only four years ago? She felt so different. Kept her hair trimmed close to her head. No hint of a tan anymore, no chance of that happening up here.

The assignment to Redwoods had come with rent-free living quarters, a Taser, and of course, a gun. At FLETC she'd trained with various firearms, learned evasive vehicle tactics, how to wield a collapsible ASP baton, handcuffing techniques, Tasering, even how to patrol with a dog. She'd undergone an additional three months of in-service training, where she'd covered Emergency medical services, search and rescue, incident command, wildland fire response and more.

Most of which she'd had no occasion to use.

Except the gun.

It was her first moment of real action in Redwoods, and marked the day she decided she wanted to work somewhere else. It was the day she shot Emil Reyes.

Emil had been spotted on various occasions by hikers and outfitters and had helped himself to more than his share of food and various belongings as overnight campers slept. He was one of the Park's feral people, individuals who made their full-time home in the depths of the woods. While some of them lived there with a purpose—transient meth labs being one of the big favorites—others, like Emil, had no such aspirations. Most didn't consider themselves homeless. They simply considered Redwoods their home, and both resented and preyed upon human trespassers.

While they all had different life paths that led them into the woods, Emil's began—or maybe continued—with a stint at Pelican Bay, the maximum-security facility near the Oregon border. He'd spent most of his term in the Enhanced Outpatient Program for mentally disordered offenders and emerged one-hundred percent un-rehabilitated. Possessing zero marketable job skills, a powerful survival instinct and a sewer rat's cunning, he faded into the primitive embrace of the towering old growth giants, the sheltering understory of tanoak and California bay-laurel, and the soft, fragrant ground cover of ferns and grasses.

Sightings of Emil gained in frequency during Shepherd's in-service training period. Twice, Shepherd accompanied her training Ranger, a rawboned cowgirl named Bobbie Bishop, into the woods to follow-up on a sighting. The first time, they found nothing.

The second time, they found trouble.

It was four years ago, almost to the day...

* * *

Shepherd followed Bishop through an arroyo thick with ferns and the rich scent of humus. Curtains of moss hung in festoons from the low-hanging

15

limbs that formed the redwoods' dark, dripping understory. Rolling waves of fog crippled visibility. As far as she could tell, they were wandering aimlessly through a soupy mist, over an endless carpet of spongy algae, each step indistinguishable from the previous.

On top of everything, the dense canopy hundreds of feet overhead effectively foiled GPS. The steep, wooded hills and valleys blocked cell reception, and even made radio communication hit-or-miss. Throw in the fog, and you might as well have been on the moon.

Bishop turned, pointed to her right. Shepherd strained to see.

"Fishhooks," Bishop whispered. "Booby-trap. Probably more out here, be careful."

Shepherd nodded. At no point during her Wildlife Management curriculum did they cover drug-addled assholes stringing predatory fishhooks. She was a suburban girl from Van Nuys, California, a high school softball star who grew up with dreams of championing forests and wildlife and rode an athletic scholarship to Humboldt State to follow that dream. An inexplicable career choice, considering the closest she'd ever come to woodlands before college were the bulldozed hiking paths through the Santa Monica Mountains.

Progress was slow as Bishop watched for a secondary perimeter of booby-traps. Shepherd pushed aside a tangle of huckleberry branches, and it was like opening a curtain. Even with the fog, she could see a shaft of light funnel into the clearing ahead.

What caused the sudden clearing became evident. A massive redwood had fallen and crushed the understory, leaving a hole in the canopy. The two women had emerged at its midpoint, with the top and base of the tree vanishing into the mist on either side. Shepherd couldn't see over the immense trunk.

She followed Bishop alongside the fallen giant, staying close to the trunk to take advantage of the cleared path of crushed vegetation.

"Look up there," Bishop whispered. She pointed to a spot further along. Shepherd saw an ugly scar gouged into the tree, a savage, amorphous slash into the heartwood roughly forty or fifty feet from its now visible base.

"Emil," Bishop mouthed. She gestured with both hands for Shepherd to keep low and unfastened her gun. Shepherd's heart hammered in her throat. She broke a sweat despite the chilling fog. She'd heard stories. Burlers tended to be unstable, unpredictable, and occasionally violent. She fumbled with the safety strap on her holster and pulled out the SIG P220 she'd been issued, a blunt brute of a handgun known more for its exceptional accuracy than its good looks.

They approached the burl scar. It was enormous. The missing burl had to have weighed hundreds of pounds. Hell of a logistics challenge for Emil, if he was the one who had carved it out of this tree. Could be worth a thousand dollars or more, so maybe he figured it would be worth the trouble of transporting it out of the woods. You could buy a lot of meth for a thousand bucks.

Eight feet ahead Bishop dropped to the ground, gun drawn, and motioned frantically for Shepherd to do the same. Shepherd dove to the right and sighted down her gun, pointing into the blanket of fog, hand trembling, breath coming fast and shallow.

She squinted to see through the dense mist. Barely discernable, a figure hunched over something on the ground.

"Emil! Get your hands in the air where I can see them!" Bishop yelled. The sudden break in the silence startled Shepherd and galvanized the squat form in the fog. Instead of standing or raising its hands, it made several repetitive, almost spastic movements. Like someone starting...

"Emil!" Bishop yelled. "Do not start that saw! Do not start that—"

The chainsaw fired to life. Emil shouted something Shepherd couldn't make out, stood and ran towards Bishop, the saw screaming at full throttle. Shepherd saw a rope-thin, ragged shard of a man emerge from the fog, eyes wide, gaping mouth a toothless hole in a wild, unkempt beard. Shouting incoherently as he ran towards them.

"Emil, put it down!" Bishop shrieked.

"Stop now, stop NOW!" Shepherd yelled. She held the gun out, arms stiffly extended. Her grip was too tight. Her vision narrowed to a tunnel. The pistol's front sight shimmied and jumped.

Emil kept coming, yowling with mindless fury, chainsaw raging, legs churning. Bishop held until he was within five yards, then fired. Emil staggered from the impact, his arms drew back, and Shepherd watched in disbelief as the shrieking chainsaw arched through the air.

Bishop's scream was forever seared into Shepherd's brain. It would haunt her dreams, wake her in a slick, guilty sweat. Her own scream was almost as loud but unheard as she finally pulled the trigger, and pulled again, and again, firing as fast as the double-action allowed, launching eight 185-grain hollow-points that blew gelatinous globs all over the fallen tree.

What remained of Emil Reyes slid to a stop two feet from Bishop. The ranger lay on her side, her hand pressed against a ragged, free-flowing gash across her right arm. The chainsaw had fallen next to her and coughed to a stop. Pure silence slapped down with the intensity of thunder...

* * *

"Shep!" her office manager, Ruby Spears, bellowed from the outer office with her usual decorum. "You asleep in there? Get line one, it's Wild Bill."

Chapter Four

Orick, California

S hepherd hung up the phone, reached for her jacket, and fit her hat over her head. As she started out the front door, Ruby looked up expectantly. As office manager of the Orick station, Ruby liked to be kept informed.

"Got to go over to Wild Bill's, granny," Shepherd said. At sixty-eight Ruby was too young to be her grandma, but Ruby was everybody's grandma. "Another bear."

"Same as the others?"

"No. This one was badly wounded by an arrow. Bill says its hindquarters were paralyzed. He had to shoot it."

"What a damn shame." Ruby looked up at the clock. "You gonna get some lunch?"

For some reason, Ruby was always concerned about Shepherd's food intake. Maybe because of the ten unwanted pounds the Ranger had added, mostly to her waist and ass, in the two years Ruby'd been on board.

"I'll get some at Herm's on the way."

"Burger again? I can hear your veins clogging up from here."

"I'll get chicken."

"You'd better."

She didn't. She'd meant to, but once she whiffed that grilled beef she couldn't resist. She'd once dated a dietician down in Ukiah who had urged her to stick with fish and poultry. "Fins and feathers," she'd say. "No cow. No pig. That's how you stay in fighting shape."

Shepherd had always kept a pretty good handle on her weight, but even at five-six, her wide shoulders and somewhat prominent hipbones made her look a little heavier than she actually was. The extra ten wasn't helping.

The dietician had also advised her to eat more fruits and veggies, so she felt suitably guilty as she stepped over to the walk-up window of the weather-beaten little diner and ordered the double-chili-cheeseburger. And a vanilla shake.

"Goin' off the diet, Shep?" Matty, the seventy-year-old owner and cook, peered out the To-Go window, which happened to also be the Eat-Here window.

"Yeah, doctor's orders. Turns out I'm not taking in enough dairy and grease."

"Well, you're in luck, we got plenty of both." Matty threw a couple patties on the grill, her eyes squinting against the rising smoke. "That gonna be *alfresco*?"

"Nah, to go. I'm heading up to Klamath, over to Wild Bill's."

"He okay?"

"Yeah. He found a bear."

"Ah gee, another one? Damn. What's going on, Shep?"

"Nothing good." She walked away from the window and plopped behind one of the three plastic tables that made up Herm's outdoor dining experience.

* * *

The half-hour drive to Klamath gave Shepherd plenty of time to finish lunch. A half-mile before town she veered northwest onto a single-lane gravel road marked only by a black, unmarked mailbox. Two miles later she pulled into Wild Bill's place; a twenty-acre ranch surrounded by pine and redwoods.

She tapped the horn a couple of times, then climbed out of the Parks vehicle. No sense wandering around trying to find old Bill. He'd show up, riding one of his forty-some-odd mules, his expression a mystery behind an untamed thicket of beard white as sunbaked bone, bisected by a yellow stain running its full length.

And sure enough, he did.

"Hey, Shep," he said, as he guided a big mule out of the feed barn.

"Hey, Bill. Came to see the bear."

"Yep. Left 'er where I shot 'er, just like you said. Arrow's still in. Little ways up a hill near my lower pasture."

"How'd you happen to see it?"

"I had to put old Mint 'n' Chip down last night. When I went out this morning to haul her away, this bear was eatin' on her."

"Oh, sorry, Bill. Should I follow you?"

"No sense beatin' up that gov'mint ride. Lemme get Pistachio for you." All Wild Bill's mules were named after ice cream flavors. He claimed it made it easier to remember.

"Okay. I'll grab my pack."

Ten minutes later they were riding Pistachio and Neapolitan down the gritty lower pasture road.

* * *

The arrow had struck too high and too far forward to hit the lungs or heart.

"Probably nicked the spinal cord, maybe even broke the spine," Shepherd said. She crouched over the body as Wild Bill looked on.

"Yeah. Bad fucking shot." He turned and spat processed chew. The beard gained some fresh color. He gave his mouth a backhand swipe.

Shepherd noted the bullet hole behind the bear's eye. "Looks like you can still shoot some."

Wild Bill shrugged.

"Her weight's real low," Shepherd said. "Wonder how long she's been dragging around like this, poor thing."

She pulled a plastic freezer bag from her backpack, placed it over the protruding shaft, and used a zip-tie to tighten the bag so it wouldn't slide off. She unclipped her Leatherman from her belt, unfolded the serrated blade, and cut a path into the bear's flesh, following the shaft. After some effort, she was able to extract the arrow, including the head.

"Muzzy broadhead, maybe one hundred grain," Wild Bill noted. "Woulda gone right through if the fucker'd placed the shot right."

"The others were pass-throughs. First time I've been able to recover an arrow."

"Hope it helps."

They stood. Shepherd pulled a towel from her backpack, carefully wrapped the arrow, and placed it in the pack. She used another towel to wipe her hands. "That should do it."

"Why all of a sudden is someone killin' bears?"

"They're taking the gallbladders and the paws. It's for Traditional Chinese Medicine, supposed to cure all sorts of things."

"I'll be goddamned." Another spit, another wipe. "Like there ain't enough Chinamen in the world, they gotta kill our bears to keep more Chinamen alive."

Shepherd winced a little, but said nothing.

"And the paws?" Wild Bill asked.

"They get sold as a delicacy over there. Very expensive."

"No shit." He gave that some thought. "How you think he's doin' it?"

Shepherd shrugged into her backpack, and together they started back up the hill to the mules. "Most likely old logging roads. Maybe coming in from the rez."

"Ha! If those Yurok boys catch him, he ain't never gonna see no trial. They love their bears."

Shepherd knew Wild Bill was right. The Reservation Police would not take kindly to a bear poacher on their land, especially one who so badly mutilated the corpses. If she was going to catch this guy, she wanted to do it before they did.

Which was why she'd already put in a call to U.S. Fish and Wildlife. Help was on the way. Because the truth was, she didn't have the first idea what to do next.

Chapter Five

Hollywood, California

FIVE MONTHS EARLIER...

After pondering all the most popular suicide methods, H.H. Goldstein decided originality had to count for something. All his life he'd lived large. If something was worth doing, it was worth overdoing.

The movies he'd produced were relentless assaults on the senses, filling the screen with wall-to-wall sound and fury. Budgets rivaling the GNP of Paraguay.

His mansion was a garish explosion of aquatic kitsch, a Byzantine labyrinth of spas, waterfalls, wading pools, hideaways and grottos, typically populated by scantily clad people he barely knew, if at all. Of course, in the past all had been carefully screened by his management and were aware of what they might occasionally be called upon to do. And they had been perfectly willing to do it. Those were the days.

His marriages—and subsequent divorces—had been cacophonous blood-baths, outrageous even by industry standards.

Scandals? Sure, he'd had them, and they were immensely scandalous. Legendary in scale, the stuff the late-night writing staffs could count on for weeks of easy material.

So why flush that whole image down the can with a mundane hanging?

Or worse, some sloppy Hollywood overdose? Talk about done to death.

He needed something bold, something with flair. Dramatic, ideally with a dash of the macabre.

Which is why he decided to tie a cinderblock to his foot and drown himself in one of his most notorious grotto pools.

Naked.

That's how you make the front page, and not just in *Variety*. The 48-point screamer in the *L.A. Times*. The instant trender on Twitter.

A decent plan, but it presented a few problems. First, there was the challenge of tying the rope around the cinderblock. Goldstein, never a handy guy, had not personally tied any of those fancy knots the sailors in *The Mutiny Cruise* had used to lash Gilda Weeks to the yardarm, or whatever that fucking thing was called. He'd made a bundle off that picture, but the only knot he ever learned to tie was the kind that affixed his two-thousand-dollar Stefano Bemers to his feet. Which turned out to be an extraordinarily difficult knot to tie into the bulky rope he'd chosen for this task. After several frustrated attempts, the resulting mess seemed to have a reasonable hold on the cinderblock, assuming he didn't struggle too hard to break free.

Goldstein hefted the cinderblock to his chest, taking care not to let the rough surface of the cement brush against his penis. He gathered the trailing rope and walked over to the deepest pool on the property, made infamous through the years by celebrity party-goers and *Playboy* as "The Croc Pot."

Fourteen feet directly under the one-meter diving board. Plenty deep.

Nobody was in or near the pool, as he'd instructed.

It was time.

Goldstein hauled himself up the three stone steps onto the diving board and walked without hesitation to the end. He curled his toes over the edge of the board, looked down through the shimmering, perfectly maintained depths to the ebony bottom, and jumped.

* * *

H.H. Goldstein's path to the end of his diving board commenced when

Closed Doors opened, dead as a lox. A hundred and eighty million to make; first weekend opened at under twenty million, down to twelve on weekend three. Disaster. That made three losers in a row. The stuff that puts the "ex" in executive producer. Insult to injury, lost him his window table at Nobu in Malibu.

Bad enough. But it got worse, as his career's death spiral sent his longtime friend and companion, the body part he treasured and trusted the most—The H.H. Hammer—on a sudden, maddening, and evidently permanent hiatus.

It's one thing to lose an ocean view while you slurp oysters. It's another to have a conked-out cock.

He tried the little blue pills. All those side effects the commercials drone about? He got all of them—except, sadly, the one lasting more than four hours.

He tried the natural route. Truckloads of Vitamin E. Hypnosis. Acupuncture, arginine, ginseng, vats of pomegranate.

No good. No wood.

He even looked up an old high school buddy, Solly "Shakes" Watson. Shakes had prospered in a different side of the film business than Goldstein and sent over a team of his finest fluffers. Their efforts, while earnest and professional, were sadly unproductive.

With his professional life in the shitter, his debts rapidly depleting his assets, and his pecker in angry revolt, Goldstein decided it was time to call it a life. Thus, the final swim in The Croc Pot.

This effort, like everything else he touched lately, was a colossal fuck-up. After twenty seconds underwater he panicked, kicked himself loose from his incompetent knots, and fought his way to the surface.

Sobbing for air, he splashed his way to the side. That's where Mr. Kim found him, clinging to the ladder, crying like a little bitch.

In great, jerking heaves he told Mr. Kim, "My cock won't work! Oh, Christ, why won't my cock work?"

In that moment, Mr. Kim transmogrified from Korean gardener to savior of souls, a saint sent from Heaven. The little man calmly reassured his boss that all was not lost. There was a cure. Mr. Kim knew of a Traditional

Chinese Medicine practitioner. In fact, a relative of his. He'd cured many men of this problem.

"*Xi Jiao*," Mr. Kim said, as he helped Goldstein climb out of the pool. "All you need, Mr. Golden."

And goddamn if he wasn't right.

Xi Jiao. Nothing like it. Nothing legal, anyway.

Rhino horn. Technically more like hair than horn. Mostly keratin. Some calcium carbonate, calcium phosphate, tyrosine, other shit. No medical reason it should work. Even the majority of TCM practitioners would tell you it wouldn't put concrete in your cock.

Which Goldstein figured was just those Chinks trying to keep it for themselves.

Ever since he'd started on powdered *Xi Jiao*, H.H. had been swinging The Hammer like John-fucking-Henry. Two, even three little starfuckers at once, upside down and sideways, a dizzying kaleidoscope of lips and ass, silicone and semen.

With those kinds of results, it was little wonder Goldstein became a devoted TCM convert. He simply couldn't get enough of the stuff.

Moreover, let it never be said that H.H. Goldstein was one to let a sweet business opportunity pass him by. Plenty of Wilting Willies in Hollywood, whether from age, coke, mommy issues, whatever. All of whom would gladly—ecstatically—part with plenty of cash and/or favors for a prescription-free, side-effect-free, junk juicer.

Which explained why, three months after his ill-fated suicide attempt, Goldstein found himself riding the spring-pocked passenger seat of his gardener's battered Datsun pick-up, tooling along Western Avenue into the heart of L.A.'s Koreatown.

"Almost there, Mister Golden," Mr. Kim said. After eight years' manicuring the two-acre lawns and gardens surrounding the Goldstein home, this was as close to the pronunciation of his employer's name as the sturdy little Korean ever came.

It was Goldstein's first personal buying trip. In the past, he'd simply handed Mr. Kim a wad of cash. The little fucker drove off to God knew where, came back with the dick hardener, and all was well with the world.

But Goldstein was on a new mission. And he wasn't about to hand fifty-two thousand dollars in crisp, rolled bills to a gardener who didn't make that much in a year. Trust is one thing, stupidity something else.

TCM had handily solved his erection challenges. It only made sense it could solve his financial challenges, too. That kind of a deal, he had to make in person.

Chapter Six

Koreatown, Los Angeles, California

Mr. Kim wheeled the ancient, foul-smelling Datsun down a cluttered cul-de-sac off Western, near 7th. He came to a grinding stop next to a graffiti-scarred apartment complex.

"Holy shit. This is the place?" Goldstein asked. His grip tightened on the handle of the leather briefcase in his lap.

"Yes," Mr. Kim nodded. "You stay. I go in first, tell him you're here."

The little man climbed out of the truck and went to the door. Goldstein watched as Mr. Kim knocked, waited, and spoke to whoever was behind the peephole.

Mr. Kim turned to the truck and waved to Goldstein. "Okay, you come in."

Goldstein felt his joints creak as he unfolded himself out of the pickup. He reached back for the briefcase, and, by force of habit, looked around for paparazzi. Nobody around except for a few random Koreans passing through dim pools of yellow from the streetlights. No one likely to recognize him, especially dressed as he was in dark jeans, a black t-shirt, black leather jacket, aviator shades and a black Dodgers cap. Still, he lowered the bill of the cap and kept his sunglasses on as he walked up to the door. Mr. Kim gestured for him to go inside.

"What, you're not coming in?"

"No. I wait in my truck. Drive you home after."

"Oh. Okay."

Goldstein pushed through the door into a dimly lit, cramped living room. The walls were lined with neatly shelved pill bottles and clear jars. On one side of the room there was a stainless-steel examination table. On the other, a low-slung table flanked by thin pillows. The room smelled faintly of boiled cabbage. Standing next to the table was a trim, bespectacled young Asian man who appeared to be in his early twenties.

"Take off your glasses, please," the man said.

Goldstein removed his sunglasses. "Who are you?"

"My name is Doctor Wu. I'm pleased to meet you." The man spoke calmly and quietly, in carefully enunciated English.

"You're the doctor?" Goldstein would've cast him as the computer nerd in a summer camp comedy.

"Yes. May I please look at your eyes a moment?"

"Sure." Goldstein bent down and looked directly into the doctor's eyes. Wu stared back without expression.

"You are drinking too much carbonated fluid," Wu finally said. "It's leaching the calcium from your bones."

Goldstein, who chain-gulped Diet Coke, was impressed. He straightened and said, "Not bad, Doc."

"So, Mr. Kim has told me that you are his employer, and that you are the one he has been purchasing *Xi Jiao* for. He also told me you are planning a larger purchase than normal."

"And he told *me* you don't usually do face-to-face business with whites," Goldstein said. "But I've got a fifty-grand roll in my fag bag here, and I'm thinking that's small potatoes compared to the kind of business you and I could do. So maybe this time you'll make an exception."

"Please. Before we talk business any further, please sit. We will have some tea, learn a little more about each other, and then discuss our transaction."

"Oh, sure, okay, you bet," Goldstein said. Christ. Asians and their goddamn formalities. Took forever to get anything done. No choice but to go with it. He looked around for a place to sit.

"Please." Doctor Wu motioned towards one of the pillows on the floor.

"We're sitting on the floor?"

"Please."

"Well, when in Rome," Goldstein said. He awkwardly folded himself onto the pillow, his legs extended at obtuse angles. A young Asian woman appeared and handed him a steaming cup of tea. "Well, hello." Goldstein said, "Kinda snuck up on me there." He peered inside the cup. "What is this?"

"This will cool the heat in your core, calm your nerves, and improve your brain function," Wu said.

"No kidding." He looked at the tea. A few leaves swam amongst unidentifiable debris on an oily surface. Looked like something the garbage disposal barfed up. "Well, here's to improved brain function," he said, and took a sip. Tasted exactly the way it looked. He swallowed with some difficulty and, unable to speak, nodded at Wu. As casually as possible, Goldstein set the teacup down on the small table next to his pillow.

"Aside from the damage you are doing with carbonated beverages, your liver is also in distress," Wu said.

"Huh?"

"Yes. I can see by the color of your skin and the coarseness of your pores. You drink a great deal of alcohol, true?" Wu drilled him with unblinking eyes.

Goldstein squirmed uncomfortably, his knees locking up. "I have a couple beers at night, maybe a glass of wine or two."

Wu said nothing.

"Okay, more than a couple. And Scotch. But only the good stuff."

"Your liver is in distress," Wu said, continuing to hold his gaze like a cobra. "What is referred to as cirrhosis in Western medicine. Quite serious."

And he'd only admitted to a fraction of what he really drank. "Really? I feel okay."

"You are not okay, Mr. Goldstein. But I can help."

"Yeah?"

"Most certainly." He turned and spoke into the dark recess of the apartment. "*Xióng dǎn.*"

The same woman who had served the tea emerged from the darkness, went to the shelves and selected a jar. She brought it over to Doctor Wu. He unscrewed the lid, closed his eyes, and lowered his head. He inhaled deeply. Satisfied, he replaced the lid.

"*Xióng dăn,*" he said.

"Which is what?"

"Very cleansing. Ideal for liver distress such as yours."

"No, I mean, what is it? What's it made of?"

"It is dried bile from the gallbladder of a bear."

"You gotta be shitting me. A bear?"

Wu nodded.

"Is it expensive?"

"When sold overseas bear bile is worth four times its weight in gold. As it happens, this is locally sourced. I am able to give you an excellent price."

"Wait, wait. People pay that kind of money for a bear's gallbladder?"

"Given the right buyer."

"And you're saying it's good for the liver, like for people who drink too much, or use drugs or whatever?"

"Absolutely."

"Wow." Goldstein's thought about all the industry assholes he knew who drank themselves into a near coma every night. Producers, actors, writers… lots of writers. All with money.

"Doctor Wu, that rhino horn worked miracles. With what I'm buying here today, I'll start distribution within my circle, the Hollywood circle. I'll establish a clientele, you understand, and you and I will make a lot of money. I'm talking long-term, repeat business."

"I assumed that was why you were purchasing such a large quantity, yes."

"Great, then we're on the same page. Now, if this bear stuff does what you say it will, I'm thinking we can expand our business discussion tonight."

He picked up his teacup and took a healthy swig.

* * *

An hour later, they had a deal. Fifty-two thousand dollars' worth of powdered rhino horn. One hundred grams of powdered bear bile, on fifteen thousand dollars' credit.

"Doctor Wu, what can I say? I appreciate your trust. I'll have your money back to you in no time. I've done a bit of this kind of work before." He didn't elaborate, but during his early years in Hollywood he'd pushed a little powder and weed to pay the rent on his Beechwood apartment.

"As long as it is within four weeks as agreed, no interest will accrue."

"Absolutely. I think this is the beginning of a beautiful friendship."

Wu remained expressionless. Clearly didn't know Bogart from Bangladesh. Goldstein began gathering his legs under him, feeling pins and needles as blood found a path back down to his feet.

"And Mister Goldstein, I'm sure I don't need to remind you that no one is to know your source of supply."

Goldstein held up his hand. "Goes without saying. And, believe me, I'll be back soon for a lot more." He stood, and reached down for the briefcase. "Okay, guess it's time to pay up." He held out the briefcase to Wu.

"Hong," the doctor said, without moving.

A figure emerged from the shadows of the apartment. A man shorter than Goldstein's five-ten, but with freakishly wide shoulders and thighs that threatened to break through his pants. He seemed almost square. A block of granite with a head.

He walked—more of a glide, really, in spite of his build—over to the men, took the briefcase from Goldstein, and slid back into the shadows.

Nice bit of theatre, thought Goldstein. Good casting, too. The guy actually made you shiver a little, he had that kind of presence. Still, he couldn't help but feel he was in the midst of Amateur Hour here. Wait 'til they got a load of what he could make happen in this town. His town.

"We will return your briefcase in a moment," Wu said, standing without effort.

"No worries, I got it from the prop room. No one'll miss it. So, thanks very much." He and Wu shook hands, and Goldstein gathered the two boxes containing his purchases. "Doctor Wu, it's been a pleasure doing business with you. We'll be doing much more, and very soon."

The young Asian woman reappeared and walked Goldstein to the door.

"Oh, and Mr. Goldstein?" Wu said.

"Yes?"

"The carbonated beverages. It really would be a good idea to refrain from them."

"Right." Whatever you say, Kung Fu.

Chapter Seven

Chatsworth, California

"I'm telling you, Mickey, this is as easy as it gets. Now's the chance to step things up, and I want you to help me make it happen."

Goldstein took a nervous sip from his beer. Some kind of twangy redneck music blared from the overhead speakers in the Cowboy Barn Saloon, a half-hour from Hollywood by freeway, but half a continent away in culture. It was a place where locals—people born and raised in the San Fernando Valley—somehow acquired a shitkicker accent and flew Confederate flags on their trucks. Or their Lexus sedans, for that matter.

"My agent says my name is in for some gigs coming up," Mickey 'The Sandman' Calhoun said. "Couple of high falls on a Tarantino Western, maybe a fight choreo job on a new Rodriguez thing. So, I don't know." He threw back a shot of tequila, bit into a lime, then took a big drag off his beer chaser. His omnipresent Stetson rode on a steel-gray buzz cut, shading a face weathered and worn as sandstone.

"Exciting stuff," Goldstein said, almost shouting to be heard above the music. "But listen. What I've got going right now, it's easy money, it's a sure thing, and I'm looking to take it to the next level."

Calhoun had been Goldstein's fight choreographer and lead stuntman on all three flicks in the western trilogy, *Outlaw Law*. At one time he could do everything but tap-dance on horseback and might have been the best high-fall guy in the business. He could fast-draw with either hand, throw a knife or an axe with frightening accuracy, had nerves of cobalt steel and a seemingly non-existent pain threshold. However, with age and injuries his temper ignited more often, fueled by a cocaine and oxy habit that cost him jobs and drained his bank account.

In Goldstein's nascent days in the business, he and Calhoun had teamed up marketing cocaine and weed to various sound stages. That was when Calhoun got his nickname, earned by his use of an innovative negotiating tool when dealing with non-payers or upstart competitors: a leather pouch packed tightly with pristine white sand from the shore of Malibu beach. Swing it hard, it made a big impression without breaking the skull, or even the skin. Most of the time.

The partnership had been fruitful, got them through some rough times. And while they had each gone on to enjoy some glory days in the industry, both now viewed those days in the rear-view mirror.

"Look," Goldstein said, "I called you because we've done some good work together, on-screen and off-screen, am I right?" He didn't wait for an answer. "And Mickey, what I'm doing now, I'm telling you, it's magic. You ever heard of TCM? Traditional Chinese Medicine?"

Calhoun's attention was elsewhere, as line-dancing assholes from nearby escrow offices and aerospace firms formed up on the dance floor. "I don't know, maybe," he said.

"It's killer stuff, I've been doing it for a couple months now, buying and selling. They've got cures for liver problems, stomach problems, you name it. If you can't get it up there's something for that. It's unbelievable."

Now Calhoun looked at him. Goldstein winced. Going eye-to-eye with the Sandman was like staring down a crocodile. "That stuff is bullshit," Calhoun said.

"Well, maybe it is, maybe it isn't. But I can tell you, it worked for me."

"Yeah? What'd it work on?"

"Never mind what, I'm telling you it worked. And my customers, they can't stop raving. Better yet, they can't stop ordering. I've been busier than a dog with two dicks."

"So, what do you need me for?"

Goldstein leaned in, although the chances of being overheard were nil; as it was, he had to shout to be heard. "I want to cut out my dealer."

Calhoun raised a hand as a waitress passed, pointed towards both drinks on the table to order refills. "I've heard this song before."

"And it worked before, didn't it? It'll work again. Instead of me ordering *from* him, I fill an order *for* him. Phase one, right? Start with a small order, next time jack it up to a larger one, get some working capital up front, figure out the fulfillment angle on the wholesale level, and bam! Now we've got supply and distribution, and our margin increases exponentially."

"And whoever 'he' is, he's gonna roll over for this?"

"He's a fuzzy-nuts kid playing doctor. He's not in our league, believe me. Hell, I don't know if he even has his green card. Trust me, he won't know what hit him 'til it's a done deal."

Calhoun took a few moments to answer. "You got him all figured out, do you?"

"Him, the whole thing."

"Uh huh. So what's the risk factor?"

Goldstein held up both hands. "Mickey, that's the beauty. Worst case, and I mean absolute worst case, we pay a fine."

"*You* pay a fine."

"Okay, *I* pay a fine.

Calhoun leaned back as a waitress delivered their next round of drinks. Goldstein sipped the foam off his beer while Calhoun salted the back of his hand, licked it, knocked back a shot, and followed with a long pull on his beer.

Goldstein was hopeful. At the same time, he shuddered at what he might be getting into. While these days he was far removed from the Hollywood producer's knitting circle, he'd still heard about some of Calhoun's recent episodes. How he'd punched out a line producer. Taken a piss on a fellow stuntman's car. Grabbed an AD by the nose after being told his scenes had been cut at the rewrite that morning. Did a little time for a bar fight that went too far.

No doubt Calhoun was volatile and unpredictable. But in Goldstein's experience, the man got shit done.

Calhoun set the beer down and wiped a hand across his mouth. "All right. Gimme the details."

Goldstein let out a breath, unaware he'd been holding it. "Okay. All right then," he said, and leaned in even closer. "Did you know that the gallbladder from a bear is worth more than gold?"

* * *

A half-hour later the live entertainment at The Cowboy Barn kicked off. Three women who clearly had just wrapped a Chatsworth porno shoot jumped on stage with chaps and cowboy hats to showcase their yodeling skills and tits, not necessarily in that order.

"Quite a place," Goldstein shouted to Calhoun.

"Works for me," the cowboy replied.

"So, what are your thoughts?"

Calhoun shrugged. "I'm looking for the catch."

"There is no catch, Mickey. None. I'll handle the pick up, the transport, the delivery, I'll do all that. The negotiations, the finances, that's all on me. Seriously, all you need to do is go merrily a-hunting, shoot some bears, get their gallbladders and paws, and when you've got the order filled, I'll take them off your hands."

"With money."

"Of course. Payment immediately on delivery."

Calhoun didn't answer, his interest captured by something on his phone.

When he finally looked up, he said, "Okay, I'm in. But I'm gonna need a second man. We'll need two to do the shooting."

Goldstein sat back. "I don't know if I like that, Mickey."

"Well, tough shit. You don't just dial up bears like hookers. I need to bring someone in with experience."

"You know someone who hunts bears?"

"Bears, deer, cougars, wild boar, wolves, hell, he's killed damn near everything at one time or another. He was one of those, whattayacallit...

outfitters. But more important, he's like a fuckin' Apache with a bow."

"He's an Indian?"

Calhoun snorted. "No, he's a bowhunter."

"You're going to hunt bears with a bow and arrow?" Goldstein sat back. This was getting complicated.

"Yeah. Where we're going, it's best to be quiet."

"What do you mean? Where are you thinking?" Goldstein asked.

"You said the order is six, right?"

"Six bladders, plus the paws."

"And you're figuring that's just a start."

Goldstein nodded. "Right. Bigger orders to come. This one's to gain his trust."

"What I'm thinking, if we're gonna do volume, we have to be where the bears are. Meaning we go up north, to Redwood National Park." He held up his phone. "I just Googled it. Biggest concentration of black bears in the whole state, right there."

"Christ. Where the hell is that?"

"Way up, northern Cal. Six hours past Frisco. Humboldt County."

"Oh, yeah, they grow a lot of pot up there. Really powerful shit." Goldstein paused, gave that a moment's thought, then shrugged it off. "That's a long way, Mickey," he said. "And why the bow? Can't you just shoot them?"

"Redwoods is federal land. Guns are noisy."

Goldstein took that in, gave it some thought. Problem? Not really. Wildlife trafficking was federal already. So, no new ground being broken by doing the product acquisition on federal land, not that he could see.

"All right, fine, if that's what you have to do. And this other shooter. We can trust him?"

Calhoun waved a hand dismissively. "I done some work with him on a couple Westerns at Universal. I think he also worked on one of the Robin Hood pictures. Name's Wheeler, Cody Wheeler. The guy's a magician with a bow, almost went to the Olympics back in the day. Hunts all kinds of stuff. When he lived down here, he hunted deer right in Griffith Park, I shit you not. Lives up north now, last I talked to him. Pretty near where we're heading."

Goldstein's head pounded from the bad music and cheap booze. "Okay, fine. Sounds great. But I can't raise your cut for a second guy, my margin will get squeezed. We'll have to stay at seven-fifty a bladder, and you'll have to split two ways."

"Three-and-a-quarter apiece?" Calhoun shook his head. "That won't work."

"Come on, Mickey. I already made the deal. I can't go back and ask for more."

"Then I guess it comes out of your share."

Goldstein sighed. "Fuck. How much?"

Chapter Eight

Ukiah, California

Ray Charles spent the better part of ten hours sleeping on Tanner's lap, his big purr a low, constant rumble. By the time they reached Ukiah, the gateway to the Northern California coastal redwood forests, Tanner's legs were sound asleep.

He pulled into a Shell station with easy access for his blue Ford Expedition and 18-foot Coachmen Clipper Ultra-Lite trailer. Gas, a stretch, and a quick walk on a harness for Ray Charles—something that never failed to catch attention.

This time it was a boy, maybe twelve, who poked his head out the window of a Subaru. "What is that?"

"It's a bobcat."

"Really?"

"Yep."

"How come you have a bobcat?"

A man, presumably the boy's father, came around from where he'd been pumping gas. "Whoa! That *is* a bobcat."

"What's its name?" the boy asked.

"Ray Charles."

"That's a weird name."

"He's a weird cat."

The man edged around to the driver's door. "Isn't that kind of dangerous?

You have to have a permit or something?"

"He's just a big pussycat. Most of the time, anyway. But yes, you have to have a permit."

"Well, that's really something," the man said, and got in the car. As they pulled away, the boy stuck his head out the window and yelled, "What's the matter with his eyes?"

They turned onto the highway before Tanner could answer.

He walked Ray Charles to a patch of spotty grass and dirt next to the station. The big cat used a litter box with no problem, but much preferred the chance to go natural whenever the opportunity presented itself. Tanner stood in the classic pet owner position: slipping on a disposable poop-glove, looking off in the distance as Ray Charles circled a few times, scratched at the ground, and took a bobcat-sized dump.

* * *

Fueled up and back on the road, Tanner drove past miles of seemingly endless conifers standing in anonymous uniformity; an army of implacable green soldiers, shoulder-to-shoulder and ramrod straight. It occurred to him that only two crayons were needed to color the landscape framing the long grade up Happy Hill toward Eureka. Forest Green, for the trees. Burnt Sienna, for the tree trunks. You could drive this stretch of highway every day and never really be sure where you were.

"You oughta see this," Tanner said to Ray Charles.

The fifteen-pound feline stirred at the sound of Tanner's voice. He stretched both forelegs, splayed his paws and yawned.

"Get a sense of humor," Tanner said.

The cat looked up at him with unseeing eyes, the lids having long been sewn shut over empty eye sockets.

The anesthetizing scenery caused Tanner's mind to wander. He thought about the boy's curiosity as Ray Charles's head returned to Tanner's knee.

It had been two years earlier, in the very different topography of Arizona's Rincon Mountains.

Tanner was on a roadrunner census with the Arizona Game Warden. They were wrapping for the day when Tanner's radio barked.

He climbed into his Expedition and keyed the mic. "Tanner here, what's up?"

"Nick, you're in the Rincons, right?" the dispatcher said.

"Affirmative."

"A pair of hunters called in. They found a bobcat corpse up there. Female. Looks like it was nursing. They marked its location."

"Tell me where."

* * *

Following the dispatcher's directions, Tanner guided the SUV up several grueling miles of fire road, and stopped at the GPS point the hunters had provided. From here he'd be on foot. The trail they'd marked took Tanner up a steep, winding deer path that snaked around savage banana yuccas and over jumbles of car-sized boulders.

True to their word, one of the hunters had flagged the location of the dead cat's body. Rather creatively, he'd sacrificed his underwear, skewered it on a stick and wedged it into the ground. Although the hunters were long gone, Tanner nodded his approval at their ingenuity—and their priorities.

He checked out the corpse. A good-sized female, clearly in nursing mode. The snarling rictus told Tanner it had died badly, likely poisoned. It was a common practice of Arizona homeowners and ranchers to spread grain pellets coated in anticoagulant to control the ground squirrel population. The collateral damage was the internal bleeding and tortured, writhing death of the bobcats, coyotes, raccoons, vultures, and occasional family dog who fed on the dying rodents.

"Where are they, mama?" Tanner asked aloud.

He scanned the surroundings. It would be a sheltered, shaded spot. Someplace reasonably protected from marauding coyotes and foxes. A cave, a hollow, even a large hole under one of the boulders.

Tanner spent the next three hours scrambling, crawling and sliding across unstable, knife-edged shale, peering under random heaps of rock and boulders, searching exposed hollows under stunted Joshua trees. The air was heavy with heat and the dank threat of rain, and smelled of sun-baked rock, cholla blooms and his own sweat. Monsoonal clouds on the horizon would soon abbreviate what little sunlight remained. He knew he was nearly out of time. Even with his flashlight, the return hike would be a rough go in the dark, worse in a downpour.

He had given up and started down when he heard the unmistakable mew of a hungry kitten.

He looked at the horizon. Figured maybe fifteen or twenty minutes before the light was gone, with the rain soon to follow. The smart thing to do would be to leave now and come back early the next morning.

When he might very well find them dead of dehydration, starvation, or some combination.

So really, there was no choice.

He turned back, tracked the sound to a ledge twenty yards across the hillside, and minutes later located the source. A sprawling Spanish Bayonet yucca formed a living, formidable ring of bristling spines around its desiccated core. The sound came from somewhere in that core.

"Gotta hand it to you, mama," Tanner said with a sigh. "Hell of a hiding place."

At the cost of what felt like pints of blood, he bulled his way through the outer defenses of the brutal plant. There was a dark hollow at its base, the mewing coming from within.

"No rattlesnakes with you in there, I hope," he said.

With that, he reached down and groped blindly into the hollow. He winced as yucca spines lanced into his armpit and side. Straining, his fingers moved over three small, furry bodies. Only one moved. It squealed as Tanner worked his hand along its back, then pinched its scruff.

He extracted the squalling kit, its eyes squeezed shut, its mouth wide in protest.

"You the only one that made it? Anyone else alive with you in there?" He gently set the kit down, took a deep breath, and reached back into the center of the yucca.

* * *

The siblings were both dead. The live kit was badly dehydrated, and unresisting as Tanner swaddled him in his jacket. Darkness slammed down when the monsoon hit, the trail now running with water and virtually invisible, so Tanner had to slide down most of the hill on his rear, collecting cactus needles like a pincushion. Back at the vehicle, he stowed the kit on the passenger seat and navigated the difficult descent down the fire road by Braille. When he finally reached pavement he stopped, used his phone to look up an emergency vet clinic, and gunned it into town.

A subcutaneous saline drip rehydrated the kitten, and bottle feeding every two hours provided the nutrition to keep it alive. But within days, both eyes were leaking pus. Antibiotics didn't make a dent in the virulent infection, and in the end the vet could see no choice.

"I've got to put him down, Nick."

Tanner stood over the metal examination table, stroking the kit's fur, feeling the low vibration of his purr. "No other options? What if this was someone's house cat, what would you do?"

"If it was someone's pet?" The vet sighed. "I'd either put him down, or stop the infection by removing both eyes, depending upon what the owner wanted." He looked down at the kit. "And in this case, there is no owner."

Ray Charles had been Tanner's constant companion ever since.

Chapter Nine

Eureka, California

The RV Tanner towed behind his Expedition had been home since the divorce and proved to be a great fit for undercover work. Wherever Tanner rolled in he was just another weekend road warrior, well under the radar of anyone who might be watching local hotels and motels for noteworthy arrivals. 'Noteworthy' generally meaning someone who looked like the law.

Tanner's phone buzzed as he motored through downtown Eureka. He checked the number and smiled. Kiera had her own cell phone now, a twelfth birthday present, which had—for at least one shining moment—made him The Best Dad Ever.

"Hey, sugar bunny," he said.

"Dad, please." She hated that nickname. Too childish. He loved it.

"I'm sorry, ma'am, you must have misdialed. I was expecting a call from my young daughter, but you sound like a mature woman on the brink of thirteen, a grizzled matron, if you will."

"Dad." She sighed, but he could hear the smile on her face.

"What's up, darling?"

"Where are you?"

"I'm in Eureka. Garden spot of Northern California."

"Chasing bad guys?"

"Always. So. A call instead of a text. To what do I owe the honor?"

"Guess what?" She didn't wait. "I got invited to be on the travelling team."

Her dream—and Tanner's fear—ever since she started gymnastics. "Oh, hey, congratulations. That's great."

"I know, right?"

"That takes a lot of time, doesn't it? A lot of practice, after school and such?" Tanner knew the answer. Four hours a day, four days a week. He'd been dreading this.

"It does, but they give you lots of time to do your homework, and you've got all those hours while you're travelling."

"Sounds pretty demanding, Kiera. You sure you want to do this?"

"Dad. Don't spoil it."

"No, no, I mean…" He tried another tack. "What does your mother think?"

"She says if it makes me happy, I should do it."

"She does."

"Yeah, and now that she and Kent are, you know…"

Tanner felt his heart bump. "Mom and Kent are what?"

A pause, an audible breath, and then, "So she hasn't told you yet."

"Told me…?"

"Well…"

"Kiera, what?"

"I didn't know she didn't tell you." Another pause, another breath. "Mom and Kent got engaged."

And there it was.

It was bound to happen. Only natural. He and Lori had been divorced, what? Nearly six years now. So why the roaring in his ears?

"Dad?"

"Yeah, I'm here." His turn for a deep breath. "Huh, they're getting married. That's, I don't know. That's great, I guess. What do *you* think?"

"Kent's nice and all."

Tanner had met Kent a couple of times a few months before, when he'd been by for visitation. And goddammit, he *was* nice. Rich, too.

"Mom's a really smart woman, Kiera. I'm sure she's making a good decision."

There was another pause, this one much longer.

When she spoke, her voice was small. "Remember when you came back?"

His stomach flipped, but he kept it from his voice.

"Absolutely." Four years ago, two years after the divorce. A couple of dates, one awkward as hell, the other not so much. A roll in the hay and somehow he and Lori were agreeing to give it another try. What added impetus was that Tanner had recently made GS-13, which meant he had the option of a desk job at the L.A. office, regular hours, home every night, weekends off, like a normal person. No more field work, no more undercover assignments that would have him gone for weeks at a time. Those long absences from home had been the primary cause of their split. Now, that obstacle no longer existed.

It turned out he couldn't do it.

Couldn't handle sitting under florescent lights in a hermetically sealed building, where the day was all about meetings, and phone calls, and spreadsheets. Where the poachers, the smugglers, the "canned" hunters, the outlaw outfitters, were all abstractions. Names on paper, problems someone else was trying to handle. Where the only hint of the wildness he'd sworn to protect were the ants that found the open jar of honey on his desk.

He gutted it out for six months before he asked to go back into the field. When he told Lori, it broke her heart. She didn't even get angry. Said she understood, said she even expected it. But it crushed her.

His first assignment took him eight hundred miles from home, to the Grand Tetons. Undercover as a buyer of "sheds," elk antlers illegally gathered from the park. The assignment lasted three weeks.

Two years earlier, there'd been screaming fights and slamming doors. This time, she simply had all his clothes packed and waiting by the door.

"It's not your fault, Nick. It never was," she said. "It's who you are. I guess I didn't remember how much it wore on me."

"Lori." He couldn't think of anything else to say.

"You love what you do. You love those animals, more than you love being a family man."

A harsh thing to say, and it hurt. But there was no getting around it. If you stepped back and looked at it objectively, if you judged solely by his actions, she was absolutely right.

Which, again objectively, made him a shitty husband. But he was determined that it would *not* make him a shitty father. He'd had one of those. His daughter deserved better.

He used all his accrued vacation time on visitations. Sent his monthly checks right on time. Sent more than the court ordered. Overdid the birthday and Christmas gifts, like the cell phone, because, well, maybe because it made him feel better. Like more of a father.

Which of course was a big load of bullshit.

He'd failed at marriage and might be heading down the road of failing at fatherhood, too. Lori was about to marry a commercial real estate broker with two kids of his own. Made lots of money, far more than Tanner, for sure. By all appearances was good to Kiera, treated her like one of his own.

Which raised conflicting emotions for Tanner. Of course, he wanted his daughter treated well. But Tanner feared the erosive powers of time and distance that wore away precious memories, leaving them stripped clean of emotion. She'd slip away as the teen years wreaked havoc, an inexorable current carrying her farther and farther from him...

"Dad? You there?"

"Yeah, sorry. Sure, I remember, hon. But, you know, that didn't work out. I loved being back with you, I think about it all the time. All the best times in my life were with you and Mom. It didn't work, but it was totally my fault, not yours, not your mom's. We've talked about this before."

"I know."

Tanner's eyes blurred. "Look. Kiera. If your mother's happy, and if you're happy, then I'm a happy guy. Nothing else matters."

"Except catching bad guys."

He didn't answer. Couldn't think of what to say.

"How's Ray Charles?" she asked.

At the sound of his name, the bobcat's head popped up, bobbing side to side like his namesake.

"He's right here. He heard you."

48

"Tell him hi, and I can't wait to see him."

Tanner wiped his eyes. "He misses you too."

Chapter Ten

Trinidad, California

After a solid fourteen hours of travel from L.A., Tanner backed into slot 15 at a small RV park in Trinidad. The overgrown, ragtag facility boasted little in the way of luxury accommodations, or accommodations of any sort. Dirt parking areas were roughly demarked by redwoods and other pines. Some featured cinderblock fire pits, all had fifty-gallon metal trash cans. Nothing fancy, but there were hook-ups, it was near the highway, and only a short drive from the Redwood State and National Parks, all of which met Tanner's needs.

He got out of the Expedition, stretched and popped his spine back into position, then began the process of moving in. First step: crack a cold one, and take a long, deeply satisfying pull.

That important task completed, Tanner hooked up the electricity and water, extended the slide-out room, rolled out the awning, connected the propane to the barbecue grill, and set up the climber and outdoor enclosure for Ray Charles.

Tanner was headed back into the trailer for another beer when a man spoke from behind him.

"Hey."

Tanner turned. "Hey, yourself."

The man seemed as round as he was tall, with a head that perched on his shoulders without benefit of a neck. Thin-framed, round eyeglasses rested on a wide nose, flanked by bulging cheeks rutted with acne scars. He wore a black nylon jacket the size of a pup tent, half-covering baggy gray trousers that sagged over worn, muddy boots. He stepped forward and extended his hand.

"I'm Joel. Joel Friedland. Otherwise known in these parts as Toad."

Tanner shook the meaty hand and resisted the impulse to wipe his palms on his shirt. "Pleased to meet you, Joel. I'm Nick."

"Seriously, dude, call me Toad. Everyone does."

Tanner smiled. "Okay. Toad it is."

"Saw you pull in. Plan on staying long?"

"I don't know, hard to say."

"No schedule to keep, eh? That's nice. Free spirit, right?"

"Only way to go."

"You got that right and then some," Toad hooked a thumb towards the other side of the park. "Me, I'm practically a permanent resident here. Help out the manager when she goes on vacay, help keep order, you know."

"So, you live here full time?"

"Pretty much, unless Dot-Dot gets a wild hair and wants to go visit her shitbird relatives in Colorado. That's my wife. Real name's Dorothy, everyone calls her Dot-Dot." He pointed at the carpeted climber Tanner had set inside a wired enclosure. "I see you have a cat."

"Sort of." Tanner went to the RV door and tapped the floor. Ray Charles emerged at the signal, and Tanner scooped him up.

"Holy shit," Toad said. "That's a bobcat."

"Yes, it is," Tanner said.

Tanner opened the small gate to the enclosure and set Ray inside. The big cat sniffed around for a moment, then located his climber and bounded to the top.

"I'll be goddamned. What's with the eyes?"

"He's blind."

"No shit. Isn't that something? Gets around pretty good, does he?"

"He does all right, yes. A bobcat's sense of hearing is extremely acute. Between that, his sense of smell, and his whiskers he does all right."

51

Toad watched out of eyes sunk in fat, like someone had pushed marbles into an amorphous glob of clay. "Wow. Wait'll Dot-Dot sees this, what a hoot. He doesn't bite or attack?"

"Not so far." The questions were always the same, but it was understandable. Tanner and Ray Charles had been guests at many high school assemblies, outdoor education schools, eco-festivals and more. Tanner believed that every introduction of Ray to the public was a great educational opportunity, and he enjoyed the interaction.

"That is something. A blind bobcat. That's a first in this park, for sure." He looked over at Tanner. "So, what brings you here, Nick? Lemme guess. Musician?"

"No, writer. Doing a piece on law enforcement in Redwoods."

"Oh, yeah? You look like a musician. Course, I don't know what a writer looks like, so there you go. Who you writing for?"

"Freelancing, actually. Hope to sell it to a magazine."

"Hey, a journalist," Toad said. "I'm something of a journalist myself. More an investigative reporter, I guess. Me and Dot-Dot are chronicling the existence and evolution of Sasquatch."

"Bigfoot," Tanner said, unsure if Toad was serious.

"Yessir. Got cameras strategically placed throughout certain sections of the Park where there've been confirmed sightings, or where I've found signs that would indicate activity."

Tanner kept a straight face. "No kidding? How's that going, have you come up with anything?"

"Oh, yeah. Most definitely. Some very compelling images. Of course, nothing that could be called definitive yet, you know, but highly compelling. We're on the right track for sure."

"Well listen, Toad, I was about to have another cold one. Care to join me?"

Toad waved a hand. "Thanks, I'll take a rain check. Dot-Dot's waiting on me, it's near bedtime. I'll catch hell if I'm late. You need anything, we're over on the other side, in twenty-two." He took another look at Ray Charles. "That's just the damnedest thing." He looked up at Tanner. "Okay then, see you."

"See you around. Thanks for stopping by."

Toad turned and waddled off, thighs scraping, arms thrust sideways to clear his hips, out of the pool of light around Tanner's trailer and into the darkness.

Tanner watched him a moment, then climbed the stairs into his trailer. Tomorrow promised to be a busy day, starting with a meet-up with the Park's Enforcement Ranger, Kathleen Shepherd.

Chapter Eleven

Orick, California

Shepherd pulled into the Ranger HQ at the start of her shift. She noticed a blue Ford Expedition parked out front as she walked in.

Standing at Ruby's desk was a lean, six-foot man who looked to be in his mid-thirties. Second glance, maybe closer to forty. Could be it was the ponytail and coarse black hair that made him look younger at first. Well-built in that loose-jointed, ropey sort of way. Flat belly. A nose that looked like it had been broken at least once. Sharp, clean jawline. Pale blue eyes set deeply under an overhanging brow. One of those guys with mix-and-match features that somehow came together well.

"Ah, there's Ranger Shepherd now," Ruby said. She looked down at the business card she was holding. "Ranger Shepherd, this here is Nick Capretta, nature author and photographer, here to write about—what is it again exactly?"

"The role of Enforcement Rangers in our National Parks," Tanner said. He extended his hand. "Nice to meet you, Ranger Shepherd."

"And you, Mr. Capretta." They shook hands. This had to be her Fish and Wildlife guy.

"Call me Nick."

"Great, and I'm Kathleen."

"Kathleen it is. I've been talking with your lovely associate here, and she tells me you found another bear. Tragic, but from the standpoint of content

54

for my article, I guess my timing is pretty good."

Shepherd played along. "I did. Up near Klamath. This time I managed to get some evidence. Let's go in my office, I'll bring you up to speed."

"Perfect." Tanner turned to Ruby. "Thank you, Miss Ruby, and may I say, you're a delight." He winked.

Shepherd couldn't believe her eyes. Ruby blushed like a little girl. "It was my pleasure, Mr. Capretta," she purred. "And you let me know if there's any way I can help."

"Oh, I'm sure there will be. I can already tell who runs this outfit."

* * *

"What's the story on these?"

Tanner stood in Shepherd's cramped office, examining the framed photos on the wall. Several showed her standing in front of a huge redwood. In each of those, the tree had a substantial chunk cut from its enormous trunk.

"Midnight burlers," Shepherd said. "Burl poachers. So, what's your real name?"

"Tanner. Nick Tanner. I nearly always keep the first name, less to remember. Tell me about these burlers. I've heard about it, haven't seen it before, though." He turned and slouched into a chair across from Shepherd, who was already seated behind her desk. "I saw, like, eight burl sculpting shops on my way through town."

"It's Orick's biggest industry. Legal industry, anyway. Tourists love the things. The sculptors are supposed to get their raw burls from legal sources, like blowdown or beaver bait—and for the most part they do. But legal burls are more expensive than illegal ones, so it's tempting."

"Beaver bait?"

"Logging trash. The superfluous stuff they can't use."

"How much are the burls worth?"

"The poachers sell by the pound. Three bucks a pound, thereabouts. A few hundred to a couple grand a burl, depending on the size."

"Not a huge amount of money."

"Not small change if you're a tweaker."

"How do you tell a poached hunk of tree from a legit one?"

"We can't, really. We have to catch them in the act or set up a sting. Sometimes we can match a burl to a tree, but that's the exception."

Tanner motioned to a photo on the wall, one with an engraved plaque. "I noticed one up there, says 'Thanks to Ranger Shepherd, from Save the Redwoods.' Looks like you caught at least one."

Shepherd looked down. "I was with my Training Ranger. We went after a guy named Emil Reyes. Mentally disturbed ex-con. He was stealing from campers, harassing hikers, just a general pain in the ass. That's what we went after him for. What we didn't know was he'd cut down a four-hundred-year-old tree to get at a burl that was high up. That burl must've weighed hundreds of pounds. He couldn't do anything with it, had no way to haul it out, but he was too greedy to chop it up. He couldn't bring it in, and he couldn't leave it. He sat there with it, was there when we found him."

"What happened?"

Shepherd shuffled some papers that didn't need shuffling. "He wasn't cooperative."

She didn't elaborate.

"Huh." Tanner felt he'd hit a nerve. There was something interesting there, but now wasn't the time. He pulled out his cell phone and touched the Record app. "Okay. Tell me about the bears."

* * *

Shepherd's summary was concise and clear. At one point she brought out the arrowhead, still wrapped in the plastic bag.

"How far in did it go?" Tanner asked.

"Maybe twenty percent sticking out."

"Okay. Long shot, but maybe enough to get something. I'm guessing this town doesn't have a police department, much less one with forensics."

"No, closest city department is down in Arcata. It's pretty small. Eureka's got a bigger one, down the coast a little farther. Up here we contract with the County Sheriff, but there's only one officer assigned to most of the area covered by parkland. Truth is, we're pretty much on our own here."

Tanner pulled the packaged arrow across the desk. "We've got an office in Arcata. I'll have them run it."

"Great."

"So, what are your initial thoughts on this? Think these burl poachers might be involved, maybe looking for extra money? What's your gut telling you?"

"Doubt it. Burlers are too high most of the time. They don't have the patience or skill to take down a bear with an arrow. I feel a little out of my depth on this one. I've never dealt with this TCM stuff. Heard about it, of course, but we never had an issue here until now."

"What concerns me about all this," Tanner said, "is you're finding these bears too easily. Makes me think either this guy is a rank amateur, or he's working fast, like he's on some kind of deadline and it's making him careless."

"And we don't even know if we've found them all."

"True."

Tanner sat back in his chair. "If one of your hikers or campers stumbles on this hunter—whole lot of empty out there."

"Believe me, I've thought about that."

Ruby opened the door and poked her head in. "Sorry to interrupt, but there's a fella here who says his, uh, husband is missing."

"Tourist?" Shepherd asked.

"Resident. From down near the college."

"How long has he been missing?"

"Shep—" She caught herself. "Ranger Shepherd, I really think you need to talk to this guy. He's got some, uh, extenuating circumstances."

Chapter Twelve

Orick, California

"My name is Alton Ruff. I'm an honorably discharged Army sergeant. I'm disabled, I'm gay, and I will tell you up front that my husband and I grow pot for a living. But I'm a citizen, I pay most of what I probably should in taxes, and I'm here for your help. My husband has gone missing."

Ruff was in a wheelchair. His oversized shoulders were hunched and powerful. Thick blue veins rode the surface of tattooed forearms forged in iron. Below the waist, his twisted, atrophied legs were in stark contrast.

Shepherd reached out her hand.

"Mister Ruff, I'm Ranger Kathleen Shepherd. This is Nick, uh…"

"Capretta. Nick Capretta. I'm a writer doing a piece on law enforcement in our National Parks." Tanner leaned over and shook the man's hand. It was like grabbing a bench vise.

"Mister Ruff," Shepherd said. "How long has your husband been gone, and have you contacted the sheriff?"

"My husband started a farm in Redwoods to help us pay the bills. Which is a federal crime. So, no, I haven't called the sheriff. I heard good things about you, so I'm coming to you. The National Park is your jurisdiction, correct?"

"Yes. But as you said, it's a federal crime to grow marijuana on Park land. And I'm federal."

Ruff waved dismissively. "C'mon. You got bigger things to worry about than our puny little plot. Cartels are out there growing thousands of acres. And to answer your first question, he didn't show yesterday."

"One day?"

The big man shook his head impatiently. "He's finishing up the harvest. He's been out for weeks, but he was due back."

"So maybe he'll show up tonight..."

"No! Something happened. I know it. I need you to go look for him."

"Sir, a grown man who doesn't show up for a day? We can't even file a missing person report with the sheriff on that."

Ruff said nothing. Shepherd sighed, pulled a chair over, and sat next to him.

"What's his name?" she asked.

"Harley Thompson. Thirty-seven years old. Five-ten, one-seventy-five, shoulder-length brown hair, brown eyes, olive skin. And I know I can't file a report yet, that's why I'm coming to you. I'm telling you, something's happened, he should've been home. It's on Park land, and I want you to find him. I want you to go out there and find him." Ruff's eyes teared up, and he angrily wiped a big hand across them. "I'm telling you, something's happened."

Shepherd shot Tanner a look.

"Sir, I'll absolutely go out there," she said. "But listen. Even if I don't find Mr. Thompson, I'll have to confiscate or destroy any plants I find. Every single one."

Tanner watched Ruff's face for reaction. There was none.

"When did he last contact you?" Shepherd asked.

"Contact how? Carrier pigeon? There's no fucking cell service out there." He slammed his hands down on the arms of his wheelchair with such force it startled Tanner. "And I can't do a fucking thing. Look, I don't give a shit if you burn down the whole farm. I'll tell you where it is, knock yourself out. But find Harley. Maybe he's out there hurt, or bleeding, maybe he had an accident, a tree fell on him or something..."

Shepherd put a comforting hand on the man's shoulder and turned to

59

Ruby. "Get me a Park map, please." She turned back to Ruff. "Sir, you tell us exactly where your farm is. I'll take a look."

Tanner watched as Ruff pointed out the farm's location. Under normal circumstances, a missing pot farmer would have had nothing to do with his duties. He needed to get the arrow to the Arcata office and get his investigation rolling.

And maybe it was coincidental that this guy Harley Thompson goes missing right in the middle of this spate of bear poaching. Probably was.

But maybe not.

Chapter Thirteen

Somewhere in Redwoods Park

Two days before his husband would report him missing, and an hour's hike from the nearest abandoned logging road, Harley Thompson cut the final plant.

He straightened and surveyed his work. Five hundred marijuana plants had filled a small clearing, maybe an eighth of an acre he'd single-handedly cleared of scrub, tanoak and alder back in February. He felt a certain satisfaction that only two redwoods had to go, very young and each less than twenty-five feet tall. The southern exposure at the base of a shallow ravine made this an ideal location. The plants had enjoyed optimal sunlight, and a creek supplied plenty of water through a gravity-fed line.

"Not too shabby," he said aloud. Especially for a lone operator.

When Alton had become disabled, Harley realized they could no longer survive on the profits from the tiny Arcata rental home they'd fashioned into a grow house. They needed to expand. From his wheelchair, Alton could still handle most of the day-to-day maintenance in Arcata. Harley would step up their game by setting up a farm in Redwoods.

It was not an easy decision. Not only because it was illegal; it was also increasingly dangerous. The pot growers in Northern California's state and national parks were no longer aging hippies growing a little weed or college kids keeping the frat house high. Marijuana was a thirteen-*billion*-dollar cash crop in California. No other crop—or state—came close. That kind of money caught the interest of Mexican cartels, who were finding it harder and harder to bring pot over the border. So, they decided to set up shop in the most prolific marijuana farming region in the country.

Their invasion was often violent and sometimes deadly, as the local mom-and-pop growers were forcibly evicted or simply scared off. Mexican field workers were smuggled across the border to handle the manual labor of clearing, planting, maintaining, and harvesting the farms. Armed guards kept watch day and night.

And they had a zero-tolerance policy when it came to competition.

Harley had done his best to protect his investment, encircling the plot with military-grade tripwire. At regular intervals, he'd connected the wire to rat traps rigged to blow off shotgun shells with the pellets removed. Nice, scary surprise for anyone approaching the area, and plenty loud enough for him to hear from his base camp several hundred yards upstream.

He gathered up the day's harvest in a large burlap tarp, tied it off and hauled it along one of his trails towards camp. He always took pains to avoid taking the same trail twice; no reason to leave a roadmap from the grow site to his camp. This time, carrying the load, he decided to take his easiest trail, one he hadn't used in a week or so.

Harley had been in the woods a long time, nurturing the plants from seedlings to harvest, but now, at last, he was nearly done. Almost time to go home. Get Alton started on the trimming. Sleep in a real bed, eat a pizza, drink some beer.

He was maybe fifty yards from his camp when he saw them.

Gummi bears.

Probably a couple pounds' worth of the brightly colored candies, spread haphazardly around a small clearing. And then the smell hit him. Anise oil, with its penetrating scent of black licorice. He'd lived around the woods of Northern California all his life. His father was an avid hunter. He knew what this meant.

Bears love the scent of anise oil. And they go apeshit over candy.

"Oh, shit," slipped out. Barely more than a whisper, but too much. He froze and scanned the trees nearby. The understory was too dense to spot

62

anything—any*one*—who didn't want to be seen. But they could easily see him, standing on his cleared trail.

Head down, eyes fixed in front of his feet, he bee-lined for his camp. Maybe he'd been seen by the poacher—or poachers—maybe not. Either way, Harley wanted to make his intentions clear to whoever was baiting bears in a National Park. *You do your thing, I'll do mine, I'm the fuck outta here.*

Load the harvest into the truck, tarp it off, grab his shit and hit the road. He hadn't seen the poacher, had no intention of doing so, but who knows how nervous the guy might be? Or crazy? Out here in the woods, miles from civilized constructs like law, order, moral judgment, any goddamn thing could happen.

Like for instance, a guy in full camo standing ten feet in front of you on the trail, pointing a drawn arrow at your heart.

A hot rush of adrenaline sickened Harley. The muscles in his legs knotted and quivered, vibrating like a tuning fork. He set down the sack and raised shaking hands.

"Oh, shit. Look, man, I got no problem with whatever you're doing. I got my own thing, y'know? I just wanna take my plants and split."

The man was a statue, his face shadowed by a brimmed hat pulled low, his features blurred with black and green camo paint. The arrowhead was still as death.

"Seriously, buddy, I don't care, okay? Whatever you got goin' on, that's your thing, I got my own shit to deal with, you got yours, and yours is none of my fuckin' business. I don't care at all, so let's go our separate ways, please. No harm, no foul, man, okay?"

"What do you think you saw?" The man's voice was unexpectedly light. Youthful, kind of twangy.

"See, that's exactly it," Harley said, sensing a drop in the tension. "Nothing, dude. I saw absolutely nothing. Not a fucking thing. Hell, I don't even see you right now. You let me get to my camp, pack my shit, I'm asshole and elbows and I saw nothing, okay?"

The man was still. The arrow didn't waver an inch.

"Look, could you lower the arrow please? I'm ready to shit my pants here, no kidding. I'm no threat, I'm unarmed. You're makin' me very fucking nervous."

There was a long moment where the only sound was Harley's own percussive pulse behind his eyes.

At last, at long, long last, the man lowered the arrow. He still had it fully drawn, but it was a start. Harley exhaled sharply. He hadn't even realized he'd been holding his breath.

"Cool, man, that's great, thanks. I've already forgotten everything, I'm gonna..." He was interrupted when a sledgehammer hit his foot. The shock was so hard and sudden the pain hadn't reached his brain by the time he looked down and saw three black feathers protruding from his boot. He instinctively jerked back in horror, and felt an agonizing tear, a rending of flesh he swore he could *hear*. His foot was solidly pinned to the forest floor. A growing circle of blood darkened his boot.

He fell to the ground, screaming, his brain on fire, his face streaming snot and saliva as he pulled uselessly at the arrow in his foot. A shadow fell across him, and he looked up too late to avoid the boot swinging toward his head.

* * *

In his thirty-two years, Cody Wheeler had done plenty of killing, but he had yet to kill a man. And he wasn't about to start now, so he nailed the hippie's foot to the ground and kicked him unconscious.

But now what? One thing to make cash money bow-hunting a few bears. A whole other thing to cross the line into murder.

Wheeler didn't know what to do. Let the guy go, maybe he tells someone about the site, maybe people start looking, finding dead bears with no galls and no paws.

Kill him? Whole other can of worms opens up there. Too many what-ifs. None of which he was being paid to consider. He was hired to kill bears and do some fast, crude butchering, pure and simple. Not this shit.

No, this was a decision for Calhoun.

The sixty-pound draw that could launch an arrow completely through a bear had easily penetrated the pot grower's boot, foot, boot sole, and drilled deep into the earth. In fact, the fucking thing was so stubbornly planted Wheeler couldn't pull it out. He ended up using the saw blade on his hunting knife to sever the shaft above the guy's boot, then pulled the foot up and off. There was a lot of blood.

With the hippie unconscious, Wheeler went back into the woods to retrieve his ATV. He thought about what he'd done. Had it felt different, shooting a man? Maybe it did, he decided. In what way, he wasn't sure. But it wasn't a pleasant feeling.

* * *

Wheeler brought the ATV alongside the now squirming, semi-sentient man, and chopped a few lengths from rope originally earmarked to haul a bear carcass into hiding. With swift, sure movements he laced knots around Harley's wrists and ankles. Harley wasn't a particularly big man, but it was still like lifting a loose sack of rocks onto the ATV's cargo carrier and took every bit of Wheeler's strength. Finally, he lashed Harley's wrists to the frame of the ATV.

Slumped sideways, Harley moaned, his eyes swimming and unfocused.

"Don't worry," Wheeler said. "You'll live."

He put one of his game bags over Harley's head, then eased the ATV forward, headed for the logging road where he'd stashed his Land Cruiser.

Chapter Fourteen

Somewhere in Redwoods Park

The abandoned logging road was one of the myriad of roads that snaked through Redwoods. They were reminders of the rampant logging that built nearly every town large and small spawned by California's gold rush. This particular road led to a remote redwood canyon along the Yurok reservation border. Alton had circled the general area of Harley Thompson's grow site on the map. "I've never been there," he'd said. "But we planned the farm together using topo maps. Knobbler's Creek runs above it, so maybe if you follow the creek from there you can find his base camp?"

On paper, it seemed as good a strategy as any. Goddamn painful in reality. Tanner endured nearly two hours of random spinal readjustments, made worse by Shepherd's apparent desire to break the sound barrier. They jolted and careened in her under-shocked SUV, scraping brush and hopping rocks along a weather-beaten, sullen excuse for a dirt road.

At last, Shepherd brought the vehicle to a merciful stop. "Knobbler's Creek comes closest to the road right about here. From now on we're hiking."

"When we get back, I'll do you a solid and shoot this piece of shit to death," Tanner said. He opened his door and eased himself out of the passenger seat, gratefully stretched his legs and arched his back. "Then you can put in for one with an actual suspension."

"Oh no, don't shoot it, you'll only make it mad," Shepherd said.

Blazing Saddles," Tanner said, smiling. "You a fellow movie buff?"

Shepherd shrugged. "I see a lot of old movies. Not a whole lot else to do up here at night."

* * *

Tanner watched Shepherd move easily into the woods. Young goddamn legs. His own were beaten beyond their years. His knees crunched like shredded wheat as they popped and stretched into working condition.

The redwood trees in this area were scattered and relatively small, allowing plenty of sunlight to reach the understory and catalyze its growth. The additional light made the trail easier to follow. The shoulder-wide clearance presumably made by Harley sliced neatly through the chaotic mass of greenery.

"Looks like this whole area was pretty heavily logged," Tanner said.

"Clear cut," Shepherd said. "This is all young growth."

"I can hear the creek," Tanner said.

"Yeah, should be just up ahead. Map showed it about a half mile in."

"Look at all this poison oak," Tanner said. "I hate this shit. I break out if I even think about it."

The two kept moving along the trampled footpath, Tanner occasionally detouring to avoid encroaching vines of poison oak. Shepherd walked right through it.

"That doesn't bother you?"

Shepherd shrugged. "I have an immunity. It's not uncommon."

"Pretty handy."

They walked on in silence. From the moment they'd left Orick, Tanner could almost see the cloud that hung over Shepherd. She did what she was supposed to, handled her duties, but it was all one note. No ups or downs, no enthusiasm or irritation. Even when she'd made the *Blazing Saddles* joke, it was dry. No playfulness, no joy.

"So, how'd you end up here?"

"I'm not sure," she answered. "Life, I guess."

"Like it?"

"Actually, I've applied for a transfer. There's a position open in New York, at Liberty Park."

Tanner laughed. "New York? You'd leave all this for that shithole?"

"Yep."

"What's the matter with here?"

"Nothing's the matter, really. It's beautiful and all. But at some point—it's pretty lonely. Like I said, not much to do at night."

"Ah."

Shepherd colored a little and looked back at Tanner. "It's not that."

"I didn't say anything."

"I know what you meant."

"You said you were lonely, I responded with a sympathetic grunt."

"Let's drop it, okay?"

Tanner looked ahead at Shepherd as they both labored up a rise in the creek trail. His thoughts went to his shipwrecked marriage, and the daughter he saw too little of.

"Maybe you picked the wrong occupation," he said. "Lonely is part of the job description."

Shepherd said nothing. It was another two hundred yards before she warned, "We've got to be getting close. Keep your eye out for tripwires."

"What do they use out here?"

"Shotgun shells, fishhooks. Sometimes even actual shotguns. If you're lucky just loud windchimes."

"Same shit, different park. Worst I ever saw was a tiger pit guarding a still in Tennessee. Pointy sticks and everything."

"Haven't seen one of those. We did have a guy who built tree snares," Shepherd almost smiled. "Only thing he caught was his own wife. We had to air evac her out."

"Now, see? That's fun stuff. Why would you want to go to New York?"

Shepherd said nothing more. No easy way to talk about Emil Reyes, and the shot she didn't take in time. Or the shots she finally did fire, too late, far too late.

"Hey, I think this is it." Tanner was ten yards behind Shepherd, indicating a break in the undergrowth. "Hey, Shep."

Shepherd shook her head clear and came back. "Sorry."

Tanner took the lead as they made their way down a sloping trail. "Watch it," he said, pointing out a fishline tripwire. "Looks like we've got the right path."

"Yeah. And look." Shepherd nodded toward a row of disturbed soil that ran straight down the hill, occasionally intersecting the path. "That's the drip line."

Within a few minutes they walked into a clearing. The compact grow field lay in front of them, studded with severed stalks and carpeted with yellowed, decaying leaves.

"Gotta hand it to the guy. Pretty tidy set-up for one man to pull off all by his lonesome," Tanner said.

"Actually, he took a huge chance with this location," Shepherd said. "He's only about a mile from where we found a four-acre cartel site about three months ago, with three guys working it."

"A cartel site."

"Yeah. Probably plenty of others around here we haven't found. But if they find him..."

"Maybe they did."

"Maybe."

"It occurs to me, if that's the case, they may also be one hundred percent aware of our presence."

"That's true," Shepherd said, looking into the woods.

"On the other hand, I suppose they'd have shot us already." Tanner unsnapped his holster strap. "So probably we're good. I'll have a look around."

Shepherd sighed and pulled out her phone. "His base camp should be real close. I'll get some pics of all this first, for the paperwork."

Chapter Fifteen

Somewhere in Redwoods Park

Having spent most of his youth and nearly all his professional life in open country, Tanner started every field investigation by tuning into the rhythm of the land. It was his observation that every National Park was unique, with its own distinctive identity forged by the composite of its flora, fauna, climate, topography, and of course, humanity.

Tanner had spent a couple of his college years playing keys in a bar band and liked to attribute a kind of musical tonality to each Park. The lazy, sultry thrum of the Everglades. The soaring, operatic timbre of Bryce Canyon. Carlsbad Cavern's darkly gothic nuances were a world apart from the plaintive, acoustic twang of Joshua Tree. The music coalesced with the land's indigenous physical properties to create what Tanner visualized as a rhythmic quilt.

A successful investigation is the discovery and analysis of anomalies in a pattern. To find the anomalies in the quilt, you must first understand the pattern.

Because this was his first time in Redwoods, Tanner spent the initial ten minutes of his search seated on a stump the circumference of a Volkswagen, registering the Park's impact on each of his senses. What did he smell? What could he hear? He focused his vision on the ground in front of him, gradually working towards the underbrush, and then up towards the canopy.

He was struck by the utter stillness. Which made sense, since only a

Herculean wind could muscle through the massive trees. But the stillness was far from silent. With so little air movement, the slightest sound was amplified. Birds chirped, insects buzzed, every noise seemed to reverberate. Like sitting in a big, empty church.

He dug his hands into the soft, spongy topsoil, brought it to his nose. The smell was a heady mix of fresh, wet pine, sodden leaves and decaying tree bark.

He looked straight up. While they were not in an area of old growth trees, the canopy was so high it seemed surreal. Too high and too dense to make out individual needles, leaves, or even the smaller branches. Glowworms of backlight fought through the growth, sharply contrasted by the dark underbelly. And Tanner knew that he was only seeing the beginning; even in relatively new growth there could be another fifty feet hidden from view.

He stood and walked the clearing perimeter, eyes down. All manner of beetles and other insects stalked the leaf litter. Powerful carpenter ants carried shards far heavier than their own body weight, carting their freight with relentless determination along well-worn trails. Softer spots revealed the passage of raccoons, opossums, and bird tracks Tanner couldn't identify. The unmistakable twin imprint of deer hooves. A single bobcat print. The quilt's intricate pattern told a daily story of struggle, survival, and death, if one knew how to look.

It wasn't long before Tanner identified several different breaks that probably marked trails back to Harley's base camp. Like all growers, Harley would have rotated the use of the trails to keep them from becoming too obvious. The question was, which one did he use most recently?

Tanner inspected each of the openings, finally deciding on one that showed signs of scattered marijuana leaves. Maybe dropped from a harvest bag? Seemed logical enough, and at any rate, all these trails should lead to a camp fairly close by, so Tanner figured he couldn't go too far wrong. The camp would be close enough to respond to encroachers, distant enough to bail if the encroachers turned out to be the law or some other threat.

Tanner followed the trail for fifty yards or so, moving methodically, looking down, left, right, ahead, down again. All senses attuned to any break in the pattern.

The redwood growth was more tightly packed here, with less understory as the canopy screened out the light. A few yards off the trail, he spotted what a casual observer might describe as a random pile of fallen timber. To Tanner, there was nothing random about it. At one time it had been carefully organized. Moreover, the area around it appeared intentionally cleared of any growth more than three feet in height.

Without question, an anomaly in the pattern.

He walked slowly towards the stack, eyes scanning the ground. The ubiquitous leaf litter was clearly out of whack here. He looked up, scrutinized the trees around him for signs of a hunter's tree blind. Had to be here somewhere. But redwoods grow like tubes, with their first branches well off the ground—sometimes hundreds of feet up. Not a great option. None of the fir or oak understory trees seemed sturdy enough, not within a twenty-yard range of the woodpile. So, if not a tree blind, maybe a ground blind?

For fifteen minutes he examined every inch of the small clearing. In the end, it was much harder to spot than Harley's trail had been, but it was clear. Twelve yards out. Flattened ground, a single boot print, and once he scuffed around a bit, a small remnant of what looked like a granola bar wrapper.

He walked back out to the log pile. He knew that it had once been a rudimentary tent-like structure made of similarly sized branches. It had been knocked around quite a bit to disguise its purpose—but not enough. Tanner searched what had likely been the makeshift tent's interior, raking his hand through the ground, sifting it in his fingers. He found something. Blew away some clinging soil.

A Gummi bear.

* * *

"A bear bait site," Shepherd said, after Tanner described what he'd found.

"Yep." Tanner slung down a large burlap sack.

"What's in there?"

72

"A shitload of weed. Found it off the trail, a little ways from the bait site."

"Uh oh."

"Way I see it, Harley's camp—I found it, it's only about 100 yards out—maybe attracted bears to the area. Smell of food, whatever. Meanwhile the poacher cuts sign and sets up. Probably has no idea Harley was around."

Shepherd looked at it. "But then they run into each other."

"Maybe. Harley's camp is still all set up. Tent, cooking stuff, more weed, a little bit of food tucked away in a bear keg."

"Not good." She nudged the bag with her boot.

"Nope."

Shepherd sighed. "Well, shit." She put her hands on her hips, looking at the open sack of weed. "We've got to get a search going."

"Yep. How's that work around here?"

"We get anyone we can get. Law enforcement, volunteers, whatever we can scrounge. We pull lots of locals together. Basically, as many bodies as possible."

"Sounds good," Tanner said. "And I assume everyone over the age of seven out here has a truck or four-wheel drive vehicle. We'll need those to transport the search party out here."

"Won't be a problem, we've done that before."

"We need to do this immediately. It's possible Harley happened across this guy, got scared and took off into the woods. Could be somewhere not too far, totally lost. Could be he ran into the poacher, maybe he's lying around injured somewhere."

"Or worse."

"Yeah. That too."

Chapter Sixteen

Eureka, California

"Ah, hell," Cody Wheeler said. "I went to a lot of trouble to bring him here."

Harley Thompson was now permanently out of the pot-growing business. He lay face-up on one of the twin motel beds, open eyes staring sightlessly at the ceiling. His mouth was locked open, his tongue distended.

Calhoun, face red and Stetson slightly askew, released Thompson's throat. He hiked a leg up, getting off Thompson's chest like he'd slide off a horse, and stood. He adjusted his hat, pulled his sleeveless vest back into position, then massaged his hands, cracking all ten knuckles.

"Started to cramp up a little."

"Was that really necessary?" Wheeler asked.

It took Calhoun a moment to answer, and when he did, he was looking down. "Yeah. Couldn't use a knife or gun here. Too much blood, too much clean-up."

"I don't mean strangling him, I mean killing him. You really have to? All I'm sayin', seems like a stupid move."

Calhoun raised his eyes, stared at Wheeler a moment, and reached into the pocket of his vest.

Wheeler had been sitting with his feet up on the motel desk, rocking back in the standard issue rolling desk chair. Thanks to the wheels and laminated floor, he rolled across the room instead of falling over when Calhoun hit him flush on the forehead with a sand-filled blackjack.

Wheeler came to a stop against the mirrored closet door and launched out of the chair like an attack dog. He dove full length at Calhoun, only to be dropped by a hammering chop on the back of the head.

Groggy but still game, Wheeler reached forward and hooked a forearm around Calhoun's ankle. He jerked back hard, and Calhoun went down like a felled tree, his arms windmilling for balance.

Wheeler crawled on top of the bigger man's legs and aimed a hammering fist for the groin. Calhoun roared in pain and bucked Wheeler to the side, then whipped the sandbag in a sidearm swing at Wheeler's head.

The blow caught Wheeler just above his left ear. Flashes of white and yellow light speared through his vision. He raised a protective arm in time to catch the next sandbag wallop, and felt his forearm go instantly numb. He folded both arms up, hands clasped behind his head, face on the floor.

"Okay, okay, stop!" he yelled. "Enough."

Calhoun disentangled his legs from under Wheeler, got to his feet and dropped onto the bed. His chest heaved for air. He tossed the blackjack on the bed beside him.

"What the fuck?" Wheeler moaned, feeling a knot already blooming on his forehead.

Calhoun pushed off the bed, knelt, grabbed Wheeler's hair with one calloused hand, and cranked his head up to eye level.

"Don't never do that," Calhoun growled. His face was twisted with rage, his words rained spittle into Wheeler's face. "Don't never question me. Don't never come after me. And don't never, EVER, compromise our operation again by being such a stupid fuck. You bring a civilian here, where he can see us?" He pointed at the dead man on the other bed. "Who is this guy? Is someone gonna miss him? Do you even know if you were followed here? Fuck!"

He came nearly nose to nose with Wheeler. "You put me in a very difficult position, Cody. Very fucking difficult."

He dropped Wheeler's head back to the floor and straightened.

"God damn it." He pulled a checkered handkerchief from his back pocket and wiped the back of his neck. "We don't have time for this shit. We're on the clock. Goldstein comes up here Sunday, that gives us two days left and we're still a gall short."

Wheeler hauled himself into a sitting position, leaning back against one of the beds. He gingerly felt another lump forming behind his ear. "Fuck, Mickey. That fuckin' sandbag hurts."

"We gotta get rid of this body, too. Shit." Calhoun stuffed the handkerchief back into his pocket. "I'll take care of that. You get your shit together and get out in the woods. And Cody, don't get seen again. You do, just shoot the fucker and hide the body somewhere. You bring anyone here again I'll shoot you myself."

He went to the other bed, grabbed the dead man by the legs, pulled him down to the floor, and dragged him towards the bathroom. Wheeler bent his legs out of the way as the body slid past.

"What are you gonna do with him?" Wheeler asked.

"Make him more transportable. Don't worry about it. Just go get us a fuckin' bear."

Chapter Seventeen

Koreatown, Los Angeles, California

H.H. Goldstein was looking for a way to turn the day's challenges into opportunities.

After a disastrous pitch meeting at Hulu—*Hulu*, for crissakes—to a bunch of shit-for-brains kids who looked like they should be popping zits for their prom photos, he stopped for an afternoon pick-me-up at the Insomnia Cafe on Beverly. It was a well-known hangout for screenwriters, so he was confident he wouldn't run into anyone important. He wanted to knock back a couple espressos in peace before heading over to meet with Doctor Wu.

Restored and caffeinated, Goldstein drove east on Beverly, then turned south on Normandie. Almost immediately, the shop signs and bus stop ads traded English for the Hangul alphabet of Korean.

Through a rare L.A. miracle, he found unrestricted curb space less than two blocks from Wu's nondescript building. Goldstein popped his trunk and pulled out a large cooler, closed the trunk and double-checked the Mercedes was locked. As he walked to Wu's, he could feel the neighborhood eyes on him. They weren't even trying to be subtle about it; one old gal even pulled open her window blinds to get a better look.

There were plenty of areas in the City of Angels where a big white guy could go and be a sore thumb minority. More and more every day. As a rule, Goldstein avoided those kinds of places, yet here he was. He noticed that the neighborhood smelled of cooking. Foreign, unidentifiable odors wafted from open kitchen windows. Take a walk down any residential street in Beverly Hills, he thought, and you won't smell a damn thing cooking. You also won't see anyone raise the blinds to watch you pass. You won't see any people at all, really. It was like the more palatial the home, the more upscale the neighborhood, the less actual living anyone did in it.

This street, on the other hand, throw in a few loose chickens and goats and you'd have a camera-ready Third World set. Dumpy yellow, brown or gray two-and-three-story apartment buildings, with an occasional runt of a house squashed in-between. Air conditioners notched into the walls or wedged in windows by plywood. Front yards the size of a welcome mat. Crappy sidewalk heaving unevenly from the roots of trees that had long outgrown the four-by-four patch of dirt they'd been jammed into decades before. Air jangling with the sounds of daytime TV, truck traffic down Western, a baby's squall, some woman screeching in what was either agony or Korean.

Goldstein reached Doctor Wu's door, knocked, and was let in by the squatty cinderblock-looking guy. Chong, Hong, something like that? He couldn't remember. Not that it mattered, no words were spoken. Hong—yeah, that was it—motioned him into the main room, pointed him to the goddamn pillow on the floor—there go the knees again—and faded into the darkness of the adjacent hallway.

The same silent Asian woman from last time appeared with a teapot. She poured into a cup nested in a saucer on the low-slung table before him. "Thank you," he said. She bowed and poured into another cup set on the opposite side of the table. So, once again they were going to waste time talking about a bunch of nonsense before getting down to business.

Goldstein glanced at his tea and winced. The usual yard trimmings *du jour*. At the sight, the three espresso shots roiled in his otherwise empty stomach.

"Welcome, Mr. Goldstein." Wu glided into the room and easily settled on the floor cushion. He kept his eyes on Goldstein as he raised his teacup to his lips, sipped, and placed it back on the saucer. "You appear well-caffeinated."

"Thanks, Doc." How did he do that? For his part, Goldstein could stare at Wu all day and have no idea whether he was healthy as a horse or dying of bird flu.

Wu nodded. "I see you brought a delivery."

Goldstein's eyebrows arched. Well, what do you know, looks like they were skipping the small talk today and getting straight to business. "I'm a man of my word." He lifted the cooler onto the table.

Unsummoned and without a sound, Hong reappeared. Wu continued to gaze at Goldstein as Hong removed the cooler and retreated into the shadows of what Goldstein assumed was probably a kitchen.

Wu took another sip of tea. Goldstein fidgeted in the silence. He wasn't about to drink that foul-smelling swill, and his knees were killing him. He didn't like being stared at, either. Wu didn't even appear to blink, he was like some kind of mental patient with that fucking stare. Really playing up the inscrutable Oriental angle, playing it to the hilt. Go ahead, you little shit, he thought. You're trying to intimidate a guy who's gone nose-to-nose with William Morris barracudas, professional assholes who wouldn't give a backend gross point to Jesus himself. Studio honchos who'd carve out your liver and feed it to their faggy French bulldogs before they'd cough up an above-the-line dollar. Your little inscrutable starefest act doesn't make a dent.

After several moments, Wu shifted his gaze. Goldstein turned and saw Hong step into the room. He carried a baggie filled with something brown, wet and shapeless, and handed it to Wu. Goldstein recognized it as one of the gallbladders he'd just delivered.

Wu opened the baggie, brought it to his nose, closed his eyes, and inhaled deeply. Held his breath, exhaled, then inhaled again.

He opened his eyes, nodded, and handed the baggie to Hong.

"All is well," Wu said.

Goldstein turned back to the table. "Of course. Where I'm from, a deal's a deal, Doctor Wu. When I say I'll deliver, I deliver."

"I appreciate that."

"Which brings me to the next stage of our relationship."

"Oh?"

"Yeah. What would you say if I could bring you a lot more of those bladders?"

Wu paused a moment before answering. "How many is a lot?"

"Twenty."

This time Wu was silent for several moments before he spoke. "Twenty."

"At fifteen grand apiece. And I'll throw in the paws."

Wu sipped at his tea, then dabbed his lips with a napkin. "The price is unacceptable. And the volume is risky."

"Not for you." Goldstein ticked off his points on his fingers. "I've got the harvesting team. I'm handling transport. I'm assuming all the production risk. All you have to do is sell or ship, whichever works. And you know you can get sixty K apiece."

Wu said nothing. Inwardly, Goldstein smiled. Elementary Negotiating 101. Thinking silence would make him uncomfortable and start giving back. This guy is so far out of his league he doesn't even know what game he's playing. Time to pile on.

"And because of that, this time I want an advance. I've got expenses to cover, contractors that need good faith money, etcetera."

Less than an hour later, Goldstein walked down the odiferous little street to his car. In his cooler were two banded stacks of bills. One stack was payment for the delivered bladders. The other, a fifty-thousand-dollar advance against the agreed-upon three-hundred-thousand-dollar fee to deliver twenty more bladders.

All in all, a good day. Goldstein felt that warm rush that always came from a deal well-made, a deal where he got everything he'd come for. Where cards were laid on the table, money paid, and the other guy doesn't know there's still a card or two tucked away.

* * *

Inside Doctor Wu's apartment, the silent woman closed the door behind Goldstein and moved to clear the teacups. Doctor Wu's gaze never left the closed door.

"Hong."

Without a sound, the man appeared at his side. Wu addressed him in Korean.

"Mr. Goldstein strikes me as a greedy man. Please monitor our investment."

Hong made no reply, other than to bow and leave the room.

Chapter Eighteen

Arcata, California

By the time Goldstein landed at the California Redwood Coast-Humboldt County Airport—a name bigger than the airport itself—he was hungry, annoyed, and had to piss like Secretariat. His head glistened with sweat, his shirt was a wet sucking leech on his back, his balls stubbornly bat-winged to his thighs.

Once he relieved himself and grabbed his garment bag off the carousel, his mood wasn't helped by the fact that Calhoun was late. Again. How was that even possible? Not like there was any traffic up here in Sherwood Fucking Forest. Twenty minutes gone, and still no sign of the goddamn cowboy. He stood at the curb, alone except for two other passengers awaiting rides and some homeless guy passed out on the only bench.

It reminded Goldstein that tardiness was Calhoun's worst flaw back in the day. Well, maybe not the absolute worst. There was also the violent sociopath flaw.

Still, he was always late. Rarely with any consequence, because few had the nerve to say much to Calhoun. He'd look at you with those slate-gray, soulless eyes, and goddamn if you didn't feel your sphincter twitch.

Finally, Goldstein spotted the raised black F250 as it swung into the passenger pick-up and drop-off loop. "About fucking time," he muttered. For some asinine reason he raised his hand, as though Calhoun would have trouble picking him out of the teeming throng.

The truck rumbled to a stop. Goldstein opened the door, tossed his carry-on on the seat. "Gee Mickey, glad you could make it," he said. He laid his garment bag carefully in the bed of the truck, and said, "Hope this doesn't blow out."

"Get in the truck."

* * *

The restored Victorian bed-and-breakfast towered four stories over the square-mile Old Town of Eureka, offering a striking view of Humboldt Bay. It stood as the centerpiece among other Victorians along the boardwalk, each painted in a dissonant yet somehow pleasing mix of quiet pastels and loud, vibrant hues.

Inside the top floor suite, Goldstein flopped onto a tufted velvet sofa, exhausted from the long climb up the narrow staircase. "You'd think when they renovate these things they'd put in a fucking elevator," he said.

Across from him, Calhoun sat in what Goldstein recognized as an elaborately carved Queen Ann. Long legs crossed, Levis riding up his boots, ever-present black Stetson low on his forehead. Couldn't be more incongruous, Goldstein thought. Not to mention what appeared to be a genuine marble-top Eastlake side table, upon which Calhoun had set a sweaty can of Coors.

Goldstein turned to his left. "You must be Mr. Wheeler."

"Yup," Wheeler said.

"Man of few words, I like that. Pleased to meet you."

Goldstein hadn't met Wheeler on his previous trips up to Eureka and looked him over. Medium height, slim build. Lank, dirty blonde hair that scraped the shoulders, inefficiently corralled by a dirt-colored ball cap worn backwards. His face looked swollen on one side, with some purpling under both eyes. Probably been in a fight over some three-hundred-pound bar fly with bleach-scorched hair, dark roots and a litter of snot-nosed kids.It struck Goldstein that Wheeler would be perfectly cast as a no-shirt-wearing, Budweiser-swigging, NASCAR-watching piece of unemployed trailer trash. He seemed boneless and vulgar, slouched in a beautifully refinished Heywood Wakefield. One booted foot rested on a cooler.

"You got any cold ones left in there?" Goldstein asked.

Wheeler hiked his foot off the cooler, reached in, grabbed a can and tossed it to Goldstein.

"Wow. You guys sure know how to live," Goldstein said. Coors. Christ. Still, it was cold, and Goldstein chugged half of it. "Ah," he said. "A rare treat."

He set the can down on the Venice Traditional coffee table in front of him—on second thought, looked like it might be a replica—and rubbed his hands together. "All right, then. Down to business."

He leaned forward. "Gentlemen. I know your time is valuable and so is mine, so I'll cut right to the chase. I'm here for two reasons. First, of course, I'm taking delivery of our current order. Reason two: we've got a fresh order."

"Reason three: payment for the current order," Calhoun drawled.

The guy sure knew how to blow a nice build-up. "Okay, okay, fine. We'll do that first." Goldstein rose, went to the garment bag he'd laid over the dining table, and extracted an envelope. He waved it in front of his face. "Full payment. And I assume you fulfilled the full order?"

Wheeler kicked the cooler. It slid across the polished hardwood floor and came to rest in front of the sofa.

"Ah. In with the beer. You boys ooze class. And the paws?"

Calhoun nodded towards another couple of large coolers stacked in a corner.

"All right, good." Goldstein dropped the envelope in Calhoun's lap, and walked back to the sofa.

Wheeler turned to Calhoun. "You gonna count it?"

"Fuckin' A," Calhoun said. He ripped open the envelope and fanned the sheaf of bills on the side table.

Goldstein opened the cooler and looked inside. He pushed a couple of beer cans aside, lifted a zip-lock baggie and eyeballed the flaccid lump of washed-out flesh inside. "Excellent." He dropped the baggie back into the cooler, slid the lid shut, and turned to his guests.

"So. Moving right along. I've got another order. Substantially larger."

No one spoke for a moment.

"We been pushing real hard lately," Calhoun said. "Mistakes get made that way." He didn't mention the arrow he'd recently lost on an errant shot. He'd never found the wounded bear, and could only hope no one else had either. And of course, neither he nor Wheeler mentioned the deceased pot farmer.

"Totally understand, you've both been doing yeoman's work, don't think for a moment I don't appreciate it. But now it's time to step it up, Mickey. This is what I was talking about, this is where we take control. We pull this off, I don't have to sell to that weird little Chinese prick middleman, I go straight overseas myself. In fact…" He settled back. Timing is everything when delivering a punchline. "I've already made contact and promised a delivery."

Neither of the other two men reacted, not even a bit.

"Tough crowd," Goldstein said. "Maybe you don't get it. This means more margin. Way more margin."

"More what?" asked Wheeler.

"He means we'll get paid more," Calhoun said. "Least, that's what he better mean."

"Of course, that's what I mean." Goldstein said.

"I like that," Wheeler said. "What do we have to do?"

"I'm glad you asked. I hope you boys are as excited about this as I am. We've got an order for—get this—twenty bladders."

Once again, the room went silent. It was Wheeler who spoke first.

"That's a tall order."

Goldstein turned to Calhoun. "Is it?"

Calhoun looked at Wheeler, then turned to Goldstein. "You ever hunted bears?"

"No. I produce movies. Why the fuck would I hunt bears?"

"Well, they don't show up just because you yell 'action.' It's a process."

"A process?" Goldstein threw up his hands. "There's what, thousands of fucking bears in those woods? You can't get a lousy twenty?" He turned to Wheeler. "You're supposed to be some bigshot hunter, why can't we get twenty?"

Wheeler shrugged. "I didn't say we couldn't. Didn't say we could, either. That's a lot of bears. How much time?"

Goldstein said, "Four weeks."

Wheeler laughed. "Four weeks?"

"No fucking way," Calhoun said.

Goldstein looked at both of them. "Really?"

Calhoun finished counting the money and handed a share over to Wheeler. "Really. That's too many bears, too little time."

"Fuck!" Goldstein spat. "I've made a commitment."

"You'd best unmake it," Calhoun said.

"God damn it." Goldstein thought a moment. It was clear there was no point in arguing. He took a breath. Deal-saving time. "Okay. All right. How soon *could* you get twenty?"

All eyes went to Wheeler.

"I been doin' two bears a week, on average" Wheeler finally said. "Mickey, he's maybe a bear every week-and-a-half at best." Calhoun shot him a look, and Wheeler shrugged.

"Okay," Goldstein said. "I guess it's harder than I figured." He thought a moment. "Three a week, give or take. I might be able to work with that. So, you're saying you need six, seven weeks."

"At best," Wheeler said. "We'd need a lot of luck."

"Make it ten," Calhoun said. "Shit can go wrong."

"Like I say, we'd need luck," Wheeler said.

Goldstein sighed. "All right, I get it, I get it, you need luck. Okay. Ten weeks. I think I can buy us that much time."

"Maybe buy more." Calhoun tipped his hat down an inch. "I don't bet on luck."

"I'll see what I can do," Goldstein said.

"So, what about that margin?" Calhoun said.

Goldstein looked at Calhoun, then said, "All right, how's this? To reinforce the sense of urgency in meeting this deadline, and to demonstrate my profit-sharing intentions, this time I'll pay one thousand dollars per bear."

An applause line if ever there was one. He paused but got nothing. Christ, the two of these guys, you couldn't force an expression with a crowbar.

"Thousand'll do," Calhoun said at last.

"I should hope so. That squeezes me, but if all goes well, I'll make it up down the line. So that's it then. I'll buy us more time. You gentlemen go back into the wilderness and do-do that voodoo that you do so well. I'll come back to this heinous village in ten weeks to collect the goods and deliver your payment."

Goldstein slapped both hands on his knees and stood. "And that concludes our business today, gentlemen. I'm afraid I must now ask you to excuse yourselves, as I have other urgent matters to attend to." Like getting drunk, jerking off, and hopefully grabbing some sleep before renting a car for the long drive back to civilization. One of the unfortunate inconveniences of this business; you can't fly with ice chests full of bear gallbladders and paws. Not even on Southwest.

Chapter Nineteen

February 6, 1885

Eureka, California

Night of "The Eureka Solution"

Fifty-six-year-old Eureka City Councilman David Kendall finished dinner at his favorite restaurant and started the short walk back to his downtown home. As he passed the few blocks that made up Eureka's Chinatown, he heard the unmistakable, and not uncommon, sound of gunshots.

According to the next day's Daily Humboldt Standard, Kendall "went to investigate," whereupon he was struck by a single bullet. He was carried home by a friend, and promptly expired.

In response, as many as six hundred men immediately filled downtown's Centennial Hall, with tempers running white hot. The good citizens of Eureka had long seethed over the invasion of "coolies," the Chinese immigrants willing to tackle hellish work for obscenely low wages. The local newspaper kept the flames well fanned:

"We have anxiously watched hordes of Mongolian paupers flooding our shores; we have seen our civilization almost subverted and our children driven from all avenues of honorable labor by aliens foreign to our tongue, religion, customs, and social relations...Such a race of people can only prove a detriment in any

community that lays claim to civilization, progress and truth. Age only seems to steep them deeper in their degraded filthy mode of life."

The killing of a white man was either the final trigger or the long-awaited excuse. The mob's first proposed resolution was to slaughter every Chinese person in the city. When that measure failed, another was brought forth: pillage Chinatown of all its property and money and drive out the inhabitants.

In the end, a team of fifteen men—without an official nod from the mayor or the police department—spent a busy night invading every domicile in Chinatown, ordering the residents to gather whatever they could carry and leave town. Gallows were hastily erected in front of City Hall, bedecked with a sign warning that any Chinaman found in Eureka after 3 P.M. on February 7th would be hanged.

The action came to be known as The Eureka Solution, and in a single day rid Humboldt County of virtually every man, woman and child of Chinese descent.

* * *

Nearly a century-and-a-half later, Hong was acutely aware of being the only Asian he'd seen since arriving in Eureka.

It didn't make him uncomfortable. It was just an observation. He had traveled extensively as Doctor Wu's right-hand man and trusted enforcer. Eureka was, it appeared, just another of the many breeding grounds for overweight, pasty white Americans.

Which made his task more challenging than usual, to be sure. However, one of Hong's many talents was his ability to blend into the background, to become a shadow. Unnoticed. The fortunate person never knew he'd been around. If someone became aware of Hong, it was because Hong wanted it that way. Or because he was about to relieve that person of all awareness, forever.

Upon his arrival a day earlier, he'd noticed the high concentration of homeless trash scattered like organic litter along the bay boardwalk and alleys of Old Town. As in every city around the world, these were the invisible people.

Hong's plan was straightforward. It had been his experience that this kind of human waste was generally limp and rotted from drugs and alcohol, and incapable of much resistance. Especially when faced with someone like him.

That first day he walked the waterfront until he found one of those lost souls lying on the pavement, backed against a chain-link fence that surrounded a sewage pumping station. The man huddled inside a foul, tattered military camo jacket wrapped over several layers of rancid shirts and sweaters. His pants were the color of diarrhea and stank of molding sweat and urine. He feebly raised his head, held out a hand and muttered incoherently as Hong approached.

Hong checked the surroundings, then reached down for the man's hand.

Moments later, he returned to his rental car, his newly acquired and rankly offensive disguise bundled under his arm.

Today he'd put his ruse to the test at the airport, when Goldstein's flight arrived. Mired in filth and stretched still as a tombstone on a bench, Hong had watched as Goldstein waited at curbside. The man lacked patience. He had none of what Hong called, "Inner quiet." The great Doctor Wu had spotted it instantly, although he had tactfully directed his comments towards Goldstein's more overt flaws.

Hong was still on the bench as Goldstein got into a truck that came to meet him. Hong observed the driver, heard the verbal exchange. Although he seldom spoke, Hong's English was impeccable.

Once the truck rolled off, Hong followed in his rental car. When they stopped in front of a large Victorian in Old Town Eureka, he pulled into an alley behind an abandoned movie theatre.

On the streets he again assumed his role. He muttered unintelligibly as he lurched along the sidewalks, seemingly at random, yet always keeping the front door of the Victorian in view.

He didn't have long to wait. He'd only been walking for about a half hour when two men emerged. The man with the cowboy hat who had met Goldstein at the airport. With him, a lean, lanky man with shoulder-length dirty blonde hair who moved like an athlete.

Hong continued to watch as the cowboy pulled away in a black truck, while the thin man in the baseball hat left in an ancient Toyota Land Cruiser. Which left Goldstein still in the Victorian. Likely, then, that Goldstein had flown here to receive a previous order, and to deliver the new, much larger order he'd promised Doctor Wu. The two men were likely the bear hunters.

Hong staggered and babbled his way back to his car, occasionally gesturing and shouting at passing drivers as he'd seen the street trash do. When he reached the alley, he ducked into his car. A pack of moistened towelettes served to clean his face. A quick, few swipes with a comb put his hair back in order. The stained, stench-drenched jacket was tossed out the window.

Pulling away, he touched the speed-dial on his cell phone for Doctor Wu. Time to report in, and receive further instructions.

Chapter Twenty

Orick, California

S oggy, bedraggled weeds fought for life in the rutted field that passed for the parking lot shared by the Orick Ranger Station and the Tall Tree Tavern. A light rain fell in the early morning gloom, largely ignored by the eclectic band of twenty-seven search party volunteers who warmed themselves with steaming cups of free coffee, courtesy of Tall Tree.

Shepherd emerged from the station and walked towards the group. It was a good turnout, with a lot of familiar faces. She headed towards a barrel of a man stooped with age but still nearly six feet tall.

"Hey, Beaver, mind if I get up in your truck?"

"All yours." Beaver Tollson was a retired logger and Orick's mayor—an honorary title bestowed at an annual beerfest, typically to the last one standing. He pushed a steaming coffee mug into a massive tangle of white beard, presumably towards a mouth somewhere within.

Next to Beaver stood chainsaw artists and renowned Saturday night bar brawlers Dave Jeffries and Frank Mazzeo, two leviathans with beards like bramble thickets and arms as thick and knotted as the redwood burls they carved for a living.

Amy Manning, husky bartender and owner of Tall Tree, had provided the free coffee and then shut the doors to the usual morning drinkers in order to join the search. With nothing to do until the bar reopened, a couple of them joined the search party as well. They stood together, chain-smoking and looking like someone ran over their dog.

Wild Bill and his wife Alice stood quietly by their truck. Bill occasionally turned to his side to hawk a muddy stream of tobacco over his shoulder. More refined, Alice spat into an empty pop bottle.

The rest of the group was a mix of locals and a few faces Shepherd didn't recognize. Alton Ruff's wheelchair kicked up wet gravel as he rolled among them all, handing out fliers bearing Harley's photo.

Tanner warmed his hands on a go-cup of coffee as Shepherd climbed up on the tailgate of Beaver's truck.

"Quite an assortment," he said.

"They're good folk."

"Could be rough going out there, with the rain and all."

Shepherd nodded. "Folks out here live hard. They can handle it."

She looked up and yelled over the general hubbub. "Thanks for coming, everyone." The crowd settled, and she dialed down the volume. "Thanks very much. And before I start, everyone give a shout out to Amy for the hot coffee. Thanks, Amy."

Hoots and whistles, as Amy took a bow.

"Okay. Here's the deal. What we know at this point is that Harley Thompson, a resident of Arcata, may be out in the woods and need our help." She held up one of the fliers Alton had been distributing. "You should have one of these. If you didn't get one, be sure to pick one up. General description, clothes he may have been wearing, and so on. Harley's last known whereabouts was out near Knobbler's Creek and the old Weyerhauser East Road, so that's where we'll be heading today."

Some groans from the group, and big Frank Mazzeo spoke up.

"Well hell, Shep. That's a long way out. What's he doin' out there, growing?"

"Yes," Shepherd said, with a quick glance at Alton. "He has a grow site."

"Out there? That ain't too bright," Frank said. The crowd murmured agreement.

Shepherd snapped another look at Alton, but the big man stayed calm. "Okay, listen everyone, we're wasting time. A man may be lost in our forest, and it's up to us to find him. We've got plenty of vehicles to get everyone there. My vehicle will hold six, maybe one or two more if we get friendly, and I'm hoping all of you who brought your trucks can pitch in, take a few people…" She trailed off.

"Don't suppose there's any chance the Ranger wants to ride with me," said Big Davey Jeffries through a lower lip distended with chew.

"Thanks, Davey, but I'll drive my own vehicle," Shepherd said, as the crowd laughed.

Shepherd waved them quiet. "Okay, now, most of you have done this before. We'll all head out together, and once we're there, we'll form a line. I'll hand out marker flags, and we'll start a sweep. We'll stay in line, and anything you see out of the ordinary, anything at all, you sing out, the line stops, and you plant a flag. You don't touch it, you don't pick it up and yell for me to come see it, you don't stick it in your pocket, you don't even take a picture of it. Just sing out and plant your flag. No touching in any way."

"So, lemme get this straight. We don't touch it?" That was Big Davey again.

"Keep your day job, Davey," Shepherd said. The crowd laughed, and she pointed to Tanner.

"Like you all to meet Nick Capretta, he's a writer doing research on law enforcement in our National Parks. He's volunteered to help out, and he'll follow behind, taking photos to document each of the flagged areas."

Tanner took a small step forward and gave the crowd a short wave.

Shepherd held up both hands, as though catching the falling water. "This drizzle is supposed to keep up all day. Some of you are already wearing your rain gear, I assume you others brought some, you'll need it. But rain's better than fog, at least we'll be able to see each other and stay in line. Any questions?"

One of the Tall Tree morning regulars raised his hand. "Yeah. Hey Amy, you gonna open up when we get back?"

* * *

Tanner found himself impressed by the search party, once they actually got down to it. They'd come off as a ragtag assortment at the kick-off, but out here they settled into a slow, serious, effective rhythm. They were clearly comfortable in the woods.

He and Shepherd had decided to start the search a full two hundred yards east of the logging road, which put the group right on the Yurok reservation border. They formed a single line, no more than six feet between them, and began a deliberate sweep.

Shepherd walked in front of the line, keeping them in order, a whistle on a lanyard around her neck. Whenever someone spotted something they wanted to mark, they yelled, "Stop!" Shepherd would give a blast with the whistle, and the line would shuffle to a stop. The person would stick a marker flag into the ground, and yell "Okay!" Shepherd would respond with two blasts, and the line would move forward. Slow, methodical, and to Tanner's eye, pretty damn well done.

Tanner trailed the line, stopping to inspect the flagged spots. He catalogued each with a photo. Some he snapped a shot and moved on; others he studied at length. Nothing seemed especially significant.

The search party trudged on, leaving the logging road, moving alongside Knobbler's Creek, past the bear bait site. The rain picked up in intensity about an hour in, turning the march into more of a slog, but no one complained.

It was Beaver Tollson who found it.

"Stop!" he shouted. Shepherd's whistle blasted, and the line came to a halt. After carefully placing the flag, Beaver yelled back to Tanner. "It's real hard to see, so look careful!" He turned back. "Okay, done!" Two blasts from the whistle, and the march resumed.

Tanner knelt next to the flag. Water dripped from the hood of his slicker as he studied the ground. A round stick protruded a few inches above the ground. The end was a straight, flat cut. Too perfect to be a random stick. Definitely manmade.

He snapped a photo with his phone, then removed a clear plastic evidence bag from his pocket. He unfolded his utility tool and excavated around the stick, digging down a surprising distance in the loamy earth. He had a good idea what he'd find, and sure enough, about six inches deep, his tool hit steel.

* * *

The group continued on, scouring the grounds leading to Harley Thompson's farm, setting numerous flags on their way to and within his camp. They finally came to a stop after covering another two hundred yards from the southern end of the logging road back to their starting point. In effect they had covered an area over eight acres in the shape of a rectangle.

Tanner caught up with Shepherd. "They did well."

"But no Harley. I don't know if that's a good thing or a bad thing. They find anything worthwhile, you think?"

"Absolutely. I've got an arrowhead. It was buried in the dirt, like a shot gone bad. But just in case, I'll run it for DNA."

"Can't imagine there's anything on it if it was buried."

"It's a longshot."

"Better than nothing, I guess." They walked for a few moments in silence before Shepherd spoke again.

"Think Harley's alive?"

Tanner took a moment before answering. "I think it depends on what he saw, or who saw him."

"Well. At least we didn't find a body."

Chapter Twenty-One

Orick, California

Shepherd was the most frightening goddamn driver Tanner had ever seen.

At least one hand, and often both, stayed busy doing everything but driving. Lip gloss. Radio station scanning. Heater on, off, on again, temperature adjustment. Check the phone. Fuck around with the rear view. More lip gloss. Rummage around in a purse the size of a saddlebag, somehow extract a pack of Lifesavers, gobble them like candy.

"You want me to drive?" he asked.

She looked at him. "No. Why?"

"You don't seem very interested."

"In what?"

"Steering."

She tweaked the heater vent a bit to the right. "We'll get there, don't worry."

He grabbed the Oh Shit handle above his head as they slid through a turn on the dirt road. "Oh, don't get me wrong. I relish life on the edge, squeezing the juice from every moment. It's exhilarating."

"Funny."

"As the great Joe Lewis said, 'You only live once, but if you do it right, once is enough.'"

She didn't even reward that with a look.

Tanner decided the least stressful course of action was to stare out the side window. Maybe if you don't see it coming, it doesn't hurt as much. He watched the hypnotic succession of virtually identical trees flash by through the rain-streaked window and thought about what they had so far.

There wasn't much. At this point, he had two arrowheads. The one from the wounded bear was a Muzzy expandable broadhead. The one he'd dug out of the dirt today was a Wasp Drone, also a broadhead, but a fixed blade.

"Two different arrowheads," he said aloud without realizing it.

"What are you thinking? Two different poachers?" Shepherd looked at him.

"Hey, watch the road, will you?"

Shepherd turned back. "Well?"

"Yeah, that's what I'm thinking."

"So, two guys to catch."

Tanner nodded. "That's just the start. These shooters, typically they're strictly small-time. They sell the bladders for peanuts to someone with resources, who can ship overseas."

"The money man."

"Right. And it can get more complicated, with a middleman in-between. Takes delivery, marks the bladders up and gets them to the shipper."

"Your basic business model."

"Exactly. Drugs, guns, wildlife, it's all the same."

"So. Start with the shooters?"

"Usually the easiest way," Tanner said. "Low men on the totem pole, no reason for loyalty if they get caught. Make the least money, take the most risk."

In Tanner's experience, the grunts doing the actual acquisition of goods—be it poison arrow frogs in the Amazon, rhino horns in Africa, tiger cubs in Indonesia, or bear gallbladders in the U.S.—were men (yes, nearly always men) with few opportunities. Dirt poor, uneducated, with a global view that extended only as far as they could see. Any twinges of conscience they might have were subsumed by the opportunity to make money.

Generally, the easiest to catch, but their capture alone accomplished little.

Never a shortage of hungry, greedy, desperate, or outright criminal recruits ready to take their place.

The key was to stop the flow of goods at the highest level possible. That would be the distributor. The final stop before the tiger cub was shipped to a Texas billionaire; the rhino horn to a Vietnamese artist; the poison arrow frog to a Silicon Valley millennial; the bear gallbladder to a family doctor in Seoul.

In many cases this kind of investigation involved months, even years of covert and undercover operations, with the participation of agencies that might include Homeland Security, U.S. Customs and Border Security, the F.B.I., and multiple local entities. Busting the elephant tusk smugglers had been a six-month operation. This bear thing smelled like it could be a long, winding trail to China or Korea.

A lot of bears would die in the meantime.

So. Priority One: shut down the shooters and stop the killing.

Priority Two: find the middle-man, if there was one. Then, turn the whole thing over to HQ, and go after the distributor from there.

This brought Tanner back to the only real evidence he had: the arrowheads. There was an extremely slim chance there'd be something on the head of the one they'd found today, assuming it had pierced anything but dirt. But maybe. And, if the lab had come up with anything from the first arrow…

"What's next?" Shepherd said. She peeled a stick of Juicy Fruit while steering with her knees.

"Next. Well, next, I start poking around. Small town like this, somebody around here either knows the shooter, knows someone who knows the shooter, or knows someone who might be the shooter."

"Maybe I can save you some time."

"Yeah?"

"You want to find out what goes on around here, your best bet's the Tall Tree. Talk to any of the boys shooting pool, playing darts, or sitting in the back booths draining pitchers like parched camels."

Tanner nodded. "It so happens that hanging out in bars is a well-honed job skill of mine. Any night in particular?"

She smiled. "If it ends in a Y, it's a drinking night in Orick." She slid to a stop in front of the stationhouse.

"Great. I'll clean up a bit and come back tonight." He opened the door and turned back to her. "Thanks for the lift. And no offense, but I'm never riding with you again."

* * *

"Anything on the arrowhead yet boss?" Fresh from a hot shower, Tanner toweled his hair as he spoke with RAIC Steve Moore over speakerphone.

"I was just shooting you an email," Moore said.

"Let's go old school. Use the magic of telephonic voice transmission."

"Okay. We got nothing."

"Shit." Tanner hung up the wet towel.

"You couldn't have been expecting much."

"No. But worth a try."

"So how's it going there?"

"Search party came up with another arrowhead today."

"You had a search party?"

"Yeah. Guy came to the Ranger here with a missing person report."

"And you're involved with that how?"

"I don't think it's a coincidence. We found a bear bait site near the missing guy's grow site."

"Ah. So from bear gall poachers you've moved on to missing persons and, literally, to pot."

"When you were young, did someone once say you were funny?" Tanner clamped the phone to his ear with his shoulder as he pulled on underwear.

"Don't they have cops up there?"

"Barely," Tanner said.

"You put the arrowhead through?"

"Tomorrow first thing."

"I'll put in a call to hurry things along. What's the plan from here?"

CHAPTER TWENTY-ONE

"It's a work in progress."

"What a shock. Can you give me a rough idea? Something I can write up for now?"

"Well, step one involves going to a bar tonight and hanging with the locals."

There was a pause before Moore responded. "That sounds a lot like every plan you ever have."

"Hey, you don't mess with success."

Chapter Twenty-Two

Orick, California

"That fucking tree!"

Amy Manning slammed down a pitcher of Great White in front of Tanner, sloshing most of the foamy head onto the bar. "You ever wonder why this town is choking to death, that fucking tree is a great example."

Looking for an easy ice breaker that would support his cover, Tanner had asked the bartender if she knew where Hyperion was. The question seemed to have touched a nerve.

"How's that?" he said.

"We've got the world's tallest tree, right? But nobody can see it, because the Park Service won't tell where it is. Those tree-hugging assholes at the college who measured it won't tell where it is. It's in our forest, but no one can see it."

She used a worn hand towel to smear the spill along the bar. "If we could cut a trail to that tree, we'd get tourists coming to see it, pump some goddamn money into this town."

"Seems like you get plenty of tourists anyway," Tanner offered.

"Not like we could. And not the right kind."

"There's a wrong kind?"

"Damn right. Look, once upon a time you could camp anywhere, right? Now you can only camp down near the riverbed at the coast, and you ain't doing that when the water's high. Which pretty much limits us to summer campers. No RVs allowed, so right there you cut out the campers with money. Fucking granola-head backpackers don't have two nickels to rub together."

Tanner bent to his yellow pad, scribbling. Nick Capretta, crackerjack investigative journalist, on the job. "Can I quote you on that?"

"Sure. Quote me on this, too. The Park Service makes all the rules, and we got nothing to say about 'em. Their headquarters is built out of redwood, did you know that? Hell, probably some my own daddy cut back in the day. But nowadays we can't cut redwood, not here. Got fishing regulations the size of a phone book. Can't hunt at all, even with all these deer and elk. All these rules, they're killing us."

"I heard something about bear poaching going on around here."

She leaned on the bar with both hands, the towel over her shoulder. "Yeah, I heard."

He waited. And waited. "And?"

"And, I don't know a thing about it. It's a damn shame, but I'll tell you what's to blame. What's to blame is there ain't enough work up here anymore. Work that's legal, anyways. People get desperate. When it comes down to it, if they gotta take a burl or grow dope or shoot a deer out of season to put food on the table, that's what's gonna happen. And now it's bears."

She picked up the pitcher and poured, the foamy head cresting above the lip of Tanner's mug. "Speakin' of which, you gonna have something to eat?"

Tanner scanned the single page menu. "How's the chicken pot pie?"

"Award-winning."

"Sounds good."

She set down the pitcher, turned, and popped a frozen chicken pot pie into a microwave behind the bar. "You want to know what would save this town?"

"What's that?"

"If you were to do an article for your magazine that says you found Bigfoot. Biggest draw we have here. Not too many come looking for the world's biggest tree, but nut jobs from all over the world come to find Bigfoot. Every

103

time we get a sighting, it's like a blood transfusion for this town. If someone were to actually find him, we could all make a fortune."

Tanner smiled and raised his glass. "Here's to Bigfoot."

* * *

"You're a writer?"

She was stringy and tall, with black hair cropped short and wide-set brown eyes. She spoke over the jukebox—Taylor Swift wailing "Why you gotta be so mean?"—and took the stool next to him.

Tanner turned on his stool and swallowed the last of his pot pie. "I am. Nick Capretta."

She shook his hand. "I'm Lysa. I overheard you earlier, talking to Amy. I've got a slightly different, um, take on things than she does."

She had looked familiar at first glance, and now he remembered. "You were on the search this morning."

"Yes."

"Well, let me buy you a drink, Lysa. What's your pleasure?"

She pointed to the now-empty pitcher. "What's that?"

"Great White."

"Sure."

He raised the pitcher. "Another one please, Amy."

"How'd you like the chicken pot pie?" Lysa asked, eyeing the remnants in the aluminum bowl.

"What's not to like? Secret recipe, lovingly prepared by the chefs at Stouffer's, superbly reheated and served in its original container here at the Tall Tree."

She smiled. "And only seven dollars."

"That's the beauty of an expense account. I can afford the finest cuisine. So, tell me about this different take of yours, Lysa."

She started to reply but paused as Amy set a full pitcher and a glass mug in front of her. The bartender's mouth was tight, her expression empty as a shark's as she cleared the empty pitcher and Tanner's plate and moved to the far side of the bar.

Tanner turned to Lysa. "What's *that* about?"

"She and my mom aren't talking. My Mom runs the convenience store, and ever since she got her license to sell beer and wine, Amy says she's stealing business."

Tanner looked around at the tavern, which was starting to fill. "Doesn't look like she's doing too badly."

"They're all locals, pretty much the same ones every night. They show up already drunk, and here they drink just enough to stay that way. Not enough to suit Amy. She keeps hoping for more tourist business, but the truth is, the locals kind of discourage that."

"Discourage how?"

"They want the pool table for themselves, the dartboards for themselves. You know those old western movies, when the stranger walks in and everyone stops and stares? It's kind of like that here."

"I didn't feel that."

"You're here early. Wait 'til the boys roll in."

"I'll look forward to it. So back to my question: what's your different take on the Park Service?"

She leaned forward, and even in the sketchy light of the tavern Tanner could see a spark in her eyes. "Did you know," she said, her tone reverential, "that the lowest branch on a big redwood is higher than the tallest branch of almost any other tree, in any other forest, on the planet? The lowest branch. From there, you've still got another two hundred feet to reach the top."

"Wow."

"I know, right? And when you're up there, it's a whole other ecosystem. Hundreds of feet up there are pockets of fertile soil in limb crotches, with salamanders, worms, even aquatic crustaceans. Full-grown huckleberry bushes are up there. Even other trees, growing out of the soil trapped in the redwood branches. I mean, is that awesome or what?"

Tanner was fascinated. "Is this something you've seen for yourself?"

"I have. I was part of a team from the college that measured trees on some of the most remote hills and basins in the Park."

"You've been up in them?"

She nodded and took a swig of beer. "To the tippy-top. You haul yourself up and drop a four-hundred-foot line down."

"Whoa! What a trip!"

"Right? That's really the only accurate way to measure them."

"You can't shoot a measurement from the ground?"

"The canopy hides the tops of the trees. You can't see all the way up. You have to climb."

"Damn," Tanner said. "I'd like to do that one day."

Behind Lysa the door opened. Two hulking, bearded men clomped in—Tanner also remembered them from the search party. As they headed to the pool tables, the smaller one—which is to say, no bigger than a Buick—spotted Lysa at the bar. "Lysa, hey! Come sit with us."

"Looks like the boys you were talking about have arrived," Tanner said. "Either that, or a set of Paul Bunyan nestables."

"Yeah, that's them all right."

"Saw them today too."

"Yeah. They're good guys, they just get kinda feisty when they're drinking."

And chatting up one of the local girls was probably a great way to set them off, Tanner thought. "Please, don't let me keep you."

She tipped up her mug, took a long swallow. "They can wait."

The Buick stopped. "Lysa, hey? Get on over here." His buddy stood by one of the pool tables, glaring at a young man and woman playing eight ball. The couple decided their game was over.

"Lysa!" Loud enough this time for the whole place to quiet down.

She turned on her stool. "Frank, I'll be there in a minute. I'm talking to this man right now."

"Oh. Oh, well excu-u-use me," Frank said, with a sweeping bow. "You're talking to that man right now. How rude of me. Where are my manners? I'd best introduce myself."

As he lumbered over, Tanner noticed the slight weave in his step. Figured him for twenty-six or so, six-three or four, maybe two-eighty. Meaty hands, oak-limb forearms straining a rolled-up flannel overshirt. Brushpile of a beard. John Deere ballcap.

Tanner stayed on his stool, extended his hand. "Hi, I'm Nick Capretta. I was at the search this morning, I saw you there."

Frank studied him a moment. "Oh yeah. The writer." He extended his hand.

Tanner reached out his hand and stuck it in an alligator's jaw. He strained to keep the pain from his face. "I am, yes. Lysa was filling me in on the wonders of the redwoods."

"Well, ain't that special. Lysa here, she's an honest to God tree-hugger, for real. Ain't that right, girl?" He threw a big arm around Lysa, and she squirmed under the weight.

"C'mon, Frank. Go on over and shoot pool, I'll be there in a sec."

"Naw, why don't you come right now? I think mister writer has all the tree knowledge he needs for one night, right mister writer?" His bloodshot eyes drilled into Tanner's.

This had all the signs of going south. Last thing Tanner wanted. Best to switch things up. "You know anything about bear poaching in the Park, Frank?"

The jolting change of subject set the man back on his heels. Confusion clouded his eyes. "What?"

"Bear poaching. I'm sure you've heard that some bears have been killed and mutilated here in the Park in the last few weeks?"

"Yeah, I heard something about—hey. You accusing me?"

"No, no. It's part of my story. Research, y'know? I figured, you're a man of the woods, you know these parts, maybe you've come across something of interest…" He trailed off.

Frank nodded his head, looking not unlike a bear himself. "Me and the boys catch the fucker that's doing it, he'll wish he never came to our park."

"Have you seen anyone out of the ordinary, anyone around town that seemed, maybe, out of place?"

"Mister…the fuck was your name again?"

"Nick."

"Nick, I carve wood with a chainsaw for tourists. All I see every day, all day long, is out of the ordinary motherfuckers."

Tanner laughed. "Okay, well, do you know any bowhunters in the area?"

Frank's eyes narrowed. "You sure you're a writer? You sound a lot like a cop."

"Do I look like a cop?"

Frank took his arm off Lysa and came up close, his hot, beery breath singeing Tanner's nostrils. "Yeah. Sure do."

"There's a guy in your Park killing bears and butchering them, taking out their gallbladders and cutting off their paws, and leaving the corpses to rot. That pisses you off, right, Frank?"

"Fuck yeah!"

"So how can we find him?"

Frank looked down, thought a second. "Fuck if I know." He raised his head and yelled over to his friend. "Hey Davey! Get the fuck over here!" He turned back to Tanner. "Davey's got some, you know, connections out there in the Park."

"Connections?"

"He means burlers," Lysa said.

"Lysa!" Frank snapped.

"Hey, any connection that helps find the poacher, that's a big help to my story," Tanner said. "I don't care where it comes from." He watched as a behemoth who was evidently named Davey shambled over. He was an XXL version of Frank, with more beard and more hair. Tanner smiled. Maybe Bigfoot was right here under Amy's nose after all.

* * *

"Goddammit! Where'd a fuckin' writer learn to shoot like that?" Frank slammed his cue stick on the table. Tanner figured it probably registered on a seismograph somewhere.

"You boys have no respect for the intellectual nature of the game," said Beaver Tollson. Beaver had teamed himself with Tanner, declaring that brains, not brawn, led to eight-ball victory. Beaver's beard served as a catch-all for an ample and continuous spillage of the pretzels, peanuts, and popcorn that made up the Tall Tree's menu of *hors d'oeuvres*. What missed the beard found safe harbor on a formidable gut that tested a pair of red suspenders beyond any reasonable limit. "It's a game of stragedy. Gotta have steady hands and keen eyes. Ain't no game for big-ass knuckleheads like you boys. Am I right or am I right, pardner?" He slapped Tanner's shoulder with a hand forged in lead.

"Yep, all about the *stragedy*," Tanner managed.

They were shooting against Frank and Big Davey. Neither could shoot pool worth a shit, though few idiots other than Beaver would tell them. Tanner figured Beaver's age—he had to be around eighty—gave him immunity. Or maybe it was a grudging respect for his position of political power as honorary mayor.

"Gentlemen," Tanner said, lining up the nine ball. "Can you help me out? This bear story'll be huge if I can break it. Nine in the side." He ticked the cue ball a bit below center. It kissed the nine ball into the side pocket, and returned halfway back to its starting point, where it lined up nicely with the eight ball.

"Goddammit!" Frank yelled again. "We're getting' fuckin' hustled!"

"It don't take no Minnesota Fats to do that, Frank," said Beaver. "Shut up and let my boy shoot. And you," he said to Big Davey. "Help this perspiring journalist out. Don't be an asshole. Hook 'im up with Little Stevie."

"An asshole?" Big Davey reached out and put a colossal hand over the eight ball, blocking Tanner's shot. "Beaver, you're tryin' my last fuckin' nerve."

Silence. Everyone listening for the burning fuse, tense against the possible explosion.

Like all experienced fighters, Tanner could sense a flashpoint, that instant where the wrong move, word, or even tone could set things off. He could feel it in the tightening of his throat, a rising heat that radiated up from his legs. There was no upside to things going nuclear at this moment, so he kept his voice calm and low, and said, "How about this, boys. I call the bank shot. I make it, I buy the next pitcher, and you introduce me to Little Stevie."

Big Davey smiled. "And if you miss?"

"I miss, you can beat the shit out of my partner here."

"We can do that anyway."

"True, but you'd have to buy the pitcher."

After some thought, Big Davey took his hand off the ball. The whole room exhaled. "All right, deal. Call the ball."

Tanner leaned down over the table and lined up the shot. "Eight ball, two cushions, corner pocket," he said, and stabbed the cue forward.

Chapter Twenty-Three

Orick, California

The next day, Tanner went to Shepherd's office first thing in the morning. Ruby smiled as he entered.

"Mister Capretta, good morning."

"A better one for me now, seeing your lovely smile," Tanner said. "Is the boss in?"

"She is," she said, and waved towards the open office door. "Go ahead in, hon."

Shepherd gave him a nod as Tanner took a seat in a visitor's chair, but her eyes stayed focused on her computer monitor.

"Hey, Shep." He waited. "Sorry, in the middle of something?"

With obvious reluctance, Shepherd pulled away and turned to Tanner.

"No, it's okay. Just got some news, that's all."

"Good news?"

Shepherd seemed to ponder that for a moment. "Yeah. I think so. Very good, I think. So, what's up?"

"What can you tell me about a guy named Little Stevie?"

"He's a part-time maintenance guy at the Sasquatch motel. Lives in a trailer out back of their parking lot."

"I hear maybe he does more than work at the motel?"

Shepherd shrugged, leaned back in her chair. "Word is Little Stevie's one of the most prolific burlers around. I haven't caught him yet, so I can't say for sure."

"What else you know about him?"

"He's close to seventy or thereabouts. Five-three or so, wiry. A Vietnam vet, he was a tunnel rat. One of those guys that went into tunnels after the Viet Cong."

"Yow. Can't imagine a worse job."

"I know. I guess you qualify by being small enough to fit in the tunnels."

"And brave enough to do it."

"Or crazy enough. Little Stevie's probably a little of both. Anyway, that's what he did, until he lost the hearing in one ear from an explosion. He's been out here forever, had all sorts of jobs. I've talked to him a few times here and there. My impression is he's a smart guy with pretty much zero ambition. Drinks beer from sunup to sundown."

"Guy I met last night named Big Davey is gonna introduce me. He thinks Little Stevie may know something about the bear poaching."

"Dave Jeffries. He's buddies with Little Stevie. Might be a good lead." She let her gaze go back to the monitor.

Tanner watched her for a moment. "So, what's your news?"

Shepherd took a deep breath, let it out. "I got my transfer approved."

"New York?"

Shepherd nodded. "New York. Liberty Park."

"Well, I guess congratulations are in order."

She pursed her lips in thought, but didn't answer. Tanner stood. "Anything else you can tell me about this Stevie character?"

"I don't know. He doesn't talk much to me. I'm a woman, and worse, I'm the law, and he's had his run-ins with both. He's pretty much allergic to anyone with a badge. Hopefully he doesn't sniff you out."

"Sounds like it's worth talking to him."

"I'll tell you this," Shepherd said. "Stevie knows this park like it's his backyard. If anyone knows anything, he does. But be careful, Nick. Like I say, he's a lot smarter than he looks, and he's got the temper of a timber rattler."

CHAPTER TWENTY-THREE

* * *

"This thing you're writin'. You gonna use real names?"

Big Davey's eyes glimmered at Tanner out of the snarled underbrush on his face. They were inside the big man's truck, parked at one end of the Sasquatch Motel lot. In front of them was Little Stevie's trailer, squatting in the center of an empty lot.

"Depends," said Tanner. "I don't have to if you don't me want to."

"Best if you don't for me."

"No problem."

"Got an ex-wife or two might be interested in finding me."

Tanner laughed. "Been there."

He looked through the front windshield at Little Stevie's home. Mobility was clearly a long-forgotten dream for the ancient fifth wheel. Weeds sprouted through the spider webs that lined its undercarriage. Weather-cracked, under-inflated tires barely kept the trailer off the ground. Rust and time had peeled the corners into ragged edges, crumbling and decrepit.

"He lives here full-time?" Tanner asked.

"May not look like much from the outside, but inside's worse." Big Davey pushed open his door. "Let's get to it."

More out of habit than conscious thought, Tanner brushed a hand over his service Glock. Tucked into a shoulder holster, it was well-concealed by his jacket, yet easy enough to reach if he needed it. Not that he should.

Five minutes later they were seated inside the RV, on bench seats flanking a laminated table, working on sweaty cans of Old Milwaukee.

"Stuff tastes like beaver piss, but it's cheap." Little Stevie popped the top on a fresh can. He took several long swallows, his Adam's apple bouncing like a trapped yo-yo. His raised arm showed leathery skin blue with faded tattoos, stretched over corded, fibrous muscles. His hair was shoulder length, straight and greasy, a washed-out shade of red that matched his full mustache. His compact body seemed hewn of knotted rope.

Tanner poured the last half can of beer down his throat, crushed the can, and reached for another. "It'll do just fine," he said. "In lieu of genuine beaver piss." He popped a new can and took a swig, wiped his mouth with his sleeve, flicked some foam off the yellow pad in front of him. "So, Big Davey told you who I am and what I'm up to, right?"

"Said you're writing something about law enforcement in the National Parks."

"That's the general angle." Tanner raised his yellow pad for emphasis.

"And you want to know about dead bears."

Tanner looked at Davey. The big man took the cue. "I was tellin' Nick here how you know pretty much everything that's goin' on in the Park, and you might could tell him something about who's out there poachin' bears."

Little Stevie drained his beer and lit a cigarette before answering. "How many has Shepherd found so far?" he asked Tanner.

"Three. Plus, a wounded one that had to be put down."

"Well." Little Stevie blew out a lungful of smoke. "She ain't found all of 'em."

"You've seen more?"

Little Stevie nodded.

"How many?"

"You didn't ask how I come to see them."

"Doesn't matter how."

Another nod, this time at Big Davey. "Maybe he really isn't a cop."

"Someone said I was?" Tanner said.

"Not that I know of." Stevie popped another can out of its plastic collar and flipped the top. It fizzed out onto his mustache as he took a long slug. "There are others," he said.

"Why haven't you told the Ranger?"

Little Stevie's eyes narrowed to slits. "Not my job to do hers."

"Okay." Tanner said. "So, you've seen more bears. Were they—"

"Butchered. Gallbladders gone, paws amputated." Little Stevie drained the beer, squeezed the can flat, tossed it in the direction of the sink. "It's TCM."

Tanner was surprised. "You know about that?"

"Mister Capretta, I'm a part-time janitor and a full-time drunk. Maybe a couple other things. But stupid ain't one of 'em."

"Sorry, no offense meant. As you can imagine, the TCM angle adds a lot of juice to my story, makes it about a lot more than simple poaching."

Little Stevie didn't respond. Davey was silent as well.

"So if you've seen anything, or heard anything…"

It took a while for Little Stevie to respond. He filled the time by popping another Old Milwaukee but didn't immediately drink from it. He stared at the opening in the can for nearly a minute, then looked up at Tanner.

"You been asking around a bit. Down at the Tall Tree. Saw you with the Ranger at the search for the missing grower."

"I saw you too. In the parking lot. I don't think I saw you on the search though."

Little Stevie shrugged. "Didn't go. Anyone ignorant enough to grow out in that part of the Park don't deserve to be found." He took a long swig, wiped his mustache, and said, "That's cartel country. Why'd *you* go?"

"My article. Law enforcement in the National Parks includes searches for missing persons."

Little Stevie nodded, looking down at the table. "Find anything?"

Tanner paused. His first instinct was always to tell people only what they needed to know. "Hard to say. There was a lot of evidence collected, and Ranger Shepherd isn't obliged to reveal anything to me. I was just along to help."

Little Stevie looked up. "Actually, I heard *you* were the one collecting the evidence." He leaned back, and locked eyes with Tanner. "I think it's time we cut the shit."

Tanner looked at Davey, then back at Little Stevie. "Meaning what?"

"Meaning I got nothing more to say." He tipped the can up, drained it in a series of violent swallows, and set the empty on the table. He looked at Tanner with flat, empty eyes.

"Davey," he said. "This guy's a fuckin' cop."

Chapter Twenty-Four

Orick, California

"Shep, it's for you," Ruby yelled from outside Shepherd's office.

"Who is it?"

"Chief Hendrix."

Chief of Police for the Yurok tribe. Hendrix was a tribal elder Shepherd knew to be fiercely devoted to two objectives above all else: the protection of the reservation's natural environment, and the eradication of the rampant methamphetamine use within the tribe. His handful of officers shared that commitment and were known to dole out enforcement within the spirit, if not always the letter, of the law.

Shepherd heard from Hendrix only on the rare occasions when an unlucky, uninformed, or just plain foolish citizen made the mistake of committing a crime on the reservation. She picked up the phone. "Chief Hendrix."

"Hello, Ranger Shepherd. Hope you're doing well." His voice was taut, the words clipped.

"Doing okay. What can I do for you?"

"Those bears you've found? The ones butchered for parts?"

"Yeah?"

"I'm sitting here looking at your poacher."

* * *

As Shepherd drove to reservation police headquarters, she tried a few times to reach Tanner. No luck. Cell service usually worked on the main roads, so she figured her calls were going through. Frustrating, because she knew Tanner would want to question Hendrix's suspect as soon as possible, ideally before the guy lawyered up. Assuming he hadn't already.

A half-hour later she walked up to the tribal police office, a flat, featureless bungalow in Klamath. Inside was a small reception area with a single desk.

"Hi, Ranger Shepherd." At the reception desk was a moon-faced, thirty-something woman with long, razor-straight black hair and mahogany skin that glistened in the overhead florescent light.

"Hi, Janet. Got a call from the chief."

"Yep, he's expecting you." She picked up the phone, pushed a single button. "Ranger Shepherd is here." She hung up, then reached under her desk. "Go ahead, I'll buzz you through. They're in interrogation."

The door buzzed as Shepherd pushed her way through and headed down the short hallway. Outside the open door of the interrogation room stood three stony-faced Yurok officers. Their expressions didn't change when they saw Shepherd. They looked up, then back into the room.

Shepherd edged her way through them and entered. Brightly lit, walls a wan off-yellow, linoleum floors worn to an indeterminate shade. Smelled like a recently bleached locker room. Snack and soft drink machine on one side, next to a sink. Three tables, two of which were pushed against a far wall. At the remaining table sat Chief Hendrix. Across from him, a lanky man with limp, shoulder-length dishwater blonde hair slumped in a plastic chair.

The source of his apparent discomfort was plain to see. His face looked like a terrain map, mottled by angry lumps and bruises of various hues, one eye swollen shut and the other struggling to stay open. He held a bloody handkerchief to his mouth, his hands still in cuffs.

"Chief Hendrix," Shepherd said.

The Chief looked over. He was a rotund man of medium height, with the soft jowls of a bulldog.

"Enforcement Ranger Shepherd," Hendrix said. Over the course of

117

her frequent interactions with the Chief, she knew him to be a stickler for formality while on the job. "I'm glad to see you. This is Mister Cody Wheeler. Mister Wheeler, meet Park Enforcement Ranger Kathleen Shepherd." He nodded at Wheeler. "Mister Wheeler here has indicated a possible willingness to cooperate."

Shepherd grabbed a chair from one of the other tables, pulled it over next to Hendrix, and sat down. She took a moment to look Wheeler over more closely. Without ever having seen him before, she'd seen plenty like him. The northern counties were full of men like this; men who, like their fathers, had once lived proudly and well as loggers, bay men, sawmill hands. Now, they were the flotsam of shipwrecked industries, bitter, hard-drinking men with scarred fists, powder-keg frustration, and few options.

The Yurok officers had worked Wheeler over pretty well. Nothing crippling, but enough to demonstrate their displeasure. Shepherd knew better than to comment on it. "That's good," she said. "Cooperation is always appreciated."

"The officers discovered Mister Wheeler traversing reservation land, heading for the old South Bend logging road," Hendrix said, his eyes fixed on Wheeler. "In his jeep was an Igloo cooler. Inside that cooler was a bear's gallbladder."

Shepherd said nothing.

"What's more, in case there was doubt about the origin of that gall, in the back of the jeep were four black bear paws." Hendrix's delivery was sterile and factual, but Shepherd noticed his hands trembling. "It would seem a good bet that we have the man who's been poaching your bears."

Shepherd leaned both elbows on the table, her fingers meeting in a steeple in front of her chin. "You're a lucky man, Mr. Wheeler."

Wheeler pulled the bloody handkerchief away from his mouth. "Yeah?"

"You're lucky because of the excellent inter-agency relationship that Chief Hendrix has fostered between his police, our county sheriff, and of course, my office." She glanced at the glowering officers at the door. "This is their land, and they're pretty serious about protecting it."

"No shit," Wheeler said.

CHAPTER TWENTY-FOUR

Shepherd leaned back in her chair. "So, about that cooperation."

"Here's what it is, okay? I just did some time, you probably already know that. I needed the money, that's it."

Shepherd looked at Hendrix, who nodded. "We ran him. Last prior was outfitting without a license up in Montana. Did six months of a year. Before that, one A-and-B in North Carolina. Out in three months. Another in New Mexico, time served."

"You get around," Shepherd said to Wheeler.

Wheeler dabbed at his running eye.

"And get this," said Hendrix, once again looking at the man. "Back in the day Mister Wheeler here was a nationally ranked archer. Competed in the World Cup. Qualified for the Olympics, but didn't go."

"Impressive," Shepherd said. "Why didn't you go?"

"Things came up," Wheeler said, tossing the bloody rag aside. "Can we skip the small talk?"

"You want a lawyer?"

"I want to walk. I give you information, I leave town, you don't see me again."

"Not gonna happen," Shepherd said.

"You killed and butchered at least one bear on our land, sir," Hendrix added. "Nobody walks free and clear for that."

"Then why the fuck would I give you any names?"

Shepherd leaned forward again, elbows on the table. "Mister Wheeler, I need you to talk to an associate of mine. If Chief Hendrix is amenable, I'll take you back to Eureka, and book you there. If you provide meaningful, useful information, I'll do what I can with the ADA. I believe my associate will do the same, and he has more pull than I do. I can't promise more than that."

She turned to Hendrix. "Are you all right with that, Chief Hendrix?"

Hendrix sighed, looked at his men, then back at Wheeler.

"Sir, please hear this. It's your lucky day. I'm about to come to an agreement with Ranger Shepherd. But let me be clear. You are unwelcome in our nation, from now until eternity. Don't test that sentiment by returning."

Chapter Twenty-Five

Orick, California

"That true? You a cop?"

Sitting next to Tanner on the cramped bench at Little Stevie's table, Big Davey turned slightly and put a heavy right paw on Tanner's shoulder.

Tanner felt the familiar icy heat in his belly, and took a long, deliberate breath to slow his pulse. "Whatever I am, Davey, you need to remove that hand."

Beneath the bush that concealed most of Davey's face, Tanner could make out a scattershot array of Dijon-hued teeth. Could be a grin. Hard to tell. Davey said, "I bring you here, introduce you to my friend, and you're a fuckin' cop?"

Tanner took another measured breath. Calm before the storm. "Again. Second time. Please remove the hand, and we'll talk."

Now it was Little Stevie's turn to smile. He spread both arms on the back of the booth, ready to enjoy the show to come.

Davey's right hand tightened like a pipe wrench on Tanner's shoulder. He shifted to slide his vastly superior weight against Tanner, intending to pin him against the wall. Tanner figured the next move would be for Davey to bring his other hand around and start pounding him into hamburger.

Sure enough, the big man's left arm raised, but it didn't get far. Tanner's right hand was a blur as he swept up Stevie's open beer can and smashed it bottom first on the bridge of Davey's nose. The can and Davey's nose exploded in a kaleidoscope of scarlet foam. A heartbeat later, with Davey's grip loosened, Tanner's left hand shot up, grabbed a fistful of wet beard, and jerked downward, slamming Davey's already damaged nose onto the tabletop, followed by his forehead. Tanner threw the crushed can across the table at Little Stevie, then hammered the bottom of his fist into the back of Davey's neck, aiming at the point where the head meets the neck. It was a solid strike. He did it again. Safety first.

The big man flung out an arm, a reflexive, unconscious swat. Tanner put his shoulder down to push Davey out of the booth, but Little Stevie cut that effort short by lashing out under the table, his steel-toed boot connecting painfully with Tanner's shin.

Tanner reached over the table and fired a backfist, but even after countless beers Little Stevie somehow ducked back and avoided contact. His reactions were just as good when he found himself facing Tanner's Glock. He froze.

Then he smiled.

"So, I was right. You're a cop."

"Maybe I'm a well-armed writer."

"Yeah. A writer who moves like a fuckin' snake and fucked up a guy who doesn't make a habit of getting fucked up." He looked at Big Davey, face-planted onto the table. "He wakes up, he's gonna be all kinds of pissed off."

"I know. And I don't want to hit him anymore. And even though you damn near fractured my leg, I don't want to shoot you. So how about we all calm the fuck down, kiss and make up, and I'll be straight with both of you."

Little Stevie sat back, his hands down in his lap. "Be straight all you want, I don't talk to cops."

"Yeah. Most of the time, I don't either. Generally speaking, I don't find them a likeable bunch."

"So why should I talk to you?"

"Well, I *am* the guy with the gun."

"That kinda makes me even less chatty. And you still haven't said who you are. You're not County, I know all those assholes."

121

"Right now, I'm a guy sitting next to a fucking mastodon who's about to wake up with a ginormous headache, a broken nose, and a serious hard-on for the guy who did that to him."

"Yeah, no doubt. But like you say, you're the guy with the gun."

"Okay," Tanner said. He eased the hammer closed and tucked the weapon back into his holster. Stevie watched with interest, then used one hand to disentangle another Old Milwaukee from its plastic collar.

"You help me move Baby Huey here so I can get out from behind this table, I'll fill the both of you in," Tanner said. "Hear me out, you can help or not, up to you. No cops."

Little Stevie popped the beer can top, dumped a little more of the pride of Pabst Brewing down his gullet, and slid out of the booth. As he did, he tucked a Smith & Wesson .38 revolver back into his jeans.

Which was when Tanner realized how close he'd come to having his balls shot off.

* * *

The three of them sat in plastic chairs outside the trailer, a large cooler in front of them that served double duty as a footrest during the brief intervals it wasn't being accessed.

Big Davey held a bag of ice on his face, lifting it regularly to sip a beer. Little Stevie, seemingly unaffected by what Tanner figured was close to half a case of beer by now, reached forward, pulled two cans out of the cooler, handed yet another one to Tanner, and slumped back in his chair.

"All right, Mister Capretta. Now that we're all sitting around like old drinkin' buddies, why don't we dispense with the bullshit and you tell us your real name," Little Stevie said.

Tanner drained what was left of one beer, then popped the top on the fresh one. The post-adrenaline rush jitters had him feeling light-headed. Or maybe it was the beer. "All right, let's do that. My name is Nick Tanner. I'm a U.S. Fish and Wildlife Services Special Agent. I'm here to catch whoever is poaching bears in Redwoods for gallbladders."

Little Stevie considered that for a moment. "Why the fuck didn't you say so right from the start?"

Tanner shrugged. "I was cleverly operating undercover."

"You need to work on that."

"Hell, *I* thought he was a writer." Big Davey picked out a piece of shattered tooth and tossed it in the dirt. "So'd Frank and them."

"See?" Tanner said.

"No offense to the big dog or any of the others, but that's a pretty fuckin' low bar, Mister Tanner," Little Stevie said.

Big Davey nodded. "He ain't wrong there."

"All right, point taken." Tanner took another swig of beer. He felt at some point the Old Milwaukee would become palatable. Despite the taste, he'd downed enough to short-circuit a consistently reliable connection between his mouth and his brain, forcing him to focus hard on an explanation.

"Look, you have to see it from my point of view. I come into town with a clean slate. I don't know anyone, so everyone starts out as a suspect. Okay, other than the Ranger. I'm pretty confident she's not involved."

He stopped to emit a throat-rattling belch. "Other than her, the process is to rule people out, one by one, while—and here's the trick—at the same time, use the clues to relentlessly pursue and track down a suspect. So you see," he said, waving his arms, nearly losing his balance in the chair, "I come at it from both directions, under the cover of my disguise, until I finally land on the identity of the evil-doers. At which point I apprehend them. With force, ideally." He raised the can in a salute, sloshing beer on his pants. "Them's my methods, Watson."

Little Stevie nodded. "Makes sense."

"It does?"

"Yeah, it does. Suspecting everyone makes sense, because damn near everyone around here is up to something. 'Cept probably the Ranger, like you say."

"She's a hero," Big Davey said.

Tanner looked over. "A hero?"

"Ever since she shot Emil Reyes and hauled her training Ranger outta the woods." Big Davey raised his arms to demonstrate. "Crazy fucker came at them with a chainsaw. Ranger Shepherd blew his shit the fuck up, dude. I heard they needed a ShopVac to get all of him back."

"Yeah, and I heard Bigfoot ate his intestines," Little Stevie said. "Goddamn, Davey, sometimes you are so full of horseshit."

"Hey, it's what I heard," Davey said. "And she did carry that gal all the way back through the fuckin' woods." He turned to Tanner. "They had to air evac the both of them out."

"Wow," Tanner said. "The training Ranger make it?"

"She lived," Little Stevie said. He shot a silencing look at Big Davey.

Tanner was still coming to grips with this new side of Shepherd. "I didn't know all that. Didn't know she had it in her."

Little Stevie snorted. "She don't, not really. She's what you call a poor fit for this job."

"I like her," Big Davey said.

"You like anything with tits."

"So do I," Tanner said. "I mean, I like Ranger Shepherd. But let's stay on track. I just told you who I am. Either of you see any reason to tell anybody else about my secret identity?"

Little Stevie smiled just a little. "I don't see why nobody else needs to know. Davey, y'hear?"

"I don't see no reason to tell."

Tanner belched again. Incredibly, Old Milwaukee tasted even worse coming up. "Now that we're all a happy family, tell me what you know about the bear poaching."

"I know there's more than one of 'em, for starters," Little Stevie said.

Tanner nodded. "We kinda figured. Found two different broadheads. One in a bear. One in the ground."

"You found one of 'em on the search?"

"Correcto. A Wasp." Tanner tipped up his beer and was surprised to discover it was empty. He crushed the can, tossed it on the dead soldier pile, and flipped the cooler lid for another.

"Where you were searching, you know that's right next to Yurok land."

"Right." Tanner popped the tab on a fresh can. "Meaning?"

"Meaning not only next to Yurok land, but not far from the Yurok landfill," Little Stevie said. "All their trash goes there." He paused, waiting to see if Tanner caught on.

"So," Tanner said, "a dump. With lots of food waste. Like a McDonalds for bears."

"That's where I'd go."

"I found a bait site where we searched. And you're right, probably less than half-a-mile from the rez..."

"Which makes it maybe a mile or so from the dump," Little Stevie said.

"So you think they're also poaching on reservation land."

"Why not?"

"Yeah," Tanner said. "We found a different broadhead, a Muzzy, in a bear up near Klamath."

"Bowhunters don't change heads. They get one they like, they stick with it. You got at least two poachers." Little Stevie crushed his empty can flat with one hand. "I gotta take a piss." He stood and wiped his hands on his jeans. "You happen to see a big Marlboro Man motherfucker around town?"

Tanner shook his head. "No. Doesn't ring a bell. Why?"

Little Stevie headed around the side of his trailer and unzipped his pants. Tanner could hear the urine splashing to the ground as Little Stevie leaned back around the corner and said, "He don't fit in. Don't look like a tourist, don't know what he is. It was me, I'd take a hard look at him." He shook himself, zipped up, and came back to his chair.

At that instant, Tanner's phone buzzed. He worked it out of his pocket, checked the number, and answered. His tongue felt thick and heavy. "What's up, Shep?"

"Where are you?" Even through his beer-addled fog, Tanner could sense her excitement.

"I'm in the middle of an investigation," he said. He suppressed yet another belch, his stomach roiling like a Maytag.

"You sound weird."

"Must be the connection," Tanner said.

"Maybe. Well, listen, we got the shooter," Shepherd said, speaking fast. "Name's Cody Wheeler. The rez police caught him and turned him over to me. I transported him to Eureka for arraignment."

The news was a splash of cold water. "Holy shit! That's great, Shep. We gotta talk to him, get the other guy's name."

"You still think there's another?"

"Yeah. Might even have a lead." He shot Little Stevie a look and a quick nod.

"Well," Shepherd said, "Wheeler wants to deal. He's already lined up with a PD, so you can talk to him tomorrow morning."

"Tomorrow's good, yeah." Tanner tipped his beer can over, pouring the last half onto the dirt. "Listen, you know where Little Stevie's place is, right?"

"I told you, by the Sasquatch—"

"I need you to come get me."

"I can drive you somewheres," Big Davey said, and burped.

Tanner put a hand over his phone. "Thanks, Davey. I've gotta discuss the developing case with Ranger Shepherd. Law enforcement business." Back into the phone, he said, "Can you come now?"

* * *

"You have any dinner plans?" Tanner asked.

"Me?" Shepherd shot him a look as she spun gravel away from the lot outside Little Stevie's trailer. "Well, no."

"Great! How about tonight you show me the best steakhouse in these parts, and I'll buy?"

"Um, okay." She thought a moment. "We could go down to Eureka, down in Old Town. Carter's is good. Oh, but wait. It's karaoke night, I think."

"Ha, perfect! I happen to be a karaoke master."

Her eyebrows raised. "Okay."

They rode in silence for a few moments. Then Tanner asked, "So. How's that transfer progressing?"

"Oh, well...Actually, I haven't responded yet."

"Really. Second thoughts?"

"Maybe, I don't know. Just haven't responded, that's all."

"I'm telling you, within a week you'd be bored shitless. Nothing but tours, tickets for littering, answering the same asinine questions day after day. You got it made out here, you got all these oddball citizens, poachers shooting bears, missing people. Much more fun. Plus, you'd probably never get to shoot anyone out there like you did here."

Shepherd reacted like she'd been slapped. "How'd you hear about that?"

Tanner was taken aback by her vehemence. "Um, it came up somewhere. Can't remember who told me."

"It's not something I'm proud of. It was horrible. It still haunts me."

"Well, I heard some crazy fucker came at you and your partner with a chainsaw, and you put him down, then carried her out of the woods. Saved her life."

Shepherd said nothing.

"You're a hero."

"No. Truth is, if I hadn't froze, if I'd shot sooner, she'd still have her job. And her arm. I'm no hero. I froze, and it ruined her life." Her hands were tight on the wheel. "You know what she's doing now? She's not a Ranger. She's dealing blackjack one-handed down in Trinidad."

Tanner let that sit for several moments. "You dropped the perp, you carried your partner to safety, you saved her life. That's not fucking up. Not at all."

Shepherd yanked the SUV alongside Tanner's Expedition in the ranger station parking lot, lurched to a stop, and continued to look out the front windshield.

Tanner opened the door. "Sorry I brought that up."

"Never mind."

"So. How about I meet you here at seven, and we head out." He smiled. "And I'll drive."

Chapter Twenty-Six

Hollywood, California

"Hell if I know. I'm just saying I ain't heard from him since he went into the woods yesterday. He didn't come to the room last night. Maybe a fuckin' bear ate him."

"Ah, shit." Goldstein wasn't in the mood for Calhoun's smart-ass attitude. To take this call he'd excused himself from an important lunch meeting at Café Del Mar with Helen Berman, who aside from being the head of Sundial Pictures was also a thin-skinned shrew with the temperament of a Rottweiler. If she felt disrespected, Goldstein knew he might as well pitch his project to the fucking lobsters in the fish tank.

"Mickey, I'm busy here, cut the comedy. You need to find him. What if he quit, just took off or something? That's a loose end we can't afford."

"I'm not joking. Maybe a fuckin' bear ate him."

"Then find that bear, and when it takes a shit, confirm that Wheeler's in it," Goldstein hissed. "I don't have time for this. Neither do you. We've got two weeks left on the contract. I do not want to be asked to refund money I no longer have."

"And I can't deliver bear parts if I don't have someone to help me shoot the fuckin' bears."

Goldstein felt like screaming. Instead, his voice went lower. "Goddammit, I'm in the middle of something here. I have to go. Find Wheeler or figure out how to shoot the rest of the goddamn bears yourself, but get the job done! Now, goodbye, and fuck off!"

He slid the phone back into his pocket and went back to his squid salad and Helen Berman. Hard to tell which was less appetizing.

* * *

Orick, California

Perched on a stool at the Tall Tree bar, Calhoun tucked the phone back into his jeans and pulled his Stetson low over his forehead. Behind him, billiard balls clacked together, triggering raised voices as he drained the last of his beer.

"Can I get you another one, cowboy?" Amy Manning grabbed his mug and stood ready.

"I'm good." He dropped a twenty on the bar.

"Lemme get your change."

"It's all right, that's yours," he said. He leaned in. "For a little information. I'm looking for a guy named Cody Wheeler. He been in today at all?"

Amy looked at the bill, then at Calhoun's dead, black eyes. She felt something dark crawl up her back and wriggle into the base of her brain. "Well," she said, "I don't know who that is. He a friend of yours?"

Calhoun nodded. "Sure, we're old buds. Thin guy, blonde, usually wears a ballcap. We were supposed to meet here."

"What's your name, cowboy? He comes in asking about you, I'll tell him you stopped by."

He slid off the barstool. "Describe me however you like, he'll know."

"Okay. Sure," Amy said, the words trailing him as he turned away. She watched him push through the doors, then scooped the Jackson and tucked it in her pocket. For no reason she could articulate, she felt if she never saw that cowboy again, it'd be too soon.

Outside, Calhoun leaned against his truck, smoked a cigarette, and thought about his next steps. He had a bad feeling. Shouldn't have taken this last order on. Too many bears, too little time. Wheeler was doing okay, he was bringing in bladders, but he was a goddam pro. He'd gotten the lion's share of the bladders on the previous orders, and the same was holding true on this one.

But they were still short. Two weeks to go. Calhoun exhaled a cloud of smoke. No way they'd make it. Hunting bears with a bow and arrow turned out to be harder than it had looked on all the online videos Calhoun had studied before heading north.

YouTube was loaded with them. It was Calhoun's observation that one could learn virtually any skill by watching YouTube. From beekeeping to embroidery to skydiving to shooting bears, it was all there.

The various hunters on the videos evidently honed their archery skills by shooting at big targets shaped like bears. "Middle of the middle," advised one man who identified himself as a hunting guide. "Place your shot further back than when you're hunting deer. Not too high, not too low. Middle of the middle." His video culminated in a montage of a dozen or so different bears being struck by arrows, followed by proud hunters posing with the dead ursines. The standard pose was to kneel by the bear and hold its lifeless face toward the camera. Second favorite was to sit with the bear's head lolling across the lap.

Calhoun had learned his archery skills as one of the nine million stunt extras firing from the top of a castle wall on *The Queen's Revenge*. Piece of shit bows, lightweight phony arrows that morphed into computer-generated imaging as they rained down on an army of shrieking day-player extras.

On the other hand, the bow Wheeler had loaned Calhoun was a Rube Goldberg-looking contraption with a puzzling array of cams and axles and stabilizers and other shit Calhoun had already forgotten the name of. "It's a compound bow," Wheeler had said. "Weighs just four pounds, has a draw weight of sixty to seventy pounds, shoots three hundred ten FPS. You need that to take down a bear."

Like every good stuntman, Calhoun did his homework. His YouTube research on the bow included the following comment on a bowhunting website: "Use this bow with a razor sharp, bone-crushing broadhead and you'll drop any bear if you stay within an effective range. I shoot 60-65lbs and have no problems penetrating any North American game, pretty much all shots are pass-through." Calhoun had discovered plenty of similarly edifying comments in chat rooms on Field and Stream, Bowhunter, and Outdoor Life.

Aside from the shooting advice, there was also no shortage of guidance on how to properly set up a bear bait station. It all pretty much echoed what Wheeler had told him.

Put the bait in a barrel to keep it dry. Cut a small enough hole in the barrel so the bear has to work for the bait, thereby staying around longer. Chain the barrel to a tree. Use a dead beaver for bait. (That raised Calhoun's eyebrows until he read further). If you can't get one, use dog food. Candy also works well. Can't get a barrel to the site, stack logs. Anything to delay the bear.

A few clicks also brought Calhoun to sites detailing the bear's anatomy. Those he had studied assiduously, committing the location of the gallbladder to memory. He'd always been good with knives and was confident in his ability to excise the organ quickly and efficiently.

And he'd been right about that part. Once the bear was dead, the butchering was quick and easy. The hard part had been the "middle of the middle" target. He'd had more than a couple shots hit too far forward, or too high, and the bear had taken off like it had rocket fuel up its ass. He'd never mentioned any of that to Wheeler; no point.

Calhoun flicked the last of his cigarette into the mud and checked his phone. He hoped to find a message there from Wheeler. Nothing. He pulled out another cigarette and fired it up.

If Wheeler had an accident and was starving to death out in the woods, or he'd fallen out of a tree and broke both his legs, or a bear really did eat him, then there was no problem. Odds were good he'd be nothing but mulch by the time someone came across him, if ever.

But if he'd quit, or was on a bender, or worst of all, got popped by the law, well, now there's a real problem. Who knew how solid the guy would be? He'd already panicked once, when he brought the pot grower into the motel instead of just shooting him in the woods.

Calhoun drew the cigarette down to the butt, still pondering his next move as a Ford Expedition rolled past the Tall Tree.

* * *

Long before the sun goes down, the world beneath the redwoods moves in dusky shadows. It was only five-thirty, but Tanner flicked his headlights on as he pulled away from the Ranger station onto the 101. His lights flared along the parking lot of the Tall Tree, throwing a passing spotlight on a tall man in a cowboy hat, head bent, hand to his mouth. Tanner caught the brief glow of a cigarette as he accelerated out of the turn.

"Holy shit." He drove a quarter mile until a curve took him out of sight, then wrenched the vehicle through a sharp U-turn. Little Stevie's words seemed printed in the air before him: "You happen to see a big Marlboro Man motherfucker around town?"

As he approached the Tall Tree, he saw the cowboy flick his cigarette onto the parking lot dirt and turn to climb into his truck. Tanner pulled in next to him, tried to grab a glimpse of the plates without looking obvious, but couldn't see them in the fading light. He thumbed his passenger window open as he came to a stop.

"Excuse me," Tanner said. "Sir?"

The guy turned. Little Stevie had nailed the description.

Appropriately enough, Marlboro Man's voice was the growl of a three-pack a day lifer. "What?"

"I've got some information you may be interested in."

The cowboy said nothing.

Tanner leaned down, looking up through the passenger window. "You're looking for someone, right?"

"Fuck off." The cowboy reached out to pull his door shut.

"Cody Wheeler."

"Who?"

Tanner felt his heart rate quicken. "Cody Wheeler. I know where he is."

The cowboy turned and fixed Tanner with an unblinking, unnerving stare. His black, soulless eyes reminded Tanner of a job he'd worked in the Atchafalaya Swamp, busting a ring of gator poachers. At one point he'd found himself waist-deep in steaming muck, battered by mosquitoes and brain-boiling heat, when a long, black stick floated nearby. It was within two feet of him when it raised its head and pinned Tanner with a stony gaze as merciless as the point of a stiletto. It was Tanner's first face-to-face encounter with a water moccasin. He hadn't seen eyes like that since. Until now.

Neither man spoke. Nearly a minute passed. Finally, the cowboy broke his stare and looked out his front windshield.

"Get in the truck."

Chapter Twenty-Seven

South of Orick, California

The cowboy wasn't much of a conversationalist. He steered the truck onto the 101 south for a couple miles, then turned right onto an unmarked road barely wider than the vehicle. The entire time, he didn't speak a word.

The road dove deep into the Park, fading light giving way to darkness, torn asphalt giving way to rutted dirt, all within the first mile. Ten silent, spine-jarring minutes passed before the truck rolled to a stop. The cowboy clicked off the engine, reached into his jacket, pulled out a Colt Python and pointed it at Tanner.

"First, who the fuck are you?"

"Whoa!" Tanner shot both hands up, his eyes wide and focused on the .357-sized hole staring him down. "Hold on! My name's Nick Capretta. I'm a writer. All I am is a writer, I'm here doing research for a series on National Parks."

"A writer."

"Yeah."

"What do you know about Cody Wheeler?"

"Well…what do I call you?"

"Never mind. Tell me about Wheeler."

"Look, all I know so far is he got picked up."

"Go on."

"That's it. I heard he got caught on the reservation. The rez cops turned him over to Ranger Shepherd, and right now he's in a holding cell in Eureka."

The cowboy's jaw clenched. Tanner could see the muscles pulsing.

"And you're telling me this why?"

"Well, see, that's the thing. Here's what I'm thinking." Tanner sped up his delivery, let a little desperation creep in. "I mean, I can use some cash, because I've got a little, um, a little gambling issue, you know what I mean? That casino in Trinidad, I mean, I couldn't catch a card all week. So, I'm thinking, I'm pretty close with Ranger Shepherd. I'm with her pretty much every day, and I can find out what Wheeler's said, if he's talked, whatever. That'd be of interest to you, correct?"

The cowboy stared at him a moment. "What makes you think that?"

"I'm a writer. Research is my thing, it's what I do."

"And what did your research tell you? What makes you think I'd be interested in Cody Wheeler?"

Got him, Tanner thought to himself. It was one of the things he loved best about undercover, that moment when the sucker finally swallows the bait. That hot burst of adrenaline was an electric jolt, a high as addictive as any drug. Plus, if they buy your story, it greatly reduces the odds of getting killed.

"Look, can I put my hands down?"

"Never told you to put them up."

"Well, it seemed appropriate." Tanner lowered his hands and slowed his speech. "When I was with Shepherd, she said she had info that Wheeler'd been seen in Eureka with someone that exactly fits your description. I saw you when I drove by just now, so I took a shot. And, unless you brought me to this romantic location to neck, I'd say you've confirmed my guess."

Not a flicker of expression from the cowboy. Gun didn't budge, either.

"Well?" Tanner said. "Do we have a deal?"

"Tell me what you know so far, and I'll tell you if we have a deal."

Tanner looked around at the darkening woods. "If I tell you what I know, what are the chances I end up vulture food out here?"

No response.

"Exactly. So how about we put down the gun, turn this rig around, drive back to what passes for civilization around here, have a beer or two, cut a deal, I'll fill you in on what I know. Fair enough?"

Another silence, as Tanner counted his heartbeats. Finally, the cowboy slid the gun under his leg, and shifted the truck into reverse.

* * *

A curtain of darkness and sudden rain signaled the end of another Orick day. By six o'clock the Tall Tree regulars were filtering in, shedding their coats and shaking their heads like wet dogs; the new shift arriving to relieve the daytime drinkers, who were heading home to rest up for tomorrow.

Four vinyl booths lined the back wall and culminated at the restrooms. Tanner and the cowboy—who still had not given his name—sat across from each other in the last one, drinking beer from frosty mugs. A pitcher of Great White sweated through a flimsy napkin, ringing the tabletop. Across the room, pool balls clacked, each shot chased by a shout, groan or laugh. On the jukebox, Del Shannon wah-wah-wondered about his little runaway. Tanner raised a glass.

"Here's to great music, right?" Tanner said.

The cowboy took a long drink, set down the mug, and stared at Tanner.

"All right, fine," Tanner said. "We'll skip the foreplay. Here's what I'm thinking." He was improvising, the thing he liked best about undercover. It had always been this way. Pressure gave him a charge, it slowed the game down and sharpened his senses. His mind worked without thinking, his instincts took over, and the idea that any mistake could be a fatal one made the rush that much better. "You ever hear of George Plimpton?"

"What?"

"George Plimpton. The writer."

"Maybe."

"Amazing guy. He embedded himself in his stories, then wrote from that perspective. He worked out as a quarterback, I think with the Detroit Lions, even got in a game if I remember right."

CHAPTER TWENTY-SEVEN

"So?"

"So that's what I'd like to do. I'd like to embed myself in your, what shall we call it? Enterprise?"

"I don't have an enterprise. And if I did, why the fuck would I want you to have anything to do with it?"

"For the money, my friend, why else? I write the piece, it gets published, I leverage that into a book deal with a fat advance, which we split in a yet-to-be-determined fashion."

"That's a stupid fucking idea."

"It gets better. From the book, we sell the screenplay rights. Ka-ching! And let's say the movie gets made. I've got a few contacts, it could happen. If it does, well hell, now we're talking fuck-you money, my brother."

Tanner saw something in the cowboy's eyes when he mentioned the movie deal. Maybe a soft spot? He went after it.

"I mean, it's perfect for a film. There's action, there's crime, there's mysterious characters such as yourself, if you don't mind me saying so, there's the hapless ranger trying to figure out what's going on."

He'd hit on something. He didn't know what, but something.

The cowboy topped off his own glass, didn't offer to do the same for Tanner. "What exactly do you think is going on?"

Tanner made a show of looking around, then leaned way in and lowered his voice. "Come on. Cody Wheeler. You. Dead bears with gallbladders and paws gone. Missing pot farmers. I've got this figured out."

"You got nothing figured out."

"Sure I do." Tanner leaned back in the booth, let the silence sit. The next move had to come from the Marlboro Man.

It did. He drained his mug and moved out of the booth. He leaned on the table with both hands, his face inches from Tanner's.

"You were gonna tell me something about Wheeler. So, what do you know?"

"I know he's in jail."

"You already told me that."

"Right, and I can tell you more. I'm thinking you probably want to know whether he's talking, maybe striking a deal in return for naming a few names…"

"And you're gonna do that. By this embedding thing."

Tanner sat back. "Exactly."

"Uh-huh." The big man looked down at the table. Then, his hand shot out like a striking snake, snatched Tanner by the collar, and pulled him nose-to-nose.

"You know what?" he said. "I think you're full of shit. Whatever you think you know, you'd best unthink it. Whatever you're planning to write, you'd best unplan it. Your smartest move right now would be to get the fuck gone."

Tanner held his gaze, neither man blinking. "So, that would be a pass on the film deal?"

The cowboy's expression tightened. "You're a funny guy."

"And you've had onions."

Tanner never saw the big man's other hand move. Knobbed knuckles formed into a fist, the forefinger and middle finger split, and clamped Tanner's nose like a rat trap. The cowboy squeezed his fist tight as he pushed. Tanner resisted his first reaction, which was to snap the man's hand off at the wrist and bitch-slap him to death with it. Instead he leaned back, allowing his nose to be squeezed like a walnut.

"You're not that funny," the cowboy snarled.

"Nick, you okay?" Behind the cowboy, Big Davey loomed like a dark, hairy mountain.

Reluctantly, the cowboy released Tanner's nose, though he never broke eye contact. Big Davey was trailed by Frank Mazzeo, who carried a pool cue fat end up, angled against one huge shoulder like a soldier's rifle.

"You need help, Nick?" Frank growled.

"I'm good, boys, thanks," Tanner managed, massaging his nose. "Me and…" He paused, but the cowboy didn't volunteer his name. "Me and Roy Rogers here were having a friendly chat. In fact, he was telling me how he was just leaving."

The cowboy turned. The two hulking loggers made no move to clear a path.

"Get the fuck outta my way, peckerheads," he said.

Frank smiled like Christmas morning. Big Davey stroked his beard, then said, "Now, that wasn't very friendly."

"That's 'cause I ain't your fuckin' friend, asshole," the cowboy snarled as he stiff-armed Big Davey's shoulder.

"Whoops!" Frank yelled, and swung the pool cue like Barry Bonds, connecting solidly under the cowboy's right ear. Big Davey followed with a straight right to the chin that knocked the man out from under his hat and dropped him to the floor.

The two stood over the unconscious heap. In spite of the runaway undergrowth on both their faces, Tanner could see their disappointment.

"Well, hell. He wasn't no fun at all," Frank said.

"Went down like a wounded rock," Big Davey said. He turned to Tanner. "You okay, Nick?"

Big Davey put a hand the size of a shovel blade on Tanner's shoulder. His eyes communicated what he'd already shown: he would keep Tanner's secret.

"Yeah, I am. Thanks, boys. You didn't have to do that, but…well, what the hell, he's a rude son-of-a-bitch, isn't he? Maybe you taught him some manners."

He folded a napkin in his hand, reached over and grabbed Calhoun's beer mug. "I believe I'll take my leave now," he said. He slid out of the booth and stepped over the cowboy's prone body.

"What do you want us to do with this guy?" Davey asked.

"Hell, I don't know. Haul him outside and let him wake up, I guess. Assuming you haven't scrambled him up too badly, I imagine he can find his way home."

Chapter Twenty-Eight

Orick, California

Before pulling away, Tanner noticed the light still on in Shepherd's office at the Ranger headquarters. He drove across the parking lot, got out and knocked on the door.

"Still here," he said when she pulled the door open.

"Paperwork is my life. Is it already time?"

"Yes, but first I have two questions for you." He held up the glass beer mug, balancing it by the base on his palm. "Can the Eureka PD office run prints overnight?"

There was a pause before she answered. "Yes. They also have electricity and indoor toilets and everything." She stepped back into the office lobby. "Come in, don't stand there."

Tanner followed her in. "I had an interesting meeting with a particularly nasty cowboy just now. Got his prints on this mug."

"You think this guy might be one of the poachers?"

"I do."

"Cool. You said you had two questions."

"Second question: why don't you shitcan the paperwork, come with me now to Eureka, we'll drop this off, then hit that steakhouse and rock a little karaoke?"

"Time got away from me, I haven't had a chance to change or shower or anything."

"Me either." He sniffed the air. "I don't detect much of an odor. Do you?"

She smiled. "Maybe a little. But not 'til you came in."

* * *

Some might think *Gloria* is a piece of cake, but Tanner knew it required, above all else, plenty of volume. Especially when you get to the "i-i-i-i" part.

It was indeed karaoke night at The Carter House, fortuitous indeed for Tanner. Even when sober, he found the lure of the mic difficult to resist. After four shots of Cuervo Gold, he could hear his fans calling. Not, it would be fair to say, a call anyone else could hear.

Shepherd watched with something between bemusement and discomfort as her dinner date reminded absolutely nobody of the great Van Morrison. Fortunately for Tanner, The Carter House had never been mistaken for a hotbed of musical talent. Or critics, for that matter. Several tables surrounded the makeshift stage, each filled with couples and groups seemingly more drunk than the next, and Tanner's performance had them rapt and raucous. It was Shepherd's observation that whatever Tanner lacked in musical ability—and that was a lot—he made up in enthusiasm and energy. She supposed his looks didn't hurt either. There was a table of three thirty-something gals who seemed particularly appreciative.

Finally, as the signature riff mercifully brought his performance to a close, Tanner threw in some mildly obscene air guitar gyrations, inspiring coyote hoots from the pack of party girls. He bowed deeply and stepped off the stage, signaling to the waitress for another round as he arrived at his table.

"That was...unique," Shepherd said with a straight face.

"Thanks! Been a while since I did that one. Had a little trouble there in the middle, could you tell?"

"I don't think anybody noticed the difference, no."

"Good. Hey, we should do a duet!"

"Um..."

"We could do that one from *Grease*, the one Travolta and Olivia Newton-John did." He looked up as their waiter set down another round of shots.

141

"Thanks."

"I'm not much of a singer," Shepherd said.

"Ahh, doesn't matter. It's just for fun," he said. "I can carry us."

"You do this a lot, do you?"

"Karaoke? Every chance I get. It's that inner rock star bursting to get out." He slid one of the shots in front of her and raised his.

"A toast. To catching the bad guys."

She smiled in return. "Yeah, all right. I'll drink to that," she said. And did.

* * *

"What do you think about gymnastics?"

The question caught her by surprise. "What do I think about it?"

Tanner tossed down another shot, followed it with a long slug of Great White. He wiped the foam from his lips with his finger. "Yeah."

"I don't guess I think about it much at all."

"You been married? Have kids, anything like that?"

"No." She paused a moment. "I'm gay, Nick."

He looked at her, then waved a dismissive hand. "You can still raise kids, right? Still get married in this state, can't you?"

"Yes. And no, I'm not married, haven't been, don't have kids."

"Well, my advice is, don't. Or if you do, make sure they're uncoordinated dorks so they don't get invited to travel around the country doing backflips and missing school."

"I'll make a note of it. You're married?"

He shook his head. "Was. For a few years."

"What happened?"

"Not just one thing. The job's a bad fit for marriage."

Shepherd nodded. "Too much travel?"

Tanner speared her empty shot glass with his fingers, did the same to his, and held both overhead, signaling the waiter.

"Nick, I don't need another. You go ahead, but I'm driving us back."

"Oh shit, then I'll definitely need another." He set down the shot glasses

142

and took another swig of beer.

"How did you meet?" Shepherd asked.

"When I got out of the Marines."

"Hey, my dad was a Marine. Were you overseas?"

Tanner nodded. "I visited various parts of the Middle East on the government dime, yeah. Spent most of my second tour with MCMAP as an instructor."

"What's that?"

"Marine Corp Martial Arts Program."

"Instructor? So, you're a badass martial artist?"

"Damn straight. Next time I ask you how my karaoke was, I better see a little more enthusiasm."

Shepherd laughed. "You met your wife when you got out…"

"I wasn't very good at marriage," he said. "And I'm not sure I'm doing a whole lot better as a father."

"You've got kids?"

He held up his index finger. "One. Twelve years old, her name's Kiera. She lives with her mom, and soon with her new and improved step-father, Kent."

"And I take it she's good in gymnastics?"

"Very."

"So…"

"I don't think it matters. I think her having a normal childhood, doing normal kid things, matters more. Am I wrong?"

"What do you mean?"

"This travelling team that invited her. Four hours of practice after school, four days a week, competitions on the weekend. Seems ridiculous to me."

"My father wanted me to be a ballerina."

"Yeah? Did you do this crazy training, all these hours after school?"

"Nope."

"Why not?"

"Because I refused. And because I knew I wasn't really any good."

Tanner drained the last of the beer and set down the glass. "But what if she is? What if she's the next...I don't know, name a great gymnast."

Shepherd shrugged. "Nadia Comăneci?"

"There you go. What if she's the next Nadia Comăneci?"

"Well...what are the odds of that?"

Tanner slapped his hand down on the table. "Exactly! I mean, what's the end game, here? The Olympics? Really?"

Shepherd shrugged.

Tanner's voice kicked up a notch. "The odds of her, or any twelve-year-old in thousands of gyms across the country, making it to the Olympics? I mean, it's like the lottery. Out of all these girls, tens of thousands, maybe hundreds of thousands, I don't know, out of all of them, what is it? Five make the Olympics? Six?"

"It's a long-shot," Shepherd agreed.

"And think about this. Tell me, right now, who got second place in the last Olympics."

Shepherd said nothing.

"Can't do it, right? Nobody can. Because nobody cares."

"I bet it's a lot of money, too."

"It's not the money, I don't care about the money," Tanner said. He moved the empty glass back and forth over a moisture slick on the table. "I'll send the fucking money."

"What does Kiera want? Does she want to do this?"

He looked at her for a long moment. "You know what? You're right. You're absolutely right."

"I am?"

The waiter arrived with the shots. Tanner slid one over to Shepherd, but she shook her head. He nodded, then knocked one back in a single swallow.

"There's more," Tanner said, setting down the glass. "I worry about her getting hurt."

"Only natural. But any sport, that can happen. I played some softball, I broke an ankle."

"It's a little different with her." Tanner spun the empty shot glass on the table, using both hands like he was sparking a campfire. "She's a cancer survivor."

Shepherd didn't know what to say.

Tanner looked up at her. "Chemo from two years old to five. You know they give kids higher doses of all that shit than they give adults?"

"I didn't."

Tanner nodded. "They take them right to the brink of death, then medicate to bring them back. They literally change their DNA. She had no immune system during the whole treatment. We had to filter the air in our house, leave shoes outside, hand sanitizers in every room."

Shepherd felt her eyes well up. "God, Nick. That must have been awful."

"The thing is…" He stopped. Looked up at her. "The thing is, seeing her there, all those tubes, it's just… All you want is to take her place. Hook me up, do your worst, but let this poor little girl…"

He picked up the remaining shot glass and poured it down. "I'm sorry. You didn't need to hear any of this."

"It's okay," Shepherd said. "The good news is, she survived."

"She did. And not because of me. I was there as much as I could be, but the bills, I mean, even with insurance, I'm still paying those off, if you can believe that. I had to work, I was gone so much…" He dropped his head. "So much of the load was Lori's."

"Well," Shepherd said. "You had to work. The bills had to be paid."

"That's what I always told myself. But I don't know. It's what really split us up, me and Lori."

"Sounds like you were both dealing with an incredible amount of stress."

"Her more than me."

"Also sounds like…no, never mind," Shepherd said.

"What? Go ahead."

Shepherd shifted in her chair. "It sounds like your daughter has a passion, and you're afraid to encourage that passion because you're worried she'll get hurt."

They both sat in silence, until Tanner blew out a breath.

"Shit," he said.

He shook his head. "All right. Change of subject. This guy I'm talking to tomorrow morning. What's his name again?"

"Wheeler. Cody Wheeler."

Chapter Twenty-Nine

Humboldt County Correctional Facility

Eureka, California

"Three-and-a-half to six years in a federal prison, plus up to ten grand I'd lay odds you don't have," Tanner said. "That's what you're looking at here, Mister Wheeler."

Tanner looked across the table at Wheeler and his court-appointed attorney.

"Agent Tanner, you're not the judge or jury." The lawyer was black and stringy-thin, with a high-school-senior face that shouted earnest dedication and looked like it had yet to need a razor. If he was nervous about dealing with a Federal agent, he wasn't showing it. "My client could just as easily get time served and a slap on the wrist, if anything at all."

Tanner tossed a two-page arrest report down on the table. "For poaching bears on Federal land? And trafficking in their organs?"

The attorney ignored the report. "There is no evidence of poaching on Federal land. My client was arrested on the Yurok Reservation by the reservation police. The bear organs found in his vehicle were found by them. Technically, they should be the ones to decide what charges to press, if any."

Tanner leaned back in his chair and took time to look around the room. Typical stationhouse interview room. Faded walls the color of nausea. Six-foot Rubbermaid foldable table. Hard plastic chairs. Two-way mirror in case anyone was interested enough to watch. Sour, baked-in scent of nervous sweat. He pulled a pack of Tums from his pocket and chewed a couple.

Wheeler sat across from him, looking older than his years next to the boy-band lawyer. "Well, maybe you're right," Tanner finally said. "Maybe I oughta kick this back to the rez police, let them deal with it." He stood, put his hands in his pockets, and smiled.

"But from the looks of you, Mister Wheeler, I'd say you've had your fill of interaction with those gentlemen. Maybe you were on the rez when you got caught, but we both know you've been taking bears in Redwoods. And maybe your esteemed attorney is right, maybe I'd have a hard time proving that. But the fact is, I don't want to. I also don't want to send you back to the Yuroks."

He leaned down, both hands on the table. "See, all I want from you is a little help. A couple names. You help me out, I'll help you out."

Wheeler sipped coffee from a Styrofoam cup, wincing as it passed over swollen lips. He set down the cup. "Yeah? How much you gonna help me out?"

"Before my client offers any cooperation, we need the exact details of the deal you're offering," said Ernie Earnest.

"Sorry, tell me your name again?" Tanner asked.

"Lionel Colton."

"Mister Colton, I suspect your client *is* gonna cooperate, because I also suspect he's not nearly as dumb as he looks."

"There's no call for—"

"Not only because he's already experienced Yurok hospitality, but because he knows what's waiting for him outside if he makes bail. I got that right, Mister Wheeler?"

He bent down further, inches from Wheeler's face. "You think they're gonna believe you didn't give them up? Whoever's behind this, they're probably already waiting, don't you think? I can help with that. Or, you can make bail, walk out the door, and take your chances."

Wheeler shifted in his seat, looking away from Tanner. "I don't know any names. That's the truth. I'd tell you if I knew, but I don't know. And get that breath away from me or I'm gonna charge police brutality."

Tanner stood, smiled, and fired his first shot. "You don't know the big cowboy's name?"

Wheeler twitched. Just a little, but Tanner caught it.

"You know who I'm talking about, right?"

Colton put a hand on Wheeler's shoulder. "You don't have to answer anything until we've agreed to terms."

Wheeler took another sip of coffee. Tanner walked back and took his seat across the table. He leaned in on both elbows, and the two men locked eyes. Time for a second shot.

"You wouldn't know anything about a missing pot farmer named Harley Thompson, would you, Cody?"

And there it was. Wheeler managed to keep his face impassive, but his eyes jumped.

Tanner leaned back in the chair. "You ever watch cop shows, Cody? The ones where they solve those cold cases with DNA? I like those shows, they have really hot female cops. They also solve some pretty tough cases with the smallest amount of DNA. I find that so cool, don't you?"

"What's your point, Mister Tanner?" Colton asked.

"Well, Mister Colton, my point is that we happened to have recovered a broadhead buried in the ground not fifty yards from the location of one Harley Thompson's freshly harvested pot farm out in Redwoods."

"What's a broadhead?" Colton asked.

Wheeler and Tanner both looked at the lawyer. Wheeler shook his head, then looked down at his hands, folded loosely on the tabletop.

"A Wasp Drone broadhead, Cody," Tanner said. "You're familiar with those, right? In fact..." He referred to the report in front of him. "Well, lookee here, the exact same kind you had with you when the rez police busted you."

Colton looked at Wheeler. "What's he talking about?"

"Cody knows," Tanner said. "What he doesn't know is we're running that broadhead for DNA, just like those CSI babes do. If it went through skin and blood, well, that'll tell us something, won't it? Or, maybe you could tell me whose it is, Cody?

"Whoa, where's this going?" Colton turned to Wheeler. "Don't say a word."

Tanner plowed on. "That head was sawed off at the shaft, about four inches protruding above the ground. So I'm thinking maybe we'll get lucky and find something on the shaft, too. Where someone might have held onto it to saw it off? Maybe, I don't know, some prints?"

"Look," Wheeler said, still looking at his hands. "I cooperate, I gotta walk, free and clear."

There was silence in the room. Tanner chewed another couple Tums. Colton shuffled papers.

Finally, Colton spoke up. "How about that, Agent Tanner? If my client cooperates, can you promise all charges are dropped?"

"Hey, we aim to please. But if your client killed Harley Thompson, there won't be any deal." Tanner looked at Cody. "If you killed that man, Cody, you'd best listen to Lionel here and shut the fuck up. But if you didn't, and you know where he is? Now's the time to get real chatty. I like what you tell me, we got something to talk about. Maybe you get to skip out the door like it's the last day of school."

Colton turned to Wheeler. "We need to talk."

Wheeler puffed his cheeks and exhaled, then looked at Tanner. "I'll tell you what I know. But the deal is, after I do, I'm gone, I'm in the fucking wind. Don't look for me to testify or nothing."

"It's possible I can live with that," Tanner lied. "Let's start with what you know about Harley Thompson."

"I don't know his name," Wheeler said. "Some dude found one of my bait sites. I didn't know what to do, so I shot him in the foot. The head got buried, so I had to saw it off."

"I'm going to intervene now," Colton said. He put a hand on Wheeler's shoulder. "Mister Wheeler don't say anymore. This has gone far beyond the poaching charges on the arrest report."

"Sure has," Tanner said.

Chapter Thirty

Humboldt County Correctional Facility

Eureka, California

Two hours later, Wheeler and his attorney were back in the same interrogation room. During the interlude Cody Wheeler was formally charged by the Sheriff with ADW, mayhem and attempted homicide.

Outside the room, Tanner was met by a Humboldt County Sheriff's homicide detective, a rotund fifty-something with a walrus mustache and fierce eyebrows. "Name's Rod Stewart," he said. "And yes, before you ask, I'm the famous singer."

"I appreciate your help on this," Tanner said.

"This guy confessed to shooting someone in the foot with an arrow? Where'd the other charges come from?"

"I think something worse may have happened. A grower named Harley Thompson appears to be missing. Cody Wheeler, the guy inside, is the confessed foot shooter. I don't know if he stopped with an arrow in the foot. If he did, I'm hoping Harley may be alive somewhere, and Wheeler can tell us where."

"You're hoping. But the reason I'm here is you're actually thinking the vic is dead." A statement, not a question.

"I'm afraid so. I also think Wheeler either did it or knows who did. So look intimidating. I need him scared."

"I can do that," Stewart said.

The two entered the room. Colton and Wheeler looked up.

"Who's this?" Colton asked.

"Rod Stewart, Homicide," Stewart said. He didn't extend his hand or even give the attorney a glance. He sat directly across from Wheeler and glared at him.

Colton wasted no time. "Look, other than a broadhead which is widely used by hunters, and which is highly unlikely to deliver any DNA evidence of any sort since it was buried in the ground, you have nothing to base these ridiculous new charges on."

"Number one," Tanner said, "two minutes ago you didn't even know what a broadhead was. Two, I'm guessing the number of cases you've litigated involving DNA and homicide can be counted on less than one hand. And third, your client already admitted to shooting a man in the foot with an arrow."

"Mister Wheeler was upset and feeling pressured when he said that," Colton said. "He has since remembered things differently."

"Differently how?"

"Like he never shot that arrow."

Tanner stood and paced the room before he spoke again. "Did you leave him there, Cody? Or did you take him someplace?"

Wheeler said nothing.

Tanner came back to the table, put both hands on the back of his chair. "Okay. Let's start again. Who's the cowboy?"

Wheeler wouldn't meet his eyes. "Who?"

"Tall, Marlboro Man looking dude. Don't tell me you don't know him, I talked to him last night. He was very interested in finding you. Mentioned you by name, several times."

Cody fidgeted with his hands for a few moments before answering. "Like I said before. I gotta walk."

Colton spoke up. "My client has indicated he'll cooperate, but all charges, including these bogus new ones, need to be dropped."

Tanner sat down. "Wow. That's a tall order, Mister Colton. Detective Stewart here, he's with Homicide, and he's itching to find out what happened to Harley Thompson. If your client knows anything about where Mister Thompson might be, or what happened to him after he shot him in the foot, he'd be smart to tell us now."

"Did you kill him, Cody?" Stewart said.

"Fuck no."

Tanner looked at Stewart. "You believe him?"

"Fuck no." Stewart stood. "I'm gonna file an additional charge of homicide. That should pretty well end your chance of bail, Cody."

"I didn't kill him. I shot him in the foot," Cody said.

"Then where is he?" Stewart sat back down. "This is your one chance to save your ass, Cody. Don't waste any more of my time."

"Who's the Marlboro Man, Cody?" Tanner said.

"He your partner?" Stewart said.

Wheeler put his elbows on the table and cradled his forehead in his hands. He was quiet for a long time, then said, "The guy's name is Calhoun. Mickey Calhoun."

"Cody," Colton said.

Wheeler looked at him. "This has to stop."

"Great," Tanner said, "Now we're cooking. He your partner in the gallbladder poaching?"

Wheeler shook his head. "He ain't no partner."

Stewart spoke up. "Does he know the whereabouts of Harley Thompson?"

Wheeler shrugged.

"Cody," Tanner said, "how is Calhoun involved? Is he shooting bears too?"

Wheeler snorted. "If you call it shooting."

"What's that mean?"

"Means what it means."

Tanner took a breath, looked at the ceiling, exhaled slowly. Shot a quick look at Stewart and decided to take a different tack.

"Okay," he said. "Let's talk about the bears. You and Calhoun are taking these bears for their galls and paws. Who's buying them from you?"

"Look, I'm just a hired hand on this," Wheeler said. "Mickey called me, says he's got a guy wants to buy galls. Hell, most states that ain't even illegal."

"It is in California. And it always is if they're from poached bears. And it especially is if they're taken in a National Park."

"Whatever."

"Whatever?"

"Yeah, I mean, it's not like they're endangered or something. There's a shit ton of black bears everywhere."

Tanner calmed himself by opening a folder and spreading its contents. "Cody, my well-honed crime-fighter instincts tell me you and Howdy Doody aren't the brains of this operation. So again, who're you selling the galls to?"

"I don't know the guy's name. I met him, but his name never got said. Mickey knows him. An old guy."

"Describe him."

"Uh, puffy, outta shape, maybe six feet tall. Head like a bowling ball."

"Okay. Anything else?"

"He looks a little off."

"Off, how?"

"Well, his mouth looks stretched, and he has this surprised look on his face all the time."

"Like maybe he had a facelift or something?"

Wheeler scowled. "How the fuck should I know?"

"Okay. And what was this old guy's role?"

"He's the money guy. Gave us all the orders. Last one was for twenty bears."

Tanner inhaled sharply. *"Twenty* bears?"

"Yeah. Fuckin' crazy, right? Said he needed twenty bears asap. He wanted them in like two weeks or something. I told him the best I could do was two bears a week."

Tanner rode out the acidic jolt that hit his gut. For an instant, he wanted to finish what the reservation police started, but kept it under control. "Two bears a week," he managed. "Just for the gallbladders."

Wheeler shrunk back in his chair. "And paws. Galls and paws."

"And how much were you to be paid for each bear, Cody?"

"He was paying a grand a bear. Even split for me and Mickey every bear, even though I was the one getting most of 'em."

Tanner took a moment before he spoke. "You went out onto federal land with the intention of shooting twenty bears in ten weeks, risking federal time, all for a grand total of ten thousand dollars each?"

Wheeler stayed silent.

Tanner stood. "Fuck it. I'm done with you, Cody." He turned to Stewart. "He's all yours."

"Now wait a second," Colton protested. "My client has cooperated. What about the deal?"

"I said there'd be a deal if I liked what he said. I didn't like a word of it. No fucking deal on the poaching," Tanner said. "Besides, your client clearly has bigger things to worry about." He gave a nod towards Stewart for emphasis.

"But he told you about the buyer," Colton said.

"He told me about an old guy with a facelift, and a guy I already tracked down myself. Where exactly is your client adding value?"

There was silence in the room. Tanner turned the doorknob.

"I saw Calhoun strangle that pot farmer." Wheeler spoke with his head down.

Tanner released the doorknob. He shot Stewart a glance, then turned and looked at Wheeler, who was once again staring at his hands.

"You did," Tanner said.

"Yeah. He tied him down on the bed, climbed on top and fucking choked him to death. Made me sick."

Tanner sat back down. "Where'd this happen?"

"Motel near here. Southside, off the 101."

"How'd the pot farmer get to that motel, Cody?"

Wheeler squirmed, had a sip of coffee, set down the cup. "I thought Mickey'd just scare him off or something. I never thought..." He moved the cup around on the table.

"You brought him there. After you shot him in the foot."

Wheeler puffed out a breath. "I wasn't sure what to do. I figured I'd take him back, and Mickey would pay him off. Or maybe scare him or something."

"But that's not what happened."

Wheeler shook his head. "That fuckin' guy is crazy."

"What did you do?"

"What do you mean?"

"While your partner was choking a man to death, a man who hadn't done a fucking thing to you two. What did you do?"

"What could I do?" Wheeler sat forward. "Mickey carries a goddam cannon, plus he wears a big fuckin' knife on his hip, and he knows how to use it. He can't shoot an arrow worth a shit, but he's good with knives, motherfucker can split a grape at fifteen yards. Used to do that shit for the movies. Strong as hell, too, and bigger'n me, and on top of that he's got this fuckin' blackjack." Wheeler slumped back. "I thought he'd just talk to the guy or something. I didn't want no part of killing him."

"But you let it happen."

"Okay, that's enough," Colton said.

Wheeler's tone rose. "Hey, I couldn't do a fuckin' thing!"

"Stop talking, Cody," Colton said.

Wheeler ignored him. "Hell, I told Mickey afterwards I thought it was a stupid thing to do, and the motherfucker jacked me upside the head so hard I thought he busted my neck."

"What happened to Thompson's body?" Detective Stewart asked.

Wheeler shrugged. "I don't know. Mickey said he'd handle it."

Stewart nodded. "Okay. You said you were at a motel. Where?"

"Right as you enter town on the 101, on the right. Sea Mist, or Ocean Mist, or something like that. Something with Mist."

Stewart said, "Bay Mist?"

"That's it, yeah," Wheeler said.

"Is he still there?"

Wheeler shook his head. "I don't know, maybe."

"All right. Room number?"

Chapter Thirty-One

Eureka, California

The Bay Mist Motel was a lime green double-decker horseshoe surrounding a worn asphalt parking lot. Room 231, as the number would suggest, was on the second floor. The "31" was perhaps more a marketing ploy than any attempt at accuracy, as there were only twelve rooms on the second floor, stacked like boxes on the twelve below.

Inside room 231, Calhoun looked in the bathroom mirror. He held a bag of motel ice against a visible knot on the right side of his head. The joint of his jawbone was also noticeably swollen and bruised. A careful probing with his index finger confirmed that all his teeth, historically strong, remained intact.

He replayed the incident at the bar and realized his mistake had been assuming that hairy gorilla was right-handed, like most people. He'd had the pool cue resting on his left shoulder, so Calhoun figured he'd kick the asshole's balls up his throat before he could get off a decent swing. But he was left-handed, or maybe a switch-hitter.

And then, getting sucker punched by the other Neanderthal. Fucking infuriating. Not something you let slide. Have to give that a little more thought.

Calhoun moved the ice aside, pushed gingerly at the knot with his finger, repositioned the ice as he walked out of the bathroom. His head throbbed, as much from his current predicament as the beat-down.

Wheeler got caught. At least, that's what the pony-tailed writer told him. The one who sounded like he knew way too much, not just about Wheeler, but about what was going on in Redwoods.

Calhoun sat on the corner of the bed. Would Wheeler tell the cops anything? All he'd be facing were some bullshit poaching charges. Yeah, on Federal land, so that upped the ante a bit, but still. Was the potential punishment for that enough to get him talking? Calhoun had his doubts. Wheeler was a tough *hombre*, he'd done time more than once. Good bet he'd clam up. Calhoun smiled. Wheeler might also be a little concerned about what would happen to him if he chose to remember any names, or that trouble with the pot grower.

And why would he even bring that up? That would make him an accessory, wouldn't it? Looking at that kind of charge, he'd keep his mouth shut. Wouldn't he?

Calhoun's thoughts were interrupted by a knock on the door.

He came off the bed, dropped the ice pack, and opened the nightstand drawer for his gun. He moved towards the curtained window next to the door, pulled it slightly to look outside, then let it drop closed. "Who the fuck?" he said under his breath.

It was an Asian guy. Not very tall, but very wide.

The man knocked again. "Mister Calhoun, please open the door. I know you are here."

"Who the fuck?" Calhoun said again, this time aloud. "Who are you?" he shouted through the door.

"My name is Hong."

"What do you want?"

"I wish to come in and speak with you. You and I are two parts of the same enterprise."

"I don't know what you're talking about."

"Please, Mister Calhoun. Open the door so we can talk."

Calhoun cracked the door open a couple inches, made sure the Python was visible, and said, "I don't think so, pal." He pushed the door closed, and nearly had his arm torn off when it suddenly smashed open. The gun flew out of his hand and slid along the floor toward the bed.

Hong entered hard and fast. He stopped, coiled, and slammed Calhoun's midsection with a sidekick that drove the air out of the cowboy and dropped him to his knees.

Hong turned and closed the door. Calhoun's mouth worked like a landed catfish, sucking at air that refused to go in.

"It would have been easier if you let me in," Hong said. He tossed a card key on the floor. "The front desk was very understanding. These things are so easy to misplace."

Calhoun looked up, unable to speak.

"So, to business. Again, my name is Hong. My boss loaned your employer a great deal of money towards this contract."

"I don't know what the fuck you're talking about," Calhoun managed to croak.

"Please. I am here to make sure the contract is fulfilled. You deliver the goods as promised. No surprises, no problems."

Calhoun finally managed to synchronize his breathing and pulled himself upright. He sat in the desk chair, leaned back and looked up at Hong. "We're fine. Everything's great. Under control." He took a deep breath, let it out. "There you go, you're a hundred percent up to speed. Now get the fuck out."

"Are you aware that your partner is currently in jail?"

Calhoun shrugged it off. "Big deal. Poaching charge. Worst case a fine, maybe a little time. No worries there."

"Perhaps, but the problem is that your clock is running out. My boss made certain commitments based on the promises of your boss. The delivery has to be punctual."

"Punctual? Tell your boss not to worry, I've got it under control. I've been out there shooting too, in case you didn't know. You'll get your delivery."

"How many do you have so far?"

Calhoun shot to his feet. "Hey, fuck you! This is my fucking show. I run it. Not you. I just said you'd get your fucking product, and you will. That's all you need to know, asshole."

Hong's expression darkened. "Here is how this goes. I ask questions. You listen, and answer. It is that simple. If I am satisfied with the answers, I leave you to your business. If I am not..."

Calhoun drove forward like a linebacker, aiming his shoulder at Hong's midsection, hoping to hit the motherfucker so hard he'd piss blood.

But in that instant—in the heartbeat of time it took to travel less than six feet—Hong shifted a half step to one side and lifted his knee, connecting solidly with Calhoun's forehead.

The cowboy's momentum carried him past Hong and down to the floor in a solid faceplant. He rolled onto his back, flailing unconsciously at an opponent he couldn't see, his body and mind in total disconnect.

"You are an idiot," Hong said.

* * *

"What the fuck?" Calhoun muttered, fighting back to consciousness as he pulled himself to a sitting position. "What'd you hit me with?" Still stunned, he dropped forward to his hands and knees, and moved feebly across the floor.

Hong stood by the door, watching Calhoun crawl towards the bed. "We expect full delivery, on schedule. Given the current situation, I would like to know how you plan to do that."

Calhoun nodded, turned and pushed himself up to a sitting position on the floor, his back resting against the bed.

He dropped his chin and raised his left hand in weary surrender. "Understood," he said.

His right hand snaked under the bed and scooped the fallen Colt Python. He brought it up, aimed center mass.

The blast thundered inside the tiny room. A .357 hollow-point punched a dime-sized hole in Hong's solar plexus and exploded a crimson mass out of his back. The force knocked Hong back against the door, then gravity took over and he slid bonelessly to the floor.

Calhoun stood. He felt a little wobbly, but all things considered, not too bad. Not too bad at all.

He stood over Hong's body. The game had changed considerably. This guy. Wheeler in jail. The time left in the contract. The fact that he would no longer have to split the money. Twenty grand. The interesting fact that Hong's boss already suspected Goldstein was getting ready to cut him out.

Yes, thought Calhoun. Things were going to shit.

But it could still be salvaged.

Chapter Thirty-Two

Eureka, California

"Good afternoon, everyone," Tanner said.

Detective Stewart had called in all four county Sheriff SWAT-trained deputies for the hastily organized mission briefing. The briefing was held at Eureka PD headquarters, where the Sheriff's team was augmented by three members of the Eureka SWAT team.

The assembled force may not have been numerically formidable, but to Tanner's practiced eye they looked well outfitted and professional. The men sat or stood at ease, in the loose-limbed, relaxed way common in men trained for action. Most had their eyes on the photocopied handout they'd each been given.

The consensus decision was that Tanner would lead the briefing, since he'd been closest to the case to this point.

"I'm U.S. Fish and Wildlife Services Special Agent Nick Tanner. I've been operating undercover at Redwoods on a wildlife trafficking case. In the course of that investigation a possible homicide has surfaced. Both the trafficking and homicide are tied to a team of bear poachers currently working the Redwoods. We've got one suspect in custody. He's provided information that we're about to act on. He reports that he and his accomplice, who he named as Mickey Calhoun, were staying at the Bay Mist motel, half a mile from here. You've got Calhoun's sheet on the handout. Forty-three, six-two, two-oh-five. Occupation listed as movie stuntman.

"We need to act immediately," he continued. "Calhoun already knows we've got his partner, so there's a good chance he'll be on the move." He was interrupted as a female officer opened the door to the briefing room.

"Agent Tanner, excuse me. Your fingerprint report," she said. She handed a file folder to Tanner, who scanned it quickly, then turned back to the room.

"Okay, we have confirmation on our boy," he said. "It's definitely Calhoun. It so happens I've made his acquaintance. He's a bad-tempered son-of-a-bitch, he's armed, and an all-around asshole. The weapon he greeted me with was a Colt Python. We have to assume he has others. His partner claims he's very good with a knife." He referred to the handout. "You can see he's racked up an A and B dismissed, A and B seven months served, a couple drug busts, one for selling. Another A and B pled down to disorderly conduct. So be aware.

"Here's how we'll do it. One unmarked will go in first, with one of you in civvies." He turned to Stewart. "Let's pick one of your guys, someone who works some other end of the county, in case Calhoun's familiar with any of the local law." Stewart nodded.

"Okay," Tanner continued. "Detective Stewart's guy goes into the motel office, IDs himself to the clerk, finds out if anyone's registered in room 231. With any luck, he also gets a description that matches our suspect. If someone's registered, he'll have the clerk call the adjacent rooms and clear them out. Once that's done, we roll. I'll go first with the city SWAT guys; Sheriff's SWAT zips the place up and takes covering positions.

He scanned the room. "Questions?"

* * *

Tanner sat in the passenger seat of the unmarked cruiser, with Detective Stewart at the wheel, parked a block from the motel. Immediately behind them were two SWAT vans. He watched through binoculars as a young couple hurried out of room 232, hastily buttoning and zippering as they hustled towards the staircase.

"Young love," he said to Stewart. "Nothing like it."

"Who can remember?" Stewart said.

Their shoulder-mounted radios crackled. It was Stewart's man, the one he'd sent into the motel office. "Room 232 guests are leaving. Apparently, they just got here."

"Ruined an afternoon quickie, looks like," Tanner said.

"Manager says 230 is unoccupied. His description of one of the guests in 231 matches Calhoun. He says there are two guests."

Tanner answered. "Odds are the other is the man we have in custody. But we shouldn't take that for granted."

"I've got a keycard," the officer said.

Tanner answered. "Roger that. Meet us up there. Okay, all. 232 occupants are clear. 230 is empty. Team one, team two, showtime."

Stewart jammed the accelerator and screeched into the Bay Mist parking lot, followed closely by both SWAT vans. The vehicles had barely come to a stop when their doors flew open. The Eureka SWAT officers led the way, Tanner just behind, and scaled the exterior stairway at a sprint. The Sheriff's team in the second van blocked the parking lot exit. The men immediately disbursed to covering positions.

The lead team had to pass the window of room 231 to get to the door. Tanner and one of the SWAT guys dropped flat and elbow-crawled under the window, then past the door. The officer with the keycard also crawled under the window but stopped on the near side of the door. Tanner stood. The other two SWAT officers lined up to the side of the window. No more than twenty seconds had passed since they rolled up.

Tanner made eye contact with the men across from him. Gun in one hand and standing clear, he reached across with his free hand and gave the door a backhanded knock.

No response.

He knocked again. "Sir, this is the motel manager, I have a message for you, the man says it's urgent," he said.

Still no response.

Tanner nodded. The officer with the keycard reached over and slid it in and out of the key slot. The indicator light went green.

He dropped the card as Tanner grabbed the door handle and threw open the door. The entire team exploded into the room, shouting, "POLICE! GET DOWN!"

The room was empty. Beds undisturbed. No luggage in sight. Tanner moved quickly to check the bathroom as others cleared the closet and under the beds. Nothing. Nobody.

"All clear," he said into his radio, and holstered his weapon.

After a moment Stewart entered and took a quick look at the room. "They cleared out."

Tanner walked over to the nearest bed and pulled back the covers. "Huh." He motioned to one of the SWAT officers and pointed to the other bed. "Check that one."

The guy pulled back the covers. No bottom sheet there either.

"And no pillowcases on the pillows," Tanner said.

"No towels in the bathroom," one of the SWAT officers said.

"We brought a lot of firepower to apprehend sheet thieves," Stewart said, smiling.

"Yeah, but they also stole the towels," Tanner said. "That can't be tolerated." He turned to one of the Eureka SWAT men. "You guys got a crime lab?"

"We don't live in caves here," Stewart growled. "We'll get the room worked."

The SWAT officers cleared out, their aimless chatter a poor outlet for the adrenaline still flooding their systems. Stewart went to the open door and swung it closed to look at the inside surface.

"Take a look at this," he said to Tanner.

There was a small indentation in the door, about midway up. The paint was chipped. Tanner got close.

"Maybe something," he said.

"We'll check it," Stewart said. He looked the door over. "We'll process this whole surface."

Tanner opened the door, stepped outside of the room, and leaned on the wrought-iron railing that lined the upper floor walkway. The air was thick with its usual promise of rain, the sky gray and flat. Even here, riding the left hip of the 101 highway, the sharp scent of pine overpowered any hint of auto exhaust.

Detective Stewart joined him. He pulled a pack of Winstons from his pocket and offered one to Tanner. Without a word, Tanner waved it away. Stewart stuck one in his lips but made no move to light it. He noticed Tanner's expression and shrugged. "Trying to quit."

"I did, years ago. But it's still a battle sometimes. Especially times like this."

Stewart turned, resting his back on the railing. "Think he's left town?"

Tanner took a while to answer. "I don't know. That'd be the smart thing to do, but this guy Calhoun, I don't think he scares easily."

"Well, other than the woods, there's only so many places around here he can hide out," Stewart said. "We'll put out an APB. If he's holed up in any of our towns, we'll find him."

"Great." Tanner thought a moment. "It's possible he may still want to get his bears. With his partner out of it, he's looking at a thousand bucks per now."

The Homicide detective pulled the cigarette from his lips and exhaled nothing but air as he nodded. "Yeah. The thing about hunting bears is, sometimes they hunt you right back." He stubbed out the unsmoked Winston and flicked it to the parking lot below.

Chapter Thirty-Three

Orick, California

C alhoun watched the wind throw sporadic jabs at a soggy drizzle, knocking it sideways across two urine-colored lights that clung weakly over the door to The Tall Tree. Two A.M. Closing time. A ragged stream of hulking, jacketed men and the occasional woman filtered out, each with a noticeable weave in their gait. Pickup trucks fired to life, headlights criss-crossed the unmarked dirt lot, mud flew as spinning tires left and bit into the paved highway.

From the darkness of an empty field across the highway, peering through the spattered driver's side window of his truck, Calhoun had no hope of making out faces. He had to base his surveillance criterion solely on dimension. Specifically, he was looking for someone the size of a grizzly.

It wasn't as easy as he'd hoped. One large, heavily bearded man after another lurched past the lights. It seemed impossible that the ramshackle board-and-bat building could hold that many people. "Like one of those fucking clown cars," Calhoun said to no one.

He tipped a pint bottle of tequila to his lips, savored the bite in his throat, felt it scorch a path down to his belly. He strained to see through the wet blur and glare, and finally rolled down the window. Visibility improved a little, but his discomfort increased measurably as the chilled moisture blew into his face like frozen BBs. This miserable place. Always wet, the air a weeping sponge, big fucking trees blocking the view no matter where you looked, the smell of mold so thick it wedged in your nostrils, permeated your skin, wove its way into your clothing. Nights like this made him long for a Malibu afternoon with the Santa Anas up, eighty degrees on the sand, waves flattened and sixty-foot viz underwater, spearfishing for halibut off Point Dume.

Calhoun popped the cork top back into the tequila when a towering figure ducked through the Tall Tree doorway and momentarily blocked the lights. Without conscious thought, his hand dropped to the center console and found the textured grip of his Colt Python.

That had to be the guy who'd suckered him with the pool cue. Or if not him, the one who threw the punch. Either way, guilty. Sticking their fucking noses in other people's business. Whacking a guy with a stick, while the other one turns out your lights. Fucking cowards.

Calhoun lifted the front brim of his Stetson and rolled up the window. He watched the big son-of-a-bitch stumble across the lot and climb into a mud-slathered El Dorado, model year around 65 BC. Calhoun grinned. Tuesday night and drunk as a whorehouse tick, driving a junkyard reject home alone at two A.M.. Living the dream, like all these Davey Crockett motherfuckers.

Calhoun knew what he was about to do wouldn't qualify as a plan of great brilliance. It wouldn't fool anybody for long. It was all about distraction, tossing a bag of shit in the water to confuse things and buy some time. All he needed was some time.

Of course, there was another important upside. He'd been jacked up in public, made to look like a douchebag in front of the whole bar. Hauled out and tossed on his ass in the gravel and mud like a bad Western, the door swinging shut but not blocking out the hoots and laughter from within.

Calhoun hadn't spent over a decade choreographing fights in everything from big budget boxing flicks to hayburners to chop-socky crapfests because he didn't know how to kick some ass. And he sure as hell hadn't survived seven months in Tehachapi State Prison at the toothsome age of twenty-three by letting anyone get on top of him.

So, good plan or not, there was no way he'd let this gorilla-looking motherfucker have the last shot.

The shitheap El Dorado finally fired to life after several false starts. It pulled all the way through the lot and onto the highway before its occupant realized the headlights weren't on. Calhoun snorted and started up his truck. Too easy.

With so few vehicles on the highway at that hour, Calhoun was able to follow at a discreet distance. Not that the halfwit driver could have spotted a tail if it was stapled to his ass, but just because you're dealing with amateurs doesn't mean you make amateur mistakes. Any stuntman will tell you that carelessness kills.

After about three miles the guy pulled off the highway, and onto a two-lane road cramped by vegetation and shrouded in overhanging trees. Combined with the drizzle, there was the most complete blackness Calhoun had ever experienced. The taillights ahead seemed to float in limbo, untethered, like two crimson fireflies hovering and shifting direction in unison.

In spite of the darkness, Calhoun considered turning off his headlights. Even a moron like that caveman up there might wonder who was behind him on this god-forsaken road at this hour. But visibility was tough enough with his headlights on; without them, he'd likely drive straight into a tree. Better to stay as far back as possible.

After about two miles Calhoun heard his tires crunching gravel and noticed the faded white lines down the middle of the road disappear. "Gotta be getting close now," he muttered. Calhoun was a man virtually without fear, but this wet, inky blackness was starting to get to him.

Up ahead the taillights were tiny red dots, bouncing and shimmying as they led Calhoun down a road that gradually devolved from gravel to rutted, slippery mud. Calhoun strained to navigate a road that grew less and less distinguishable from the underbrush alongside. An unseen bump snapped Calhoun's head to the side, rattled his spine and jolted loose a string of curses. The truck started to slide, so he let up on the gas and came to a stop.

He took a deep breath, readjusted his Stetson and peered ahead.

The taillights were gone.

He eased the truck forward in a crawl. The fucker had either stopped, turned off the road, or turned off his lights and kept going. If it was the latter, there was nothing Calhoun could do but leave. It meant he'd been spotted, and while that asshole knew the road, Calhoun didn't.

If the car had stopped, it was also because he'd spotted the tail, and maybe was lining up the barrels of a twelve gauge on the oncoming headlights. All these hicks out here had guns, of that Calhoun had no doubt.

If, however, the car had turned off the road—it probably meant he was home. Right where Calhoun wanted him.

So, slow and steady was the plan. Scrutinize both sides of the road. Find a break that would signal a driveway. At the same time, be wary of a stopped vehicle.

Easier said than done. The dirt road seemed to meld into the surrounding mud and underbrush. Calhoun frequently thought he'd spotted a break, only to aim the truck's headlights at another dripping wall of undergrowth and trees.

"Fuck it," he said, and switched on his high beams. At this point the gorilla either knew or didn't know he'd been followed. If he'd made a turn into a driveway, he might not even notice the lights, or find them remarkable in any way given the conditions. Anyone driving in this darkness and sloppy rain would have the high beams on.

Calhoun nearly missed the driveway.

It was a scrawny thing, little more than a widened footpath. But there it was, flanked by two four-foot poles and a plain pipe-metal gate. The gate was hinged to swing inward, and in the headlights Calhoun could now see it was slightly ajar, the chain and lock swinging freely from the end.

A little way past the gate, some lights suddenly blinked on. Calhoun quickly switched his off. Those weren't car headlights up there. Those were house lights.

Calhoun smiled. "Welcome home, pal." He pulled his truck off into the ditch alongside the gate, grabbed his Colt and a small flashlight, and slid out of the truck. He took a moment to check the package in the truck bed. He'd come back for it later.

He stepped around the gate and headed up the driveway towards the lights.

Chapter Thirty-Four

Orick, California

By the time Amy Manning chased out the last of the regulars and closed the Tall Tree, it was nearly three in the morning. And still so much to do.

She double-checked her calendar, just to be sure she had it right. Yep, sixty-seven days since the last one. A hundred forty-two since the one before that. No pattern, perfectly random. Way she figured it, only way it was credible. Space them wide apart, but often enough to keep the fire stoked, the believers believing.

Not that she needed the calendar to tell her the time had come. The receipts in the register made that real clear. Insurance going up, fuel surcharge on deliveries going up, hell, as owner of the bar and the land it sat on, even property taxes were going up. Meanwhile, tourists drank less booze, bought fewer souvenirs, stayed fewer days, visited less frequently.

"Goddamn it, where are you?" she said aloud, and took a seat on a barstool. She slid an ashtray over and fired up a joint. Took a deep, lung-expanding drag, held it, expelled a cloud of smoke.

The regulars were exactly that. Regular. Came in every night, nursed a beer like it was liquid gold, hungry eyes watchful for anyone drunk enough to splurge on a round all 'round. Not like the old days, when logging crews rolled in at quitting time, looking to cut the dust that caked their throats like wet mortar. Their pockets full on Fridays, Amy couldn't tap fresh kegs fast enough.

Same with the randy, boisterous brawlers fresh off the salmon boats, back when you could practically walk on the backs of schools out in the bay. Young guys working summer jobs, crusty old-timers with missing fingers and hook scars, hired muscle who didn't know fish from fowl but could haul line like human winches—after offload they'd all crash through the doors like a force of nature, and Amy would keep pouring until the last one fell.

The loggers, the fishermen, they were still out there, but far fewer in number, and a different breed. Worked like Clydesdales dawn to dusk, then went home to their families. Seemed like the only time she'd see them in the Tall Tree was when one had a birthday, or when something bad happened that needed a good drowning.

But pining for the old days wasn't going to put cash in the kitty, Amy knew that. To survive, you had to take action. Do whatever you could to get an edge.

She sighed, stubbed the embers of the roach in the ashtray, and lit another fatty.

Big Davey wasn't the most dependable guy on the planet, but he hadn't let her down yet, going on two years now. Weird thing was, he hadn't been at the Tall Tree at all that night. Sucking down suds, shooting pool, raising hell. Frank had been there, Beaver had been there, a couple of the others. But no Davey.

She hadn't asked about him. Didn't want to give anyone any ideas. Of course, she could've asked Beaver if she'd gotten him alone, but the chance never came up. Maybe he wondered where Davey was too, but if so, he didn't let on, and didn't say anything to her.

Amy checked her phone. Shit. The world wouldn't end if it didn't happen tonight, but goddamn it, a schedule is a schedule. She hit her speed-dial for Davey's land-line, listened to the call dump into voicemail—"Big Davey here, if I wanted to talk to you I'd've picked up"—and hung up. Tried his cell, with the same results.

Ten minutes and a finished joint later, Amy's irritation softened into concern. After all, the big guy made a living slinging chainsaws and carving knives, turning huge hunks of shapeless wood into everything from bears and bunnies to highly polished coffee-tables and wall décor. Not exactly unheard of for burl carvers to accidentally take a chunk out of themselves. Be one thing if it happened at his shop, right there on the highway, somebody'd know about it.

But if it happened at his house? Or out in the woods? Amy knew as well as anyone that Big Davey wasn't averse to the occasional burl poaching if he saw one he really liked and could get it out of the tree without doing too much harm. And, of course, he was buddies with Little Stevie; a bad influence, in Amy's view. Maybe the two of them had gone out, and there was some kind of trouble?

She grabbed the ashtray, went around the bar to the sink. As she dumped and washed out the ashtray, she came to a decision. What was that saying about the mountain and Mahatma, or Muhammad, or whoever the hell it was? If the mountain won't come to you, you go to the mountain, something like that.

She went to the ancient safe behind the bar, a classic 1910 Schwab stand-up, dialed the combination, and lifted out a bulky, shapeless bundle in a large plastic trash bag. Checked the clock over the bar. Nearly four. Figure twenty minutes at least to Big Davey's, another fifteen getting ready, and half an hour to get the job done. She shook her head. They'd barely make it before daylight, if at all. Daylight was no good.

"Davey," she muttered to herself, "you better have a damn good reason."

She locked the Tall Tree door behind her and headed for her truck.

Chapter Thirty-Five

Orick, California

It was still dark when Amy arrived at Big Davey's place. So damn hard to find, even when you knew where it was. Middle of goddamn nowhere, but that's how Davey liked it. He wasn't renowned for his people skills.

As her pickup crunched up the dirt driveway, her headlights bounced off Davey's ancient El Dorado and swung left to illuminate the clearing and pebbled path that led to his front porch. No lights on in the house. No lights in his barn-slash-workshop either, so he wasn't up early working.

"Goddammit. Probably passed out," Amy said to no one. She leaned on the horn. It blasted like a screamed obscenity, unnaturally loud as it ricocheted off the black wall of trees ringing the clearing.

"Wakey, wakey, eggs and bakey big fella," she said.

There was no response. No movement. No light. Nothing.

An acidic bubble rose and popped in Amy's stomach. She tried the horn again, held it longer. The blaring was so dissonant, so jarring she felt suddenly isolated and frightened. She let up on the horn; the utter silence that followed was no comfort.

She reached over, popped her glove compartment, and pulled out her Ruger .38 Special, a blunt-nosed, ugly hunk of metal, heavy and cold in her hand. She thumbed open the cylinder. Five slots, each filled with hollow points. Pushed the cylinder back until it clicked solidly in place. Grabbed her lithium Tech-Lite, a palm-sized flashlight with a spotlight's brilliance.

Amy made sure to leave the key in place. She opened the door and climbed out, the dome lamp casting a long shadow ahead of her. She left the door open, because you never know.

She thumbed the flashlight to life and waved the beam over the front of the house. "Davey! Davey, it's Amy! You here?"

She took a step towards the house, had a sudden thought and turned back to the truck. Reached in for her cell phone and checked the signal. Zero bars. Tossed it back on the seat. "Worthless piece of shit," she muttered.

Flashlight leveled, she made her way up the pathway and onto the front porch. A life-size grizzly bear loomed over her, the redwood burl sculpture exquisitely detailed down to the fur lines. Next to him, a beaver, gnawing on a fallen limb, lacquered eyes reflecting the glow of Amy's flashlight.

She pounded on the door. "You okay in there, Davey?" she shouted. Her voice was like breaking glass, startling and unnerving in the dark stillness. Still no answer. Tried the door handle. Locked.

She walked along the porch and played her flashlight through the picture window off Davey's living room. The powerful Tech-Lite blasted into the room, harsh and merciless, exposing every detail of the bloody, macabre scene inside.

Something primal and wholly unintelligible erupted from Amy's throat. She flipped her pistol, gripped it by the barrel, and smashed the picture window to bits. Didn't even notice the cuts on her hand and arm, the bleeding, the pain. Just barreled through and headed for the landline she knew was in the kitchen. She heard wordless, sobbing screams as she ran through the living room, and realized they were coming from her.

Later, she couldn't remember making the 9-1-1 call, but knew she must have, because the police eventually came. They found her where she had frozen: hunkered down on the tile floor of the kitchen, back to the cabinets, knees up to steady the gun she held in both hands, cocked, aimed and ready.

* * *

If there was a downside to having a blind bobcat as a travelling companion, it was the snoring.

Maybe it had something to do with the missing eyeballs, some kind of sinus misalignment resulting from the sunken sockets. Or maybe it had to do with being overfed and lazy. Whatever the cause, Tanner was certain a regular, run-of-the-mill wild bobcat did not sound like this.

But Ray Charles did, pretty much every morning starting around five-thirty, so Tanner was already wide awake when the call came from Eureka PD. The processing of the motel room had led nowhere; it had been scrubbed clean. Too clean.

"Damn. I'm not surprised. But damn." Tanner pulled a box of Shredded Mini-Wheats from the kitchen cabinet and dumped some into a bowl. "Okay, it was worth a shot." He grabbed a carton of milk from the fridge, gave it a quick sniff, and poured some over the cereal.

"We've issued an APB with the Chippies and every PD down the I5 and the 101 on Calhoun and his truck. Figuring he's most likely heading south, given the North Hollywood residence," said the officer.

"Right." Tanner's call-waiting beeped. He took a quick glance at the phone screen. Shepherd. "Hey, I've got another call coming in. Thanks a lot, keep me posted," he said, and switched over. "Hey Shep."

"Good, you're up. I just got a call from Detective Stewart. Meet me at the station."

Chapter Thirty-Six

Orick, California

"How'd Stevie find out about this already?" Shepherd said to Tanner as she wheeled up Big Davey's driveway. Just ahead, they could see Little Stevie chin up and nose-to-nose with Detective Stewart, each of them red in the face and jaws working like pistons.

They exited Shepherd's vehicle just as Little Stevie turned away from Stewart, spat on the ground, and started back for his truck. He stopped when he saw Tanner and Shepherd, set both feet and pointed a trembling index finger.

"You find out who did this," he said. "You find out. Just know this, okay? I'll be looking too. I find the son-of-a-bitch first, he ain't never going to jail."

Without waiting for a response, he flung open his truck door, climbed inside, and slammed the door closed.

"Jesus Christ on a cracker," Detective Stewart said as Tanner and Shepherd approached. "Like this ain't enough of a mess as it is, I gotta deal with that." Behind him, a Sheriff's Deputy finished sealing off Big Davey's house with bright yellow crime scene tape.

"How'd he find out so fast?" Shepherd asked.

Stewart shrugged. "Can't say. I'm guessing Amy called him. She's the one who called us."

"What was she doing out here?"

Stewart popped an unlit cigarette into his mouth. "Says he didn't show up at the bar last night, she got worried, came out to see if he was all right."

"That sound right?" Tanner asked.

"It's what she says." Stewart took the cigarette from his lips, exhaled nothing but air, put it back. "Maybe they had something going on, who knows?"

"She's not a suspect, is she Rod?" Shepherd asked.

"Hell no."

"Wonder why she called Little Stevie."

"Don't know that she did, I'm just guessing." He lifted the crime scene tape and invited them to duck under. "Reason I called you, there's some, um, details in here I think you should see. I'll take you in, but we're just starting to work the scene. Grab some gloves and booties," he said, indicating a box on the porch. "We can't go in the room where the vics are, but we can see it all from the kitchen. We'll go around to the side door."

"Vics plural?" Tanner asked.

"Plural. Two of 'em. Big Davey, and an unidentified Asian male."

"Aw, hell," Tanner said.

Shepherd raised an eyebrow. "An Asian?"

"I know," Stewart said. "'Course my first thought is tourist, but how he ends up here with Big Davey, and how it jibes with the rest of what's there…" He shook his head, replaced his soiled booties with a fresh pair, waited until Tanner and Shepherd had their gloves and booties on, then said, "Let's go have a look."

* * *

Stewart said, "Near as I can guess, Big Davey was tortured. Manages to somehow break loose, shoots the Asian guy with the crossbow, then dies, probably from blood loss."

"Aw, geez," Tanner said as they looked at the living room.

Big Davey's giant bulk sprawled sideways across a blood-soaked recliner. He was shirtless, his skin flayed and caked in hair and gore, countless deep slices revealing layers of tissue, muscle and fat. His eyelids were open, eyes staring sightlessly at the three of them. A crossbow was on the floor near his feet.

"My God," Shepherd breathed. She turned back for the door and made it outside before losing her breakfast.

Tanner hadn't seen anything like it, not since Kandahar. The big man looked like he'd been hacked to death with a machete. He pulled his eyes away from Big Davey and over to the Asian, who lay on his back, legs curled oddly. No apparent injuries to him, other than the short shaft of an arrow protruding from his chest. A bloodied hunting knife lay a few feet from one outstretched hand.

A crime scene technician measured the distance between the two bodies and recorded the result into a handheld device.

"Not much blood from that arrow," Tanner said to the tech.

The tech nodded. "Arrow's a decoy. His back's blown open."

"So he was shot." Tanner said. He nodded towards an Igloo cooler next to the Asian man. "What's in there?"

"Don't know for sure yet," the tech said from behind his mask. "Globs of some kind of meat, maybe an organ."

"That's why I called you here," Stewart said.

"Galls?" Tanner asked.

"Could be. Never seen one before."

"This Asian guy is the connection…and Big Davey was one of the poachers? They had some kind of falling out, maybe, and…"

Shepherd came back and interrupted. "No way," she said.

"How you doing?" Tanner asked.

"I'm okay."

"You're still kinda pale, you feel…"

"I said I'm okay. And no way Big Davey would poach bears. He's a hunter, most everyone up here is, and legit hunters despise poachers. On top of that, in the Park? Not a chance. A burl, yeah. But not a bear."

"Well," Stewart said, "I stopped being surprised a long time ago at what people will do for money."

Shepherd shook her head and turned to Tanner. "No way."

180

Tanner met her gaze. "You think someone set this up."

"Absolutely."

Tanner nodded slowly, then looked over at the gruesome scene. "I don't know. Maybe Davey was in on something, maybe not. What I know for sure is Calhoun and Davey mixed it up at the Tall Tree."

"Calhoun," the detective said.

"I wouldn't put this past him."

"All right," Stewart said. "We'll work the room, see if anything ties Calhoun in. Prints, DNA. They'll be on file, he's done time," Stewart said. "Meanwhile, we'll get a cause of death and an autopsy from the coroner. Which reminds me." He called to the crime scene tech. "Joey, you ready to release the bodies? Sandy's due to roll in pretty soon."

"I need maybe twenty more minutes," the tech answered.

Stewart waved Tanner and Shepherd towards the side door. "Let's get outta here." They followed him outside, removed their booties and gloves and tossed them in a lined trash can marked *Property of Humboldt County Sheriff.*

"So," Stewart said, "Who's the Asian guy, and what's he got to do with Big Davey?"

Chapter Thirty-Seven

Somewhere in Redwoods Park

Calhoun navigated his truck along a fire road that snaked deep into Redwoods. It was slow going at first but got easier as darkness gave way to a miraculously cloudless dawn. Upon arrival at his pre-set landmark he pulled the truck off the cleared road and under the concealment of the tree line. Before getting out, he popped a couple crosstops—he hadn't slept much in the past twenty-seven hours and had a long day ahead of him.

It took him nearly ninety minutes to pack his gear along the rugged trail he and Wheeler had blazed a week earlier. Back then, Wheeler had cut for sign and found fresh evidence of bear activity.

They'd worked together to create a small clearing for a bait site and built a jumbled stack of fallen logs and limbs. They'd also constructed a crude tree stand, fifteen feet up and about twenty yards from the site. "All that's left now is bait 'n wait," Wheeler had said.

Calhoun unpacked several bags of Gummi bears and scattered them around and within the log pile. For good measure, he tossed in some lumps of ground meat he'd dug out of that Paul Bunyan asshole's freezer.

Finishing that, he shouldered the small backpack, tied his bow and quiver to a rope, and climbed up to his tree stand. It was crudely constructed; a pair of two-by-four stubs nailed to the trunk as footrests to help support his weight as he sat on boards wedged into a natural crotch of the tree.

CHAPTER THIRTY-SEVEN

He hauled his weaponry up, settled into position, and began the wait.

* * *

She was over fifty pounds lighter than she'd been in April, nearly six months ago. Not that she was dieting. The reason for her relatively svelte physique was threefold; a trio of active cubs that had skyrocketed from a birth weight of under a pound to more than fifty times that, all due to a ravenous intake of her protein and fat-rich milk. Recently weaned, they had become little four-legged vacuum cleaners, non-stop eaters who set an exhausting pace for a protective mom.

The cool afternoon mist gleamed on the thick, coarse fur that overlaid her insulating undercoat. She clicked her tongue and grunted, signaling her brood to follow her down an arroyo that led to Devil's Creek, near the southern tip of Redwoods. The family descended haphazardly through a carpet of dripping ferns, their shuffling steps the only sounds that corrupted the wet, leaden silence.

She paused to allow her dawdling brood to catch up and huffed air. With a sense of smell seven times greater than a bloodhound's she easily detected a family of beavers at work over a half-mile away. She could clearly discern the pungent musk of a river otter prowling the Devil's Creek banks, and even farther downstream, a black-tailed deer doe and her two fawns.

But there was something else. She raised her nose and huffed again, casting her head right and left to get a sense of location. There. The faint but unmistakably fragrant aroma of sugar. Upstream, where the understory of California rhododendron and thimbleberry thinned, giving way to carpets of decaying pine needles under the overcast of old-growth trees.

Over her five years of life she'd spent lots of time in close proximity to humans and recognized an easy meal when she smelled it. Whether it was a backpack full of granola and protein bars left in the back seat of a car, packed-in food hung not quite high enough in a tree overnight, or her regular stop at the Yurok dumpsite, she'd enjoyed her share of tasty, leisurely meals courtesy of humans.

Her cubs followed as she changed direction and chased the sugar scent upstream. The understory grew sporadic and scrawny beneath the shade of two-hundred-foot behemoths. Soon the only obstacles in their path were the occasional fallen giants. Two of the cubs scaled one and chased each other along its length, nearly twelve feet above their mother.

* * *

Hours had passed, each one ratcheting Calhoun's discomfort up to new levels. His legs were numb from lack of circulation. Mosquitoes mined the exposed skin of his face and hands. His stomach was empty, his bladder straining, the powerful muscles in his upper back and shoulders knotted in searing cramps. Due to a bear's exceptional sense of smell Calhoun wore no bug repellent of any kind, much to the delight of not only the mosquitoes but the insistent face flies that dove for the moisture in his eyes and ears. In choosing this location, he and Wheeler hadn't noticed the ant trail that ran up the tree, but he was well aware of it now as they detoured up his pants leg.

But through all this, Calhoun moved only his lips, allowing himself an occasional sip from his CamelBak. The compact hydration backpack also held his Colt, and the gun had shifted, the barrel now poking forcefully into his back.

Wheeler and all the YouTube hunters had been adamant about the need to stay still and quiet, to virtually melt into the tree. Calhoun was a tough, hardened man. Even so, he hoped a bear would come along soon.

* * *

The sugar smell was strong now, overpowering nearly everything else. At this point, her cubs were also locked onto it. So intent were the little ones that they raced ahead of her into a small clearing. She growled at them, warning against such careless behavior, but it was no use. They were already at a pile of logs, snuffling and scrounging for the bright red candy scattered around and within the pile.

She huffed the air as she approached the pile. There was also a smell of meat, and the unmistakable scent of human, but there always was when she smelled sugar. While always cautious, she saw no reason for alarm. With a final huff, she joined the cubs and pulled a large log out of the way so they could more easily reach the candy.

* * *

Calhoun focused on controlling his heartrate. It was exciting to watch the prey, ever cautious, eventually decide she was safe. A triumphant feeling of outwitting a wild beast, of going back to a time when man was a part of nature, a cunning and dangerous predator. It was an atavistic thrill, and Calhoun reveled in it.

He sat motionless in the tree, watching them approach. Mama bear and three cubs. Four thousand dollars on the hoof; galls fetched the same price, whether from adults or cubs. Take Mama down first, the cubs will stay close to her. Then pick them off one by one. Calhoun realized he probably wouldn't get them all. Sooner or later one or two of the cubs would take off. But you take what you can get.

As the family approached the bait site, Calhoun inched through the procedure. First, slowly, ever so slowly, nock an arrow. Even more slowly, almost imperceptibly, raise the arms, get the hands to nose height. Keep the grip hand—the one holding the bow—directly in line with the target.

Peer through the Ultra Bow Sight. Inhale as you draw back the string. Bring the release hand toward your face. Rotate your shoulder until you reach "the wall," the point where you can draw back no further.

And now...hold for the shot.

Chapter Thirty-Eight

Somewhere in Redwoods Park

A ll the YouTube videos had advised to wait for a broadside shot, if at all possible. Wheeler had emphasized it as well.

The idea was to hit the bear in its midpoint, between forelegs and hind legs. At over three hundred feet-per-second the arrow would punch through the ribs like toothpicks, rip a destructive path through the lungs, shatter the opposing ribs, and burst out on the opposite side. The bear would instinctively run, but with a clean through-shot like that would suffocate and drop dead within a minute.

Calhoun held firm, right arm pulled back, left hand steady, eye sighting. The cubs were first, bounding to the bait site without caution, gobbling candy and ground beef. Mama took her time, huffing and grunting, and at one point seemed to look directly at him.

Moments passed, and the only movement was the involuntary jumping and quivering of the fatiguing muscles in his right arm.

The big bear finally broke her gaze, walked all the way into the clearing, and began nosing around at the food. The cubs gamboled around her, confusing the target area. She would turn broadside, and a cub would suddenly be in the way. Hitting a cub first would be a mistake, Calhoun was sure of that. Either they'd all take off, or who knows, maybe Mama would get pissed off and find him, climb the tree and haul him down before he could load a fresh arrow. Better to wait.

Sweat stung Calhoun's eyes, his shoulder burned, the fingers of his right hand had gone numb, but still he waited.

And then, there it was.

She moved a large log aside, and the cubs scrambled at the mounds of newly revealed treats. She was a separate, clear, broadside target, unimpeded. Calhoun breathed out audibly and let the arrow fly.

What Calhoun hadn't yet mastered was that shooting from above requires adjustments. The arrow hit the bear high and just behind the shoulder, thumping solidly into muscle. She staggered, then squalled loudly to her cubs as she bolted for the trees. The cubs screamed in terror and followed, crashing blindly through the undergrowth to keep up. Every step for her was agony, a searing jolt of hot pain as branches and vines snagged the arrow's protruding shaft, pulled against the buried head, tore at muscle tissue. Yet she continued running, if only to get her cubs to safety.

Calhoun's heart raced as he half-climbed, half-fell from his perch. He recovered, nocked another arrow, and hastily followed the bear's trail. Bear hunting was a fucking blast! He was happy to see large swatches of bloodied leaves and tree bark. Maybe an indication his shot had been effective, and he'd find her soon. With any luck, the cubs would stay close, and he'd get the chance to kill one or more of them as well.

For a short time he could hear them up ahead, branches snapping and cracking, but they moved far more quickly than he could. He needed to step up his pace, but as they left the cover of old growth trees the understory and ground growth increased. Tracking the bears through the walls of ferns and dense thickets proved more challenging than he'd imagined. In his past successful shots, the bears hadn't traveled more than a hundred yards or so. This time, as the minutes passed, he was sure he'd gone much farther than that. He hoped it wasn't another of his misses; he didn't have time for that shit.

He continued to bull his way along, scanning the undergrowth for signs of blood or obvious disturbances, stopping occasionally to listen for sounds of their flight.

A fallen redwood blocked his path, its trunk over ten feet in diameter. It looked impossible to climb. He had no choice but to detour alongside and finally reached a formidable tangle of torn roots at its base. After fighting his way past those, he stopped to re-orient himself. He listened for the bears. Listened for several moments. But heard nothing.

Had she died? Calhoun hoped that was the case, and she was somewhere nearby. But where? He looked up to find the sun, hoping to get some idea of direction. No chance; it was impossible to pinpoint beyond the canopy.

He spun around, searching for some clue to the direction he'd been heading before being detoured by the fallen tree. He could see nothing but trees. Seemingly identical trees, a bewildering, claustrophobic crush of trees.

His heart quickened, and he felt his anger rise. Goddammit! He'd done everything right. Get these four fucking bears, he'd be just four shy of the complete order, with some time to go. He was not going to let this one get away. That wasn't happening again.

He closed his eyes, inhaled deeply, blew it out. Took a more measured look around. It occurred to him then that time would quickly become a concern. The tree canopy darkened the ground, and as the afternoon progressed visibility was only going to get worse. He needed to find his dead bear soon, while there was still enough light to get the butchering done. He chastised himself for not bringing a flashlight.

After several forays down what seemed to be trails but led nowhere, he finally stumbled on what looked like blood spoor. He followed it into an increasingly overgrown area, and while it was even more difficult to make forward progress, he could more easily spot the disturbed ground and broken branches marking where the bears had probably gone. The undergrowth was so thick in places he was forced to drop on all fours and crawl along what he felt was the path.

This was not going well. He was moving far too slowly. If he didn't find the dead bear soon, he'd have to turn back.

He reluctantly conceded there would be no time to kill and butcher any of the cubs. Besides, the bow and the arrow quiver had become too much of a hindrance. He laid them, along with nearly all his gear, against a tree trunk, mentally marking the spot so he could find it upon his return. He still had a knife on his belt, the gun and some water in the CamelBak, and a folded bag in his pocket to store the bear parts. He looked up, still hoping for some glimpse of the sun to gauge the time, then pushed forward, deeper into the woods.

Chapter Thirty-Nine

Eureka, California

Thirty days suspended, five-thousand dollar fine reduced to five hundred, no probation. Hell of a deal, Wheeler thought as he walked out of the Eureka courthouse and into another cold, gray, soggy day. Got to give it up for that Poindexter lawyer. He worked the cooperation angle like a champ. Likely the Fed guy put in a word, too.

In any case, he was out, and now the plan was to get gone ASAP.

No waiting around for Calhoun. That dude was on his own, and good luck to him. This whole gig had been pretty much ass-fucked from the start. Mickey was game enough, but as good as he may have been at high-falling, gun-slinging and knife-throwing, he wasn't much of a hunter. What he was, was a fucking psycho.

Wheeler felt no regrets or compunction about giving up Calhoun. Fuck him. Killing that pot farmer, that was beyond stupid. Completely unnecessary. *Not to mention knocking my ass around with that fucking blackjack.*

The thing to do now was salvage something out of this clusterfuck. Wheeler had spent his brief time in the can thinking about nothing else and had arrived at a plan based on a simple realization: once Wheeler had met the money man face-to-face, Calhoun became superfluous. Dead weight.

Having retrieved the belongings he'd had on him when he was arrested—including his bow—Wheeler walked the mile-and-a-half from the courthouse to the Bay Mist motel. As he expected, the room had been processed by the cops and cleaned out by management. He stopped into the front office on the off chance they were holding the few articles of clothing he'd travelled with.

"Sorry, friend," the pimply-faced clerk said, sounding not at all sorry. "One of the cops told me that room was a hundred percent empty when they got there. Guess you gotta check with the other guy, he musta took your clothes."

Which of course meant the ice chest was gone, and with it the twelve galls. Most of which could—and should—be credited to Wheeler's work. No doubt riding around now in the back of Calhoun's truck.

No matter. Wheeler had devised a plan, the success of which rested on two simple facts.

Fact Number One: Wheeler had lived in L.A. for several years, and at any rate spent zero time living under a rock, so in spite of his denial to Tanner he'd immediately recognized the bald asshole money-man as a big-time movie producer. Knew it from the moment Calhoun brought that douchebag into the hotel room. Seen him interviewed on *Access Hollywood* or some show like that. Also a big spread on him in *Playboy* once, about his mansion and all the Hollywood parties and such.

Fact Number Two: One of Wheeler's long-time hunting buddies, an ex-outfitter from Montana, had for some years settled near the central California coast, where he ran a very successful pig farm.

Wheeler called up an Uber ride to take him over to the police impound yard so he could reclaim his Land Cruiser. On the way over, he put a call in to his pig farmer friend. Got voicemail and left a message. Next, he meandered through Google, researching the current residence of one H.H. Goldstein.

* * *

The four-point-two-liter straight six engine under the hood of Wheeler's Toyota devoured the curves of the 299 and roared onto the I-5, thundering due south. A brand-new cooler sat on the passenger seat.

He pondered his next moves as he ripped through California's agricultural heartland, past vast, dormant vineyards; past seemingly endless orchards of almond trees; past eighteen-wheelers humping everything from tomatoes to tractor parts to wrecked cars; past solitary drivers and packed SUVs; past the downtowns of Sacramento and Stockton; past empty stretches where cattle searched for fodder on rolling brown hillsides.

Bug juice spattered the windshield, highway seams pock-pock-pocked under his tires in a hypnotic rhythm, radio reception waxed and waned.

None of which earned more than a cursory notice from Wheeler. He drove on instinct, his mind focused on what needed to come next.

If he drove hard and the roads stayed clear, he figured to make Buellton in about nine hours. The plan was to spend the night there at his pig farmer friend's place, then back on the road by four A.M. That should get him to his second stop around seven in the morning.

After that, things were going to get real busy.

Chapter Forty

Trinidad, California

Dusk had faded to darkness as Tanner pulled into Harbor Trailer Park. It had been a long and frustrating couple days.

Yesterday, after leaving the crime scene at Big Davey's house, he and Shepherd had grabbed some lunch—more accurately, he had, she had no appetite—then headed back to the Ranger station. Tanner claimed squatter's rights on the seasonal ranger's desk and spent a few hours on the obligatory paperwork that would document his investigation and, most importantly, justify the budget expenditure for Steve Moore. The Resident Agent-in-Charge demanded meticulous accounting, always something of a challenge for Tanner.

That completed, he drove back to Eureka to meet with the Assistant District Attorney assigned to Wheeler's case. She was a knockout, and he spent more time than was probably necessary outlining the vague offers of leniency he'd extended to Wheeler in return for his cooperation. In the end, the only hard evidence against Wheeler was on the poaching charge, and the over-worked ADA was fine with reducing the penalty she'd request in exchange for a fast guilty plea. He left her with his thanks, and his phone number. In case she had any questions later.

He'd spent most of the next day with Shepherd in a fruitless search of roads and trails, following up on a morning call from Chief Hendrix. A mother bear with cubs had been spotted at the reservation landfill. She had an arrow protruding from a shoulder.

"This is a bear the locals know." Chief Hendrix's anger was clear, even over the speakerphone in Shepherd's office. "She's a regular at the dump."

"So, the arrow's recent," Tanner said. He paced in front of Shepherd's desk.

"The last day or so. The guy who called it in said he'd seen her a couple days ago, and she was fine. So, how many of these assholes are there?"

"We think there's still one out there."

"He'd have to be incredibly stupid to keep trying, after we caught Wheeler," Shepherd said from behind her desk.

"In my experience the average trafficker can't put two thoughts together with duct tape and a manual," Tanner said.

"I heard you struck out in Eureka," Hendrix said. "So maybe they're smarter than you think."

* * *

That evening, Tanner's headlights swept across his trailer and Ray Charles' enclosure as he came to a stop, illuminating the big cat perched on a carpeted cat climber. His head lifted as Tanner's car rolled to a stop.

Tanner grabbed a halter and leash, then unlatched the enclosure gate. "Sorry I'm late, pal," he said. Ray Charles lazily stretched and yawned, making him wait.

"I said I was sorry. Come on, I'm hungry. Let's get this done."

Clearly punishing Tanner for his tardiness, Ray Charles took his time climbing down from the top of the stand. Tanner fit the halter into place, grabbed a doggie-waste bag, and the two headed down the path that led to the park's edge.

"Hey, Nick!" The voice was unmistakable and detonated the quiet of the night like a trumpet. Ray Charles dropped into a defensive crouch, his head rocking like his namesake, trying to locate the source of the sound.

Tanner turned to see Toad in full-speed waddle. A fresh cigarette hung from his lips, the smoke curling unheeded into his eyes.

"Toad. How you doing?"

"Livin' the dream, big guy. How's that lion of yours?" The cigarette bounced in Toad's lips, yet somehow stayed in place.

"Long day for both of us, but we're fine."

"I was starting to worry about him, wondered if I needed to come over and feed him or something."

"Yeah, work went a little late for me, thanks. I always leave him plenty of kibble, he'll eat it if he gets hungry enough."

Toad stood next to Tanner now. His plastered hair topped out at Tanner's chest level and smelled like a wet ashtray. "Go ahead with your walk," Toad panted. "I'll walk with you."

They strolled together alongside Ray Charles, who sniffed with little interest at the pathway, heading instead for the richer scents near the creek that bordered the park. "We may have to do a little cross-country, Toad. Ray likes to, uh…"

"Shit in the woods," Toad said.

"Yeah."

"Well hell, who doesn't?" He smiled, his eyes nearly disappearing behind over-stuffed cheeks.

They followed Ray's lead to a patch of loamy soil at the base of a young redwood where his sniff-and-scratch preparations cued both of them to turn away.

"So how were things around here today?" Tanner asked.

"Oh, pretty uneventful. Few newbies showed, that family from Oregon packed up a day early and left, same ol' same ol'. Except one thing, this was kind of unusual. It's what I came to tell you about."

"Oh?"

"Yeah, had the strangest thing happen today. I was out in the south park, way down by Devil's Creek, you know, checking the camera there and whatnot."

"Oh yeah?" Tanner was half-listening and felt the leash stop moving. Which meant soon it'd be time to beat a hasty retreat. Ray Charles could clear an amphitheater. "What was that?"

"Well, I check the camera, and I scroll through the video captures in the viewfinder, y'know, see if I've got anything worth saving. Most of the time it's deer, or coyotes, once in a while a bear. The motion sensors, they don't know, there's no intelligence in the design, they pick up whatever's there."

"So you checked the camera," Tanner prompted.

"Right, yeah. I check the camera, I move through the clips, and I'm not seeing anything but, like I said, deer and such. And then, ba-boom! Waddaya think I see?"

"Bigfoot?"

"Not this time, brother, but I wish." He paused and moved away, waving a hand in front of his nose. "Lord above, that's fierce."

Ray Charles was enthusiastically tearing up the underbrush, covering the evidence of his deed. Tanner let him finish, cleaned up afterwards, and disposed of the waste bag. The pair joined Toad a few yards down the drive.

"What's that boy eat, skunk butt?"

"Hey, he's got feelings, Toad. What did you see?"

"What it was, was a man."

"Well, I guess there are hikers all over the park."

"Maybe, but not way out there. My cameras are set up specifically in remote areas, where I'm most likely to get a sighting. You don't think Bigfoot hangs around campgrounds and hiking trails, do you?"

"I guess I hadn't given it much thought, but sure, that makes sense."

"He wouldn't, right?"

"Right," Tanner said. "That would explain why so few people have seen him."

"Exactly. And here's the kicker. This guy's got nothing."

"What do you mean?"

"I mean no gear. Just a little back-packy thing, and a big-ass cowboy hat." Tanner stopped. "By himself?"

"Far as I could tell. I'm thinking I should tell the Ranger."

"Toad. Tell me you still have that video."

* * *

The quality of Toad's video was quite good, and Tanner said so.

"It ought to be." Toad said. Inside his surprisingly well-appointed RV, he sat in front of an oversized high-definition monitor. Tanner hovered behind, watching over Toad's shoulder. Toad indicated the camera that was plugged into his computer's USB port. "1080p HD, motion sensor, controllable though my smartphone—though of course out in the Park smartphones are mostly just useless hunks of plastic. Here, it's coming up."

He slowed his scroll through the footage, and Tanner leaned in. Although tinged with green, the image was amazingly clear. Trees, undergrowth, a slight breeze moving the leaves...and then, a man came into view.

Tanner couldn't see the face. Tall, well-built. Big Stetson. Walking with uncertainty, occasionally stumbling, his arms wrapped across his chest.

"Freezing his ass off, looks like," Toad said. "Knucklehead isn't even wearing a jacket."

"How long ago was this?

"It's time-stamped," Toad pointed to a digital readout in a corner of the frame. "See? Two-thirty-three in the morning."

"This morning."

"Yep."

"Over seventeen hours ago. Okay, can you show me where this camera was positioned?"

"Sure, no problem. Got a map of the park right here, shows where all my cameras are." He rummaged in a desk drawer. "Why?"

"I think there's a chance this man may be a criminal the police are looking for. During the course of my research here, I came across a bear poaching ring."

"You did?"

Toad shifted his weight, the springs in his swivel chair groaning in protest, and looked at Tanner.

"You're some kind of writer," Toad said.

Chapter Forty-One

Somewhere in Redwoods Park

C alhoun had never been so cold.

He'd long ago given up on finding the bear, his gear, or even the path he'd originally taken in pursuit of the bear and her cubs. The map he and Wheeler had used when planning their bait sites showed dirt roads crisscrossing seemingly everywhere, but damn if he'd been able to find a single one in last night's darkness.

The relentless drizzle had continued all night and soaked through his jacket, his clothes, his hat, his hair, his shoes, even his underwear through his pants. Everything was saturated and frigid. He'd given sleep a half-hearted try, huddling in the shelter of a huge fallen tree, but between the pervasive dankness, relentless mosquitoes, and the wriggling insects that lived their lives turning fallen vegetation into sodden mulch, he found no comfort, and had decided to keep moving. At least that way he thought he might stay warm. Or at least less cold.

It was a bad decision.

The grasping scrub and hidden stumps dealt him a savage beating all night. Angry, oily red bumps erupted from his forearms and ignited into fire if he scratched. The utter darkness, the unfamiliar night noises, the disorientation sparked a primal fear he'd never experienced.

When he heard running water somewhere below him, he reasoned that a good strategy would be to follow the downstream flow. Had to lead somewhere; someone's campsite, maybe back into town, maybe the fucking ocean. At least it was a direction.

Calhoun took a seat and began sliding downhill towards the water. He dug his heels hard into the muddy ground, controlling his speed. The earth was soaked and slimy, the hillside ribbed with slick, algae-caked stone outcroppings that gave his boots no purchase, like sliding on greased marble. As he neared the water the hillside steepened, and Calhoun laid flat, grabbing blindly at ferns, grassy clumps, anything to slow down.

The water roared beneath him as he shot off a ledge and into the darkness, arms flailing, images flashing in his mind of sharp, deadly rocks and torrents of merciless water. Instinct honed by years of training triggered his body to streamline into a feet-first entry, and he was nearly vertical when he hit.

* * *

The gun was lost.

It was somewhere at the bottom of Devil's Creek, along with his CamelBak and his jacket.

Some fucking creek. More like a goddamn river.

Calhoun sat on a bed of pebbles next to the rushing water, heaving for air. He'd actually been lucky, all things considered. He'd hit a deep pool when he fell, went down maybe eight feet from the force of the fall. The cold sucked the wind out of him, an involuntary gasp that sent icy water knifing into his sinuses, coursing into his lungs. His throat constricted, and he fought the urge to cough, knowing it would kill him. He was an instant away from taking that one, final breath of surrender when the swift-moving current brought him back up, banged him around rocks like a pinball as it carried him downstream, tossed him over a short drop, and slowed enough to where he could muscle himself to the shoreline and haul out.

He huddled there, a wet, miserable ball of exhaustion and pain. The shivering was uncontrollable, violent. He knew hypothermia was just around the corner, if not already there. His right ankle was tender, swelling painfully against the top of his boot. He was bruised, sore, disoriented, and

199

most of all, pissed off at the unfairness of it all.

He forced himself to control his breathing. In through the nose, out through the mouth. Slow the heart. *Hell, you been hurt before. Won't be the last time. Suck it up.*

He labored to his feet, tested the ankle. Probably not broken. Sprained. Hurt, but reasonably workable.

Thing to do is, remain calm. There was always a solution to every problem. There would be one to this. And he still had his knife. Few were as talented with a knife as he was. Axes, too, and tomahawks. He laughed, a sharp humorless yawp that surprised him. *If I'm near the reservation, maybe I can find me a tomahawk.*

He felt for the scabbard, ran his fingers along the hilt of his knife. Would it be enough? Enough, say, to stop a bear? What if the arrow hadn't killed her, and she was out there right now, in the blackness, in pain and enraged, tracking him for revenge? He was barely able to see the length of his arm. She could be out there, right now, claws ready to shred his skin, jaws aching to crush his skull.

And what about wolves? Did they have wolf packs in the redwoods? He remembered seeing something on the news about California reintroducing grey wolves. Why would they do a stupid thing like that?

And snakes. Were there snakes? He knew snakes didn't do well in the cold, that their cold-bloodedness made them slow and passive. Still, if he were to inadvertently step on one...

His cell phone was soaked and unresponsive, but it didn't matter. Through-out the night he'd looked in vain for a signal. And besides, who would he call? The only thing the phone had been good for was to occasionally light his way with a flashlight app. He tried to use that sparingly so he could keep moving throughout the night, but it had given out long before he'd gone for his brief swim in Devil's Creek.

With an involuntary groan he straightened, tested his ankle, and set himself to the task of following the creek.

He walked, crawled and fought throughout the night, guided only by the sound of the water, moving if only to keep from freezing to death. The stars were invisible to him, shining somewhere beyond the suffocating canopy and a deep mist that hung over the water. It was like wandering blindfolded in a subterranean cavern.

When the first glimmer of daylight finally came, the blackness leeching gradually to a monochromatic gray, it brought little solace. On all sides, the monstrous tree trunks loomed around him, closing in, as rigidly straight and coldly indifferent as the bars of a prison.

Chapter Forty-Two

Somewhere in Redwoods Park

"Good morning," Tanner said, his phone Bluetooth-connected to his vehicle as he drove. "Do you know anyone around here with some horses we can use?"

"Huh?"

"Rise and shine," Tanner said. He wheeled the Expedition onto the highway and gunned it north. "We've got a time-sensitive situation here, Shepherd."

"And you need horses?"

"There's a guy lost in the park, got caught on camera. Big cowboy hat. Could be our boy Calhoun."

"How do you know?"

"Guy I met hunts Bigfoot with cameras. He got him wandering in the woods the night before, showed me last night."

"Bigfoot?

"C'mon, Shep, wake up."

"Okay, okay. So, the horses are because you're going after this guy in the Park?"

"*Correcto.*"

"Where in the Park?"

"Down at the south end. The Devil's Creek clearing."

"Okay, but if you're going into the woods down there you don't want a horse. Terrain's a mess, the growth can get real thick. You want a mule."

"Okay, can you get me a couple mules?"

"A couple?"

"Of course. You're going with me."

"Shit. Yes, I can get mules."

"Great. I've packed some water, snacks, first aid and such. I'll meet you at the clearing."

"We should call in the sheriff."

"Not yet. One, we'll be on mules, not in squad cars, those boys will slow us down. Two, we don't know for sure this is our man, or how long we'll have to track him. We'll call them in when we've got something solid. It's me and you, Shep."

"All right, all right. I'll get in touch with Wild Bill. It'll take a couple hours to get them trailered up and get there."

Tanner glanced at his dashboard clock. "Say, nine-thirty?"

* * *

Calhoun plunged his knife into the icy water of Devil's Creek, pinning a foot-long suckerfish to the pebbly bottom.

Another morning had come at last, and with it, some measure of hope. The fog had cleared, replaced by sun-stoked steam rising from the mulched forest floor. It was still far from warm, however, and Calhoun had yet to stop shivering. His clothes stuck to him like wet compresses. He reached into the water and pulled out the wriggling bottom-feeder.

With a few flicks of the knife, he descaled and gutted the fish, then chomped the slimy meat like a bulldog, crunching leftover scales and bones.

Today he needed to find a road and follow it out of the park. He had no desire to endure another wet, frigid night. He was exhausted, but he would regain energy with breakfast, and he would walk as long and far as necessary until he was out of these woods. And once out, he vowed never to return.

The contract was dead. Fuck it. He had twelve galls and forty-eight paws back in his truck. That'd have to do. Goldstein didn't like it, fuck him. He could damn well take what Calhoun was able to get, he wasn't getting any more. Besides, with Wheeler out of the picture Calhoun would get the whole share, which actually put him ten grand fatter than if he and Wheeler had split the full order.

But first, of course, he had to get to his truck.

Calhoun swallowed the last of the fish, washed his hands in the sharp chill of the stream, and straightened.

That was going to happen today. Today he'd get the hell out of these woods, and never come back.

* * *

For the thousandth time that day he looked up, searching through the canopy. Occasional glimpses of the sky revealed a clear and cloudless day, but the mottled ceiling of interlocking branches kept the exact location of the sun a secret, and frustrated Calhoun's attempts to orient himself.

He was still staring up through the pines when a sudden sound dropped him to a crouch. It cracked sharp and hard, like a gunshot. Calhoun knew well that there was no hunting, and certainly no gunfire, sanctioned in the Redwoods. The sound rang out again, and this time he realized it wasn't from a gun. Something else.

A hammer? No. An axe. Someone, somewhere up ahead, was swinging an axe. It came again, sounding close, but the reverberation pin-balled through the trees and masked its location.

Calhoun spun in slow circles, eyes shut, ready to zero in on the sound should it ring out again. For minutes, there was nothing.

Then, the angry buzz of a motor as it coughed and sputtered to life, then revved up to high RPMs. Chainsaw. Which at the moment meant one thing above all else: another human being nearby. Food. Transportation.

Renewed hope dumped scalding adrenaline into his veins and drove his legs like pistons. He barreled through soggy mulch that sucked greedily at his shoes, slid down slick, mossy hillsides, clambered over the great shafts of fallen trees, wrestled through the tentacles of vine maples and poison oak. With each bit of progress gained, the sound grew louder, his resolve stronger.

When he spotted the clearing, it was sudden and surreal. A brightly lit oasis, glowing, warm and welcoming. It was like seeing his first sunrise, and Calhoun nearly cried out loud with the thought of relief from the suffocating, towering trunks and the utter, prehistoric stillness. With a final surge he bulled past the last few trees and crashed toward the light. He gave no thought to the reason for such a clearing.

He was so close. He pushed his way past a dense stand of alders and was perhaps five yards from the final ring of greenery when the world exploded.

* * *

The sound of the first shot startled a flock of scrub jays, their sudden screeching nearly as unsettling as the apparent proximity of the blast. Shepherd abruptly reined her mule, Vanilla Bean, to a halt. Tanner's mule, Chocolate Swirl, trotted up behind.

"Whoa!" Shepherd said. "Definitely a gun."

"Yeah," Tanner said. "Big one, by the sound of it. You get any kind of bearing?"

Shepherd waved a hand towards the northwest. "Can't be sure, there's so much echo. But it seemed like up that way."

"That's the way I heard it too. Same direction as the chainsaw, right?"

"I think so, yeah."

"You know of a trail, or are we still bushwacking?"

Shepherd waved at the scrawny path they were following. "This is it. Deer trails."

Tanner thought a moment. "The camera caught this guy by Devil's Creek. In my experience, lost people follow water." He gestured in the direction of the gunshot. "The creek head that way?"

"It could. It twists around a lot, eventually ends up in the ocean up near Orick."

Tanner was about to speak when another shot rang out, as loud as the first.

"Holy shit," Tanner said.

"This way," Shepherd said, and urged Vanilla Bean northwest into the woods. "We'll follow the creek."

They moved along an elevated ridge, Devil's Creek below them. The mules' hooves sucked at the algae-covered loam, the sound almost lost beneath the dancing music of the creek. Tanner worried that the ambient racket would keep them from hearing something they might need to hear. He was wrong. It was easy to hear the screams.

Chapter Forty-Three

Somewhere in Redwoods Park

At the sound of the first shot, field worker Gumaro Lopez pushed his face into the plowed earth and flattened his chubby body into what he hoped was invisibility behind five-foot high rows of leafy cannabis.

Minutes later, when the second shot cracked the stillness, he dug his elbows into the soil and slithered alongside the row, head low, aiming for the cover of the trees. He didn't know what was going on and didn't care to. He was there to keep the plants alive, not to defend them. There were others for that, well-armed and experienced in violence. Let them deal with whoever or whatever this was. If this was a police raid, he needed to vanish to avoid being deported. If this was a rival cartel raid, he needed to vanish to avoid being fed a mouthful of his own genitals. Either way, his choice was clear.

Three other undocumented workers followed Gumaro's lead. On the other hand, the reactions of security guards Hector and Luis Chairez were quite different. The first blast woke them from their customary afternoon *siesta*. By the second blast both had already raced to pre-planned positions, AK-47 rifles at the ready.

As he settled into his shooting trench, Hector spoke to his twin brother through a small headset microphone linked to his brother's radio. *"Dos trampas."*

"*Si*," Luis said. Two blasts, two shotgun-shell traps tripped, which could very well mean multiple intruders.

"*Esperamos. Tal vez están muertos.*" Hector felt no need to rush things. There was a good chance whoever had set off the traps had been sawn in half. If so, the situation was already solved. If not, they'd find out soon enough.

The two men trained their guns at the treeline. A transient whiff of gunpowder was quickly overwhelmed by the thick aroma of over three open acres of healthy marijuana, richly fertilized soil, and diesel fumes from a generator. The generator powered lights inside the makeshift greenhouse, an old shipping container packed with hundreds of seedlings. In all, a farm with a potential yield of over ten million dollars, one of several operated by the cartel that hired the Chairez brothers and imported the labor.

"*¿Crees que quizás los Búlgaros?*" Luis whispered.

"*No se.*" Bulgarian gangs had overrun the Emerald Triangle of late, checkerboarding the woods with big, sloppy grow sites of their own, and forcibly co-opting sites from independent locals. They hadn't made a move on any of the Mexican cartel farms yet, but it was likely just a matter of time. Maybe this was them?

Hector sensed the field behind him emptying of their laborers. He shrugged that off. There was nowhere for those *putas* to go. They all knew they weren't getting paid a dime until the harvest was in. As long as they didn't go too far into the woods and get lost, they'd be back.

He lightly stroked his index finger along the curve of the trigger. Maybe he and his brother would be lucky. Maybe the booby traps hadn't finished the job.

* * *

The first blast shredded Calhoun's right shoe and pulped his foot. The pain caused his vision to go white, but instinct and sheer athleticism drove him to drop, roll away, and scramble for cover behind the massive trunk of a towering redwood.

He had no idea who had shot him, or where the shooter was. He'd need to find out, but first things first. He stayed concealed and quiet as he gingerly removed the remnants of his shoe, then peeled away the blood-soaked rag that was his sock. Jaw clamped, teeth grinding against the pain, he wrenched the laces from his other shoe, pulled off his shirt and used his knife to slice off a sleeve. He wrapped the sleeve around what appeared to be the worst of the injury, then bound it tightly with the laces. It was like driving a knife into the sole of his foot, and he fought a rush of nausea. Pressing on, he sliced off the other sleeve and tied it off just above his ankle, a crude but serviceable tourniquet.

With great effort, Calhoun forced himself to think through the situation. Who had shot him, and why? Could law enforcement have tracked him down? They'd shout a warning first, wouldn't they? Maybe not. Out here in the woods, who would know if they did or didn't? He'd be a lot easier to bring back dead than alive.

But who could have seen him? He'd wandered the deep woods for two days now, never saw any sign of a road, a structure, or another person. How would anyone know where to find him, much less set up an ambush?

It was hard to think clearly. He was hungry, thirsty, and with every movement he felt someone drag the teeth of a saw across his foot. The pain was less when he remained still, but Calhoun knew staying still was not an option.

He scanned his surroundings, searching for a defensible position, an area of concealment at the edge of a few feet of open space. Enough to put the shooter in the clear.

His current spot was no good. Too many obstacles, too many branches and bushes. The shooter would have a clear advantage.

Ah. There. Maybe six, seven yards behind and to his left. A fallen tree on a slight incline. It appeared to have hit and rolled downhill, crushing the growth, leaving a clearing perhaps ten feet deep and three times that in width. From behind that fallen tree, he could watch as the shooter tracked him into the open space.

Time to move. He steeled himself against the agony to come, rolled onto his stomach, and began crawling. He intentionally kept to the thickest of the growth, hoping it would provide enough cover, knowing he still had to move quickly.

The ground was liquid and smelled of decay. His exposed torso was slick with cold mud, yet on fire from poison oak welts red and angry as whip scars. With each push forward his injured foot fired bolts of hot acid up his leg. Bushes gouged his face and poked at his eyes.

He paused for a breath, and to once again steel himself against the pain. He knew he was reaching the end of his endurance and strength, and he was both angry and ineffably sad. To be wounded and pursued in the deep forest was not a fate Calhoun had ever envisioned for himself. He was a hardened man, a veteran of brawls real and staged. Not so long ago he was every stunt coordinator's first call when the fall was high, the risks uncertain, the action brutal. Those calls were less and less frequent as age and an increasingly short fuse soured his appeal, but goddammit, he was still a tough motherfucker.

And yet, here he was, reduced to being little more than a wounded animal. Lost, hurt, and yes, frightened.

A sudden sob bubbled up and burst from his lips. He realized with surprise and reflexive embarrassment that he was crying. Pathetic. He rubbed a filthy forearm across his face. Just a few more feet to go. It wasn't over for him, not yet.

He couldn't risk crawling through the clearing itself, so he had to battle through forest growth and the stiff, tangled branches of the fallen tree. It seemed that nature was against him, fighting back every inch of the way, snagging his clothing, tearing his skin, reaching out to inflict more damage to what was left of his foot. He thought of simply giving up; of freezing like a terrified rabbit in the bush, hoping the hunter simply passed him by.

Yet still he crawled, and at last his fingertips touched the scaly bark of the fallen log. Relief was a wave that triggered new tears, and this time he let them flow. He took a deep, readying breath, knowing that his next movement—surmounting the log and dropping to the other side—needed to be swift and sure, in spite of the pain that was sure to come.

He raised himself to his knees. If he could make it over the log without being seen, he would have a chance. A chance was all he asked. He coiled himself, then launched. As his head rose to lead the way over the log, he felt a thin line of pressure crease his forehead.

The blast spun him sideways off the log and back to the ground.

Chapter Forty-Four

Somewhere in Redwoods Park

At the sound of the screaming, Shepherd saw Tanner hold a finger to his lips, point to his left, and signal that they should dismount. Her heart banging against her ribs, Shepherd slid to the ground and looped the mule's reins around the base of a giant fern. Tanner did the same.

Tanner cinched his backpack of supplies a bit tighter, pulled his Glock and moved close to her. He spoke in a whisper. "Nine o'clock. Really close."

Shepherd nodded. She suddenly felt violently cold, even as sweat drenched her armpits and boiled from her forehead.

"Your gun," Tanner said.

She continued to nod. It seemed to be all she could do. It was so cold.

"Shep. Your gun."

She looked down, then back at Tanner, her eyes confused and clouded. Her jaw trembled, her body shuddered with a single convulsive shiver.

Tanner put a hand on her shoulder. He focused on her eyes, held them with his own, as though willing them into clarity. "We gotta do this, Shep. Stay with me, now." He reached down and unsnapped her holster. "Grab it."

Shepherd drew a sharp, sudden breath, blew it out, and pulled the Sig from its holster. She held it against her leg.

Tanner leaned in, his voice low. "Put one in the chamber."

She nodded yet again and racked the slide. Tanner looked her in the eyes.

"We're good, right?"

"We're good," Shepherd said. It felt like someone else's voice, in someone else's body.

Tanner's eyes stayed locked on hers. "Stay in the bush, five or ten yards to my right. Move only when I move. Stop when I stop. Clear?"

Shepherd could find no oxygen in the air. She tried to speak, but there was a golf ball in her throat. All she could do was nod. She had a brief flash of one of those baseball bobble-heads inanely bouncing in a car's rear window.

Tanner smiled. "We're having some fun now, right? Stay with me. If I shoot, you shoot." He gave her a squeeze on the arm. "But hopefully no shooting, right?"

"Right," she managed.

Tanner peeled away toward the creek and motioned for her to move into the underbrush and follow. On legs of rubber, her Sig pointing skyward, her pulse throbbing in her neck, Shepherd pushed off the trail.

* * *

After the second blast, Hector waited a full five minutes before he waved his brother out of hiding. Neither spoke as they worked their way cautiously towards the edge of the clearing, moving from one strategically placed hay bale bunker to the next.

Multiple shotgun booby-traps surrounded the perimeter of the farm. Set between two and three feet off the ground, they were meant to either cripple or, for the unfortunate height-challenged intruder, disembowel. Way out here they were rarely triggered, and when they were it was typically by deer or elk. And never two in succession.

Hector spoke softly into his headset mic. He told Luis that they would enter the woods together at the site of the second blast. He needed to say nothing more. They moved with the choreographed precision of a team with over four years of success as cartel hitters in Sinaloa.

The second blast most certainly came from their southernmost trap, one Luis remembered setting along a large fallen redwood. As the two men moved into the trees, a fresh trail through the underbrush was clearly visible, culminating at the massive trunk. Random globs of tissue and blood glistened like hurled paint on the furrowed bark. The only sounds were their footsteps as they moved softly towards the trap.

Hector motioned to Luis that he would move further down the length of the trunk before climbing over. Luis nodded. He aimed his own gun at the top of the seven-foot high trunk, where it was clear the intruder had been hit. The blast had probably blown him off the top of the log. From the amount of blood and general gore on the tree, Luis doubted there was anyone alive on the other side.

That was the thing about Hector that occasionally frustrated Luis. His brother was always worried, always so cautious. In Luis' experience, once a man is blistered with a load of buckshot from ten feet away, he has no fight left in him at all. He rolls into a fetal position and dies, or screams in agony until he's finished with a double-tap to the head.

Waiting around and doing nothing while Hector made his way through the underbrush and tangled branches of the tree, then climbed over the trunk, and then finally told him it was okay to move forward? It seemed like a waste of time. Meanwhile, their laborers were scattering to parts unknown, and he and Hector might have to spend hours rounding them back up.

After a few minutes, he whispered into his headset. *"Dónde estás?"*

His brother's response was in English, something he always did when he was frustrated. "Fucking bushes and shit, I got hung up. I'm about ten yards out, I'll go over in a second. The fucking trunk is even higher here, I gotta find a way up."

"Fuck it, I'm gonna look," Luis said.

"No, I can't back you, wait."

"We gotta get back, those *pendejos* all took off, it's gonna take us forever to find them. I can climb over here real easy."

"Wait, I'll come back."

Luis smiled and shook his head. *Vieja.* Sometimes his brother was such an old woman. He slung his gun over one shoulder, put both hands on the top of the trunk, hauled himself up, and lay prone on the giant trunk. He listened for a moment, then crabbed his way to where the log curved down on the other side.

Keeping his body hidden, he sneaked a quick peek, and saw a human leg. Even with that brief glimpse, the damage to the leg was unmistakable. One end of the femur was clearly protruding through the flesh, and there was nothing from the knee down but a bloodied mess.

He whispered, "I see his leg. It's fuckin' trashed. This fucker's dead."

"Wait! I'm almost there."

"I'll take another look."

Luis slid further to the edge of the curve, and carefully poked his head far enough to where he could see the man's entire body. The body was on its back, sightless eyes staring straight into the canopy. From the waist down, he looked like he'd been through a meat grinder.

"I told you. This motherfucker's cooked."

"*Bueno*. Tap him twice to be sure."

Luis snorted. Like he needed to be told that. He pulled himself up to a standing position, levelled his AK-47, and looked down the sights at the man's head.

Faster than the eye could follow—certainly faster than Luis could react—the dead man's hand snapped forward. Luis dropped his gun, both hands clutching the hilt of a knife that had entered the hollow of his throat and severed his esophagus. Oxygen-foamed blood erupted from the wound, and Luis fell soundlessly, unable to cry out. He collapsed backwards on the log and tumbled to the ground as Hector's voice—no longer a whisper—called to him through his headset.

Chapter Forty-Five

Somewhere in Redwoods Park

Hector Chairez was standing over his brother, screaming with rage, when Tanner and Shepherd came to the clearing.

Tanner shielded himself behind a tree, took aim and shouted, "Federal officer! Put down the gun!"

Hector never hesitated. He pivoted, squeezed the trigger of his AK-47, and an uninterrupted swarm of rounds hammered into the thick trunk of the giant redwood that hid Tanner. With the gun firing on full auto, Hector walked towards his target, punching out a half-dozen rounds at a time, effectively pinning Tanner in place. A few more steps and the gunman would get an angle for a clear shot.

"Shepherd, shoot him!" Tanner screamed. He huddled at the base of the tree head tucked against the exploding shrapnel of shredded bark. "Shoot the fucker!"

For Shepherd, hunkered fifteen yards away behind the relatively thin trunk of a Douglas fir, it had all happened with surreal speed. The man hadn't paused. Showed no sign of fear. Just turned and unleashed a thundering hail of bullets at Tanner, then walked towards the big tree, chewing its trunk like a chain saw.

It was Emil Reyes again, a maniacal demon emerging from the fog, face twisted in rage, mouth wide open, howling like a wounded beast...

Shepherd heard her gun go off. Saw the shooter stagger, then drop to a knee. Watched frozen as the man brought the AK-47 around. Heard her own gun go off again, and again. Saw the man spin to his left, one arm dangling. Felt something pounding into the tree trunk. Then an anvil slammed into her forehead, and she fell back.

More shots. Different. Then silence.

Shepherd looked up at the tree canopy. No fog today. A clear view all the way to the top. Bright blue sky beyond, visible through the leaves. A rare day. No wind to speak of, even though the treetops seemed to be spinning a bit. Kind of cold, too. Her mouth suddenly felt so dry. Could definitely use some water.

Then the canopy was blocked. Tanner was over her.

"You're hit." He spoke in a whisper.

Shepherd felt her heart accelerate. Her pulse pounded deep inside her ears.

"I'm hit?"

Tanner didn't answer. He used his shirtsleeve to wipe the blood from Shepherd's face. A ragged slash ran from her right eyebrow up into the hairline.

"Where?" Shepherd felt a cold sweat break out, her guts cramp and spasm.

"Shhh. Keep your voice low." He wiped a sleeve across her forehead. "Not on your head, that's just a cut." Tanner looked Shepherd over, then reached over for her right hand. "Your hand."

"My hand's hit?"

"Looks like."

Shepherd had trouble focusing but was relieved she wasn't shot in the head. "That's good. Good it's not the head." Her eyes widened. "Is he dead?"

"Yes, he is."

"I shot at him."

"You got him, partner. You saved my ass." Tanner dropped their supply backpack to the ground. He brought out a roll of bandages, a handful of gauze packets, and some tape. He tore open a packet and placed an absorbent gauze square on Shepherd's forehead. He brought Shepherd's left hand up and placed it on the gauze.

"Hold that there. I'm gonna work on your hand."

Shepherd held the gauze. Tanner's face was in a fog and seemed to move around, making her feel quite dizzy. She blinked, tried to focus. "I killed him?"

Tanner stopped and looked in her eyes. "No. You hit him. I killed the fucker while he was shooting at you."

Shepherd closed her eyes. "I don't remember aiming."

"Well, you hit him." Tanner wound a roll of tape around the bandaged hand, securing it tightly.

"I'm not a very good shot."

"Good enough."

She had a quick jolt of panic. "Is it bad?"

"I think one of his shots must have hit your gun, blew it out of your hand," Tanner said, talking fast and low. "The gun hit your head and cut it pretty good. You might have a concussion too."

"But what about my hand?"

Tanner leaned in close to her ear. "Good news is, you're gonna live. Bad news is, we'll need to find your finger."

"My finger's gone?"

"We'll look for it. But first, I've got to clear the area. Maybe there's more of them."

"Oh. Yeah, you'd better." Suddenly she felt quite sleepy.

Tanner helped her sit up and brace her back against the tree. "Here," he said, handing her a canteen. "Stay here. Stay awake, and keep drinking, okay? I won't be long."

* * *

Eyes scanning, Tanner crept back into the clearing and hastily searched the man they'd shot. No ID. Same was true for another man Tanner found next to a large fallen tree, right where the shooter had been standing when it all started. This guy had a knife buried an inch above the top of his sternum, blood still bubbling out. On the ground near him was an AK-47.

Clearly a security team, most likely for a drug farm nearby. So, the immediate question was, who killed this dude? And more importantly, where was he now?

Well, technically this guy wasn't dead yet, but it wouldn't be long. His eyelids fluttered weakly, and air escaped along with the blood from the puncture to his esophagus. In any case, he wasn't going to be much help pointing out his killer.

"Bad day for bad guys," Tanner said to the dying man. "But don't worry. It'll be over soon."

The trunk of the fallen tree was a couple feet taller than Tanner. It appeared this guy had fallen from the top. Meaning whoever nailed him with the blade had been waiting on the other side. And might still be there.

Tanner decided Shepherd and her missing finger had to wait a little longer while he cleared the other side. He moved ten yards down the trunk and pushed his way into some of the tree's branches. He used them as a ladder to climb up, then bellied along the top of the trunk, back towards his starting point. Halfway up, he stopped. Gun leading, he risked a peek down.

Calhoun was in a semi-sitting position, painfully hauling himself backwards into the woods. Using what looked like a torn shirt, he'd lashed a branch to a shattered, mangled leg.

Tanner leveled the gun. "Hold it, Calhoun. Federal officer. Stop there."

Calhoun looked up, then put more effort into his slow-motion escape.

"One more butt scooch and I'm gonna blow your other leg off."

Calhoun stopped, his chest heaving, then collapsed flat on his back in pain and exhaustion.

"That was a pretty neat trick with the knife. Got any more?"

Calhoun rocked his head on the ground, side to side.

Tanner sat up on the log, gun still trained on the cowboy. "I'm afraid I fibbed to you before about who I am. I'm Nick Tanner, U.S. Fish and Wildlife Services Special Agent. And you are Mickey Calhoun, dirtbag bear poacher and probable murderer."

Calhoun stared skyward.

"Sir, I've got a logistics predicament I'm hoping you can help me with.

See, on the one hand, I've got a partner that needs medical attention right away. Lost her trigger finger, which I'm sure you can appreciate is kind of important in our line of work.

"On the other hand, I've got you, a wildlife trafficker who, as I say, is also a murder suspect. More than one murder, in fact.

"And then, on yet another hand, I've got two dead guys who are probably cartel security for a drug farm. Pretty sure that's what you stumbled onto, by the way. Guarded by shotgun booby traps."

Calhoun moaned, whether in pain, anger, frustration or all the above, there was no telling.

Tanner continued. "Actually, one of them might still be alive. Either way, I bring those boys in, the Sheriff will likely kiss me right on the lips for saving him the trouble.

"Which leads to my conundrum—I've only got two mules. Five people and/or bodies. Two mules. See my problem?

"It's incumbent upon me to prioritize. I have to decide who gets a ride out, and who has to wait until I can get some help out here, which I can pretty much guarantee won't happen 'til tomorrow. That's an awesome responsibility on my shoulders, Mister Calhoun, and I take it seriously. So let's think it through together, you and me.

"Certainly my wounded partner gets a ride, that's a given. That's one mule, which my mastery of arithmetic tells me leaves just one more.

"Now, since you clearly aren't walking anywhere, I guess you'd appreciate a ride on that second mule. You may be thinking I could set you on mule number two, and I ride double with my partner. I have to agree that's a viable plan."

Calhoun was silent, his chest still heaving from exertion and pain.

"Or…and here's where you can help with the decision…or, my partner and I can ride the two mules out of here, and leave you and those cartel guys as a feast for coyotes and turkey vultures, maybe even a particularly pissed-off bear. That would be easiest by far. Smacks of justice, too. Kind of ironic justice in your case, wouldn't you say?"

No answer.

220

"To be honest, I'm leaning pretty hard in that direction." He held up a finger. "Unless. And this is important, sir, so listen up. Nod if you can hear me."

A slight head movement from Calhoun.

"You tell me who sent you and Cody Wheeler out here to poach and butcher my bears. Who you're selling these bear parts to. Tell me that, you earn yourself a mule ride, and I'll ride double with my partner like I'm her best beau."

Tanner looked at his watch. "Now, I hate to pressure you, but I've got to go find my partner's finger, and then get her to a hospital. Time's a-wasting. So, I'll give you thirty seconds from—now—to decide if you're riding out." He looked at Calhoun. "You're going to prison, friend, or you're ending your life as critter shit. Your choice." He looked back at his watch. "And now, twenty seconds. Fifteen. Ten."

* * *

The finger was surprisingly easy to find. It rested on a bed of pine needles, a few feet from Shepherd's mutilated handgun. Aside from being disconnected, it seemed fairly intact. Tanner wrapped it in sterile gauze, popped a couple of instant ice packs, sandwiched the severed digit between, and taped the package tight.

After fetching the mules, he helped Shepherd onto Vanilla Bean, then climbed onto Chocolate Swirl.

"How you feel?" Tanner asked.

"Dizzy," Shepherd answered. "And it's weird. My finger hurts like hell, but it isn't there."

"You're doing great."

Together they worked the mules through the woods and around the fallen tree, then rode to where Calhoun still lay prone, eyes fixed on the sky.

"Is he alive?" Shepherd asked as they approached.

"I give it fifty-fifty," Tanner said.

Shepherd saw the blood, the mangled leg, the lack of color in Calhoun's face.

"You all right?" Tanner asked. "Not gonna barf, are you?"

"I'm okay. But he's got to be shocky. The ride out might kill him."

"It might."

They came up next to Calhoun, who showed no awareness of their presence. Tanner dismounted and kneeled next to the injured man.

"All right, cowboy, time to giddyap. A deal's a deal."

Chapter Forty-Six

Somewhere in Redwoods Park

Having discarded the saddles on both mules, Tanner and Shepherd rode Chocolate Swirl bareback and tandem for nearly three hours, retracing their way along Devil's Creek. Vanilla Bean trailed behind on a lead rope, her burden balanced and lashed in place.

At last, Tanner guided his mule into the clearing and onto the old logging road where Wild Bill had met them. Sitting behind him, Shepherd said, "I can probably get out here," and thumbed her radio to life.

"Ruby, come in. Ruby, you there?"

Static crackled, then Ruby's voice came through so loudly it buzzed the speaker. "Shep, where are you? I was just about to leave."

"Ruby, we've got an emergency. I need you to call in an air evac to Mad River Hospital. Two patients, immediate care needed."

"Shep, you okay?"

Shepherd blinked hard against another bout of dizziness. "I'm okay, but I'm one of the patients. We've also got a suspect." She looked behind, where Vanilla Bean stood with Calhoun stretched lengthwise along her back, his hands cuffed around her neck. Tanner had done his best to immobilize Calhoun's leg, but the pain had finally caused the big man to lapse into unconsciousness. "He's badly wounded by shotgun blasts and looks to be unconscious."

"Holy shit. Gimme your twenty."

"The old South End logging road, that big clearing near Devil's Creek. Wild Bill can tell you exactly. I need you to call him to come pick up his mules."

"Mules?"

"Right. Also Tanner's with me, he'll drive the vehicle back."

"Who?"

"I mean Capretta. Nick Capretta."

"What's he doing out there?"

"Ruby."

"What?"

"Just get on it, okay?"

"Okay, sorry, okay. Over."

"Thanks Ruby. Over."

Tanner kicked his leg up over Chocolate Swirl's neck and slid off. He turned to Shepherd.

"You need a hand getting down?"

"I'm good." Shepherd kept her throbbing hand overhead and dismounted, legs wobbling as she hit the ground.

"Go sit down," Tanner said. "I'll take a look at our passenger."

He walked Vanilla Bean to a small scrub oak and tied off her lead. Calhoun was motionless, his breathing shallow, fast and ragged. Skin cold and clammy. Pulse racing.

"He's in full-blown shock," Tanner said. "Don't know if he'll make it."

"There are some blankets in my truck."

Tanner thought about it a moment, then gave in. "All right." He went to the truck and extracted a couple of blankets. He threw one over Calhoun, then took the other to Shepherd, who had taken a seat on a stump.

"You're shivering," he said. He helped her wrap inside the blanket.

"I'm all right. A little dizzy still. The shivering comes and goes."

"We're gonna get you out of here. How's your head?"

"Hurts."

"It'll take some stitches. Think your hospital has a surgeon that can reattach your finger? We can fly you down to Frisco."

224

"I think they can do it here. Mad River's got a good trauma center."

"All right." Tanner squatted down and looked Shepherd in the eyes. "You did really well today, partner. I said it before, I'll say it again. You saved my ass. You know that, right?"

Shepherd didn't say anything.

Less than ten minutes passed before the unmistakable sound of helicopter blades broke the silence.

* * *

Three hours later Tanner was splayed sideways across his bed, sound asleep and spooning with Ray Charles, when the cell phone went off. Ray growled as Tanner reached over him to grab the phone.

"Yeah?"

"I checked with the hospital. Ranger Shepherd is in surgery." RAIC Moore actually sounded cheerful, which for some reason irritated Tanner.

"You called to tell me that?"

"That, and it looks like Calhoun might live."

"So I'm batting five hundred."

Moore laughed. "County Sheriff's sending a team in tomorrow morning to locate and remove the two DBs you left behind. I told him he could issue you a littering ticket, but he should let you slide on account of they're biodegradable."

Tanner sighed. "Keep your day job, Groucho."

"You're in a mood."

"It was a long day."

"What, you were asleep? You sound like it. It's only eight. Wake up, go out and celebrate, you done good. Once Calhoun comes to, we can drill him on the buyer."

"I already got that."

"Say again?"

"I got that. Before he passed out."

"Sounds like you need to file a report."

"Not tonight."

"How'd you get something from him? Anything I need to worry about?"

"He was nearly tits up. The woods had beat the shit out of him, he'd tripped two booby traps, his leg was hamburger. I told him I'd leave him as bear chow unless he helped me out with a name. He made the right choice."

There was silence for a moment, before Moore spoke. "Okay, that sounds surprisingly legal. What'd he tell you?"

"I gotta go to Hollywood."

"Hollywood."

"Yeah. But also not tonight. Tonight, now that you woke me up for no apparent reason, I'm taking your advice. Don't call again." He started to hang up, then said, "Unless you hear more about Shepherd."

* * *

"Yo, Nick!" Frank Mazzeo, at the bar filling his own pitcher, was the first to spot Tanner as he came through the door at the Tall Tree. He yelled down the bar, "Amy, this man don't pay for nothin' tonight!"

"Nick!" Simultaneous yells from the pool table, where several of the locals, including Beaver Tollson, raised their cues to the ceiling.

Frank carried the pitcher over to Tanner, sloshing a good portion on the floor as he threw a tree limb of an arm around Tanner's neck in a playful headlock. "You're a goddamn hero, pal, you know that?"

"What are you talking about?"

"No modesty, brother. I already heard." He waved a hand at the room. "And now they all heard too!" He laughed and clapped Tanner on the back.

Tanner weathered the blow and said, "Believe me, I'm no hero."

"Yeah, but Ranger Shepherd ain't here, so you're the next best thing. 'Sides, you helped, you got her outta there, the fuckin' guy who murdered Big Davey and poached all those fuckin' bears is caught, a couple fuckin' gangsters are dead, and you didn't get your ass shot in the process. That's hero shit, buddy, and you drink for free."

"How'd you hear all this already?"

226

"Chopper pilot's my cousin." His voice dropped, his tone suddenly somber. He brought Tanner in close. "C'mon, Nick. Help us drink a couple toasts to Ranger Shepherd, and to Big Davey's memory. We need to do this."

He hauled Tanner over to the booths near the pool table. Tanner noticed Little Stevie sitting in a darkened booth, a glass and a bottle on the table in front of him. They gave each other a nod. Amy Manning met them there with a fresh glass and another pitcher.

"Lemme pour this one up for you, Nick," she said. "You two done damn good. We can always use some good news around here."

Tanner took the beer stein Amy handed him and drained half of it faster than a frat boy at a house party.

"Thirsty, huh?" Beaver laughed. "You earned it, son."

Frank Mazzeo bent over the pool table to take a shot. He pushed the cue forward, missed the shot. "Goddammit!"

"Frank, you don't never make a shot. Why you're surprised every time fuckin' eludes me," Beaver said.

Frank straightened. "I gotta admit, I always figured writers were big pussies," Frank said. "But ol' Nick here, he come through, didn't he?"

"He did, and that's for sure," Beaver said. "You have yourself a few, Nick, and then you're gonna have to tell us the whole goddamn story. We kinda know the basics, but we want details, brother."

Tanner raised the glass to his lips and drained the rest in a continuous succession of hard swallows. He finished, wiped his lips, and said, "I'm gonna need a few of these first, boys. It was hairy out there, and I'm still kinda shook up."

He shot a quick look at the darkened booth. It was tough to see in the dark, but it looked like Little Stevie actually smiled.

Frank raised a foamy glass high. "I want us all to toast Big Davey... mountain man, burl sculptor extraordinary, big-time ass-kicker and great fuckin' friend!"

Shouts all around, glasses emptied and refilled, and Frank was ready with another toast, this time tearing up a little towards the end.

"And to Ranger Shepherd, who shot the shit out of some drug dealers and captured the rat bastard motherfucker who killed my best friend." Frank took a moment to compose himself, then rallied. "And to Nick, who turned out to be more than just some pussy-ass writer!"

Chapter Forty-Seven

Hollywood, California

E ver since he'd had to let nearly all the help go, Goldstein was forced to personally handle some of the more mundane and bothersome tasks around the house, not the least of which was getting out of bed to answer the intercom when someone was at the gate.

"Yes?"

"Open up Mister Goldstein. I have your order."

"Uh huh." The voice was not Calhoun's. "I don't know what you're talking about."

"Yeah, you do. I'm hauling a big cooler."

"And you would be?"

"It's Cody Wheeler. We met in Eureka. Let me in."

Goldstein felt his stomach drop. "Where's Mickey?"

"Long story, which I ain't gonna tell to this fucking squawk box."

Goldstein started to key in the gate code, then paused. "You're early. I hadn't planned to come up there for another couple weeks."

"Well, look at the great service you're getting. But hell, you don't want 'em, I'll go to Chinatown right now and find someone who does."

Now that he was fully awake, Goldstein was seriously pissed off. Something had definitely gone wrong. Where was Calhoun? Why was Wheeler making the delivery?

God damn it to hell. This should have been so simple. Kill a bunch of fucking bears, bring the parts back, get paid. It wasn't rocket science. And in that sense, Calhoun and his trailer trash sidekick had seemed the ideal operatives. Neither would qualify as brain donors, but Calhoun certainly had a skill set, and Wheeler had come off as someone who knew his shit.

"Today would be good," Wheeler said.

"Sorry, trying to remember the code. Gave Jackson the day off, he usually handles the gate."

Goldstein thought a moment. On the one hand, getting the order early was a good thing. Gave him even more time to lock in a direct deal overseas and cut Wu out of the picture.

On the other hand...God damn it, something felt hinky. The wrong guy showing up two weeks early, that just wasn't right. He searched for a way to stall, buy some time, see if he could reach Calhoun.

"You don't open this fuckin' gate I'm driving through it."

"Okay, okay." He punched in the four-digit gate code on his phone. Might as well deal with it.

It being a little before nine in the morning, Goldstein was still in his silk pajamas. He threw on a billowing scarlet robe, took a quick glance at the bedroom mirror as he walked past, ran a hand over his scalp, and reached the foyer as a car rolled up to the front door entrance.

He waited behind the door for Wheeler to push the doorbell, then waited another thirty seconds before pulling it open.

"Come in," he said, although Wheeler already had, rolling a large Igloo cooler behind him.

* * *

"Speaking for myself at least, a Bloody Mary is in order. Follow me."

Goldstein led Wheeler outside, to the pool where this had all started, the pool where his inept attempt at suicide had led to the revelation of TCM in all its dick-stiffening, liver-curing splendor. There was a time this path would have taken them past a bevy of nubile models and actresses, sunning themselves in a manner that would obviate tan lines. Now there were only two sunbathers, a pair of newly arrived Ukrainians on loan from Shakes Watson, his porn producer friend. Goldstein noticed that Wheeler didn't spare them a glance. Bad sign.

They came to a faux bamboo-and-thatch gazebo sheltering a bar that had once featured new craft brews on a daily basis; a selection of wines from France, Spain, and Napa; and a dizzying selection of liquors, liqueurs, and mixers. Nowadays, not so much.

Goldstein scooped ice into a couple of glasses, poured two fingers of Stoli into each, then looked at Wheeler. "I use V8 in mine, for the vitamins. You okay with that?"

Wheeler waved a hand and grabbed a glass before any mixer was poured. "Got any blow?"

Goldstein looked at him a moment, saw he was serious, and reached under the bar for a small ceramic container. He spooned a measured amount on the glassy surface of the lacquered hardwood bar. "Here." He tossed down a matchbook. Wheeler used it to guide the coke into a reasonable line and snorted it up like a Dyson.

"Achh, good," Wheeler said, pinching his nostrils.

Goldstein poured the V8 juice into his own glass. "So, where's Mickey?"

Wheeler chased the coke by draining the Stoli from his glass and wiggled a finger at Goldstein.

"He's a fucking psycho," Wheeler said. "He killed a guy. I wanted no fucking part of that, so I bailed."

Goldstein felt a belt cinch around his chest. He had to work to breathe. "You know this? You know for a fact he...did this?"

"Saw him do it."

"Oh my god." Goldstein drank his Bloody Mary in greedy gulps, then filled the glass again, this time eschewing the mixer. "What the fuck happened?"

"You could call it unforeseen complications."

"Like what?"

"Like you don't want to know. Complications."

"I see." Goldstein's heart was tap-dancing in double-time, but he kept his voice calm. "Where is he?"

"The dead guy?"

"No, Mickey."

"Told you, I fuckin' split. I don't know where he is, and I don't want to."

"I see. But you came down here with the order."

Wheeler indicated the cooler. "There's twenty galls in there."

"The deal was galls and paws."

"Yeah, well. Gonna have to be just the galls."

Goldstein said nothing. His hand shook as he picked up his glass and took a long drink.

"I don't know if my buyer will consider that a full order."

"Not my problem. You pay me, I'm gone. How you work out the deal about the paws is on you."

"Oh, sweet fucking Jesus." Goldstein slumped back onto a barstool. "Was there anything about this job you two did right?"

Wheeler's expression darkened. He jabbed a finger at Goldstein. "Fuck you. Sometimes shit goes sideways. Sometimes you gotta cut your losses." He downed the rest of his drink, set the glass down hard. "Speakin' of which. I'm gonna want the full twenty."

"You're only entitled to half. At best."

"Fuck that. Calhoun can't spend it when he's in the can, and that's where he's headed. So I get his share."

"Minus what I deduct for no paws," Goldstein snapped.

"No. I'm gonna need full payment."

Goldstein's faced flushed red. "Out of the question," he spat.

He never saw Wheeler do more than twitch, but suddenly there was a big, black hole staring him in the face. The hole was at the barrel end of perhaps the largest pistol Goldstein had ever seen.

"Whoa, whoa, come on, what are you doing?"

"Think of it as clarifying my position. This ain't a fuckin' negotiation. I need you to pay me. The deal was a thousand a bear, for twenty bears. Twenty grand."

Goldstein swallowed. "Look, please, I wish I could, but—"

He was interrupted by a concussive swat to the side of his head. "Ahhh!"

He held one hand to his head, the other outstretched like a crossing guard. "What the fuck?"

Wheeler brought the cannon closer. "I took the risks. I earned it. I need it now. And besides, think of it like an investment in your future. If I have the money to get in the wind, I don't get found, like, if they need someone to testify against Calhoun. If they don't find me, I don't make an immunity deal and name you as an accessory to murder. A murder I personally witnessed."

"All right, all right, stop with the threats." Jesus fucking Christ, had Mickey really killed someone? What an epic shitstorm this turned out to be.

Goldstein raised his hands, palms out. "Cody, if I had it, I'd give it to you. Haven't I paid up before?" He rubbed his face with both hands. "But this was a big order. I was going to pay you guys out of the proceeds when I delivered the goods to my buyer. I mean, look. Truth is, I've got a cash flow problem right now, no bullshit. I've got nothing out there, nothing shooting, nothing in development. My fucking agent just dumped me after thirty-five years, if you can believe it." He stopped, his breath coming in hard wheezes.

"Well, hell," Wheeler said. He grabbed the Stoli bottle, tipped it to his lips, and took several long swallows, without breaking eye contact or lowering the gun. He set the bottle down. "We got us a real problem then."

* * *

Doctor Wu stood in the small apartment's kitchen, cell phone to his ear, listening to the ring tone kick over to voicemail. Another call to Hong, unanswered.

Hong had been a more than reliable associate. He had earned Wu's trust many times over. Any failure to promptly communicate was simply not in his make-up. The truth was inescapable: something had gone very wrong.

Wu went back to the living room. A patient rested there in the dark, face down on a long cushion, festooned from head to toe with dozens of long, thin needles. Wu stood over his instrument table. Using forceps, he extracted a cotton ball from a jar filled with almost pure alcohol. He flicked a lighter, igniting the cotton. He set it into a small glass cup and as quickly removed it, then placed the cup on his patient's back.

On the third cup, his cell went off. He checked the display. Goldstein.

Chapter Forty-Eight

Koreatown, Los Angeles, California

Goldstein guided the big Mercedes down Western and glanced over at Wheeler. "I still feel this is a bad idea. Doctor Wu doesn't know you. Better if I go in alone, show him the goods, explain the paw issue—"

"No chance. I'm on you like a fuckin' deer tick 'til I get paid."

"Where am I gonna go? You stay in the car, I'll do the deal, ba-da-bing, we're done."

"I'm going in with you. In case there's a problem."

"Oh, there'll be a problem all right. The problem will be I brought *you* in, someone they don't know, that's gonna be the problem. Where's that goddamn street? Ah, there." He made a sharp right, the wheels crunching over broken asphalt and crushed glass as he turned off Western and rolled past Wu's apartment building.

"That's it," he said.

From the passenger seat, Wheeler surveyed the area. "What a shithole."

"Right? The guy's probably rolling in it, but this is where he lives. Or maybe it's just where he conducts business, I don't know. Shit, there's never any place to park."

Wheeler said, "We're not gonna be long. Double-park it and put on your fucking blinkers."

"This car? In this neighborhood?"

235

Wheeler's look stopped him.

"Fine." Goldstein backed down the street until he was in front of Wu's building, put his emergency flashers on, and switched off the engine.

Wheeler got out. "Pop the trunk." He went around to the back, impatiently helped the trunk hood open, and hefted the oversized ice chest. "Okay. Let's go."

"Hang on." Goldstein slid a small tube from his pocket, sprinkled a mound of coke on the back of his hand, and sniffed it up. "Ah, Christ," he said. He grabbed a tissue to dab his eyes and clean up under his nose, then got out of the car. He triggered his key fob to close the trunk and lock the car. Ran his hand over his scalp. "I still say this is a bad idea."

"We don't have to do this. Gimme the twenty grand, I'm done here."

Goldstein sighed. "This way."

Wheeler trailed a few steps back as Goldstein led them up the short stairway and rang the doorbell. A few moments passed, and Goldstein turned to say something but was interrupted when the door opened a crack.

"Oh, hello," he said, although no one's face was visible.

"Who's with you?" The voice from inside was road gravel.

"This is my associate. He and I are here to make a delivery to Doctor Wu. I phoned ahead."

"Wait." The door closed. Goldstein turned to Wheeler and shrugged.

Thirty seconds passed, and the door opened. The man who gestured them inside was an unusually tall Hispanic with a weightlifter's build. His head perched like a cherry on overdeveloped trapezius muscles. He wore a loose-fitting gray sweatshirt with the sleeves torn off. Not a square inch of unadorned skin showed on his arms; even the backs of his hands were tattooed. The ink sprouted from his collar line and crept up his neck, covering his gleaming, shaved head all the way down to his thick eyebrows.

"What's in the cooler?" he said.

"Product," Goldstein said. "Keeping it on ice, nice and fresh the way the good doctor likes it."

"Show me."

Goldstein felt the sweat pop on his forehead. "Out here? In front of God and everyone? Come on, my brother."

The man stood unmoving, his expression blank. Goldstein looked back at Wheeler.

"Okay," Wheeler said. He set the big cooler on the ground, opened it, dug through some crushed ice, pulled out a baggie. Inside, a bloody organ sloshed around as he shook the bag. He set it back into the cooler and closed the lid.

"There, you see?" Goldstein said. "We're all kosher. Now, maybe it would behoove all of us to take this business inside?"

* * *

"You are much earlier than expected." Doctor Wu sat on a floor cushion, legs crossed. A small, short-legged table sat between him and Goldstein, who had also folded himself into a sitting position. Two tea settings were on the table, with a small pot on a burner to one side.

Wu gestured to Wheeler, who stood directly behind Goldstein. "Please. Sit."

Wheeler hooked a thumb towards the tattooed bodyguard standing behind him. "He stands, I stand."

Wu looked at him a moment, then nodded once. "Very well." He swiveled his head to Goldstein. "Please, have some tea, Mister Goldstein."

"Listen doc, I know you have your way of doing things, and I respect that," Goldstein said. "And I apologize for being rude, but unfortunately, we're in a bit of a time crunch here. I was hoping we could skip the tea, cut to the chase, and get the deal done. Can we do that?"

Wu looked closely at Goldstein. "I believe your blood pressure is even more elevated than last time. Your face is flushed. Your pulse is rapid, I can see it in your carotid artery."

Goldstein put his hand to his neck. "Yeah, I gotta get healthy, start working out. Yoga or something. I appreciate the concern, but in the meantime…"

"It's just that you seem very nervous."

"No, not nervous. Excited, I guess. I mean, it's payday, right?" Goldstein spread his hands wide and laughed. "Who doesn't love payday?"

Wu smiled. "Of course." He wiped his lips with a napkin and looked towards the ice chest. "And in there, you have twenty gallbladders for me?"

"I do. All twenty."

"And the paws."

"They're coming. We had some space issues, they didn't fit in the cooler, it's the only cooler we had, etcetera, etcetera. Long boring story. Bottom line, they're home in my freezer, I'll round up another cooler and bring 'em to you next time around."

Wu took a few moments to answer. "I see." He looked at Wheeler. "And what do I call you, sir?"

"Oh, sorry about that," Goldstein said. "That's my associate, Mister—"

"Calhoun," Wheeler said. "Mickey Calhoun. You can just call me the Sandman."

"How colorful," Wu said. "Like a comic book."

Wheeler didn't answer.

"So, Mister Sandman," Wu said. "How about we see what's in the ice chest?"

"How about we see the money?" Wheeler said.

Wu smiled slightly. "I could simply have Mister Hernandez take it from you."

"He could try."

The room was silent. Finally, Wheeler put the ice chest on the floor, and opened it. "Okay, I'll show you mine if you show me yours." He reached in and came out with an organ-filled baggie. "Here's one."

Wu raised his hand, beckoning Wheeler forward. "If you don't mind."

When Wheeler was slow to respond, Hernandez snatched the baggie from Wheeler's hand and put it on the table in front of Wu.

Wu opened the baggie and put it under his nose. He sniffed deeply, held his breath, exhaled, and sniffed again. He nodded, resealed the baggie, and set it on the table. "Another, please, Mister Hernandez."

Wheeler reached into the cooler, but Hernandez grabbed his arm and held it. The big Mexican rummaged under the top layer of galls, pulled another out at random, let go of Wheeler's arm, and handed the baggie to Wu.

"What the fuck?" Wheeler said, rubbing his arm.

Wu said, "Do either of you gentlemen know why the bear gallbladder is so highly prized in Traditional Chinese Medicine?"

"Huh? For the liver, right?" Goldstein glanced around the room. He could feel his clothes sticking to his skin. "Anyone else warm in here?"

Wu opened the baggie. "A bear's gallbladder is unique and medicinally valuable due to its production of ursodeoxycholic acid, or UDCA," Wu said. "No other creature, mammalian or otherwise, produces UDCA to such an extent." He held the opened baggie to his nose and inhaled deeply. "Ah," he said, and carefully resealed the baggie. "It is therefore imperative that the gallbladders are, in fact, bear gallbladders. There are many ways to confirm this. I've found the most expeditious is to detect the odor exclusive to bear galls. The distinctive odor—and I think you'll find this interesting—is similar to opening a fresh jar of dark honey."

He paused. "These galls have no such odor."

Wheeler reached into the cooler. "No kidding? Well, here, why don't you test another?" He fished briefly around in the ice, came out with a Smith & Wesson .44 Magnum, and thumbed back the hammer. "Well, lookee what I found."

Chapter Forty-Nine

Koreatown, Los Angeles, California

Wheeler swung the gun around and pointed at the bodyguard. "How 'bout you move on over there next to the doc."

"What the fuck are you doing?" Goldstein asked, his eyes wide.

Hernandez didn't flinch but looked at Wu. Wu nodded slightly. The big man moved across the room and stood next to Wu, his eyes never leaving Wheeler's.

"So, Mister Calhoun. Your plan is to rob us?" Wu took a sip of tea.

"Oh, fuck me," Goldstein moaned.

"My plan is to get paid for everything I went through up there. You've got your bladders, I want my money."

"The agreement was for bear galls," Wu said. "These are not bear galls. If I had to guess, I'd say they're from pigs. That's often the case."

"What?" Goldstein's stomach dropped. "Hey, Doc, I didn't know. I barely know this asshole. His name isn't Calhoun, it's Wheeler. He told me they were bears, how the fuck would I know bears from pigs?"

"Shut up," Wheeler said.

The room went silent.

"Exactly what is your role in all this—Mister Wheeler, is it?" asked Wu.

"My role is I'm the guy who killed all the fuckin' bears," Wheeler spat. "All those galls and paws you got up 'til now, that was almost all me. I'm a fuckin' professional, but I got pulled into this thing by this clueless asshole and his buddy Calhoun, who it turns out can't hunt for shit."

"So where are the genuine gallbladders?"

"Calhoun has 'em I guess, I don't know. That psycho motherfucker killed someone up there, so I took the hell off."

"Killed someone?" Wu looked at Goldstein.

Goldstein's head gleamed with flop sweat. "I knew nothing about this, I'm as blown away by all this as you are, Doctor Wu."

"Look," Wheeler said. "I want my money." He waved the gun at the baggies on the table. "You know as well as I do you can sell those as bear. Half the galls in Chinatown right now are probably pig. The idiots who use this shit don't know the difference."

Wu nodded. "You're not incorrect. And if my business model was to sell to the unsophisticated in Chinatown, or Koreatown, or Little Saigon here in the U.S., I would agree. But my clients are overseas, and quite discerning. Sending them fraudulent product would be a very bad idea. And I'm certainly not going to pay you for something I can get from the local butcher."

If Goldstein had taken a moment to think, he probably wouldn't have done it. But sometimes instinct takes over—with a little help from fear and cocaine—and in the silence that followed Wu's speech, Goldstein saw a way out of his predicament. Even better, a way he could come out on top.

"You know Doctor, I think I will have some of that tea," he said, and reached for the pot. He grabbed the handle, turned slightly, and tossed the boiling contents behind him, directly into Wheeler's crotch.

What happened next was exactly what Goldstein would have scripted. As Wheeler took an involuntary step back, Hernandez cleared the small table like a panther and tackled Wheeler, his left hand tightly wrapped around the pistol's cylinder, freezing its action. Wheeler brought his knees up as they fell, trying to wedge some space so he could bring his hips around and escape, but the bigger man smothered that and rammed a stiffened ridge-hand strike into Wheeler's throat.

Choking, Wheeler jabbed his spread fingers at Hernandez' eyes, and felt one hit home. He used that moment to twist his head and bite hard into a tattooed forearm, hoping to free his gun hand. Hernandez hammered a flattened hand over Wheeler's ear, blowing out the eardrum. Wheeler released, and Hernandez hit him again, this time with a ham hock of a fist to the temple that effectively disconnected brain from body.

Hernandez pulled the pistol out of Wheeler's limp hand and stood. He looked at Doctor Wu.

"I have questions for him," Wu said. "Regarding Hong."

Hernandez nodded. He emptied the gun, tossed it aside, and left the room.

"Wow," Goldstein said. "That big son-of-a-bitch can really move."

"I also have questions for you," Wu said.

Hernandez came back into the room with zip ties. With workmanlike efficiency he bound Wheeler's hands and feet, then rolled him on his side and looped his hands to his feet, behind his back.

Goldstein unfolded himself and started to stand but stayed in place when he felt Hernandez' huge hand on his shoulder. He looked up, then at Wu.

"So, here's what I'm thinking," Goldstein said. "You folks will want to have a chat with Mister Wheeler, so I figure I'll get out of your way. You've got the pig bladders, if that's what they are, which again, I had no way of knowing. But it sounds like you can move 'em and recoup your investment, and I'll throw in the cooler, you can keep everything at no charge of course. Consider it all my gift, my way of making good on a business deal that didn't work out."

"Do you know where Mister Hong is?" Wu hadn't moved a muscle from his seat on the floor cushion.

"Your other sidekick, the guy that's usually here? I wondered where he was. Why, is he missing or something?"

Wu looked at Goldstein a long time without speaking. Finally, he said, "I want you to understand something. I'm going to allow you to walk out of here because I believe you were forced to come, and because you took action to stop this man. That, and your disappearance could bring attention to areas of business I'd rather keep private. However, you and I will never work together again. You will forget who I am, and where I live. None of this ever happened."

"Understood." With a cautious glance at Hernandez, Goldstein creaked to his feet.

"Be aware that I will have eyes on you," Wu said. "I'll know if you do something foolish. I won't be so generous a second time."

"Look, Doctor Wu, think about it. Who am I gonna tell? Anything I say's gonna come back and bite me as well, right? You go your way, I'll go mine, never the twain shall meet as far as I'm concerned."

He edged his way towards the door, his eye on Hernandez. A young woman magically appeared behind him and opened the door.

"Okay. G'bye." He wasted no time in getting to his car and, and as he gunned the Mercedes into a U-turn, he couldn't help but wonder: where the hell was he going to get more rhino horn powder now?

Chapter Fifty

Mad River Hospital

Arcata, California

"I brought you a couple beers." Tanner twisted the top off a bottle of Rolling Rock and handed it to Shepherd.

"Thanks," Shepherd said, rubbing her face. She was in a semi-reclined position on the hospital bed, her right hand suspended above her head, wrapped in what looked like a gauze boxing glove. "Isn't it late? How'd you get in?"

Tanner hooked a thumb towards Ruby, who hovered just behind him. "All her."

Shepherd nodded. "Yeah, everyone knows Gramma Ruby." She took a short swig of the beer. "Ahh. My mouth's been so dry."

"You been sleeping okay? 'Til now, anyway?" Tanner asked.

"On and off. Not the most comfortable position."

"They knock you out?"

"No. A local for the surgery, pain meds after. Thanks for coming, both of you."

"You had me scared to death, Shep," Ruby said, her eyes wet.

"Ah, sorry Ruby. I'm all right. You shouldn't have come so late, what time is it?"

"Never mind. Darlin', you look a mess."

244

"Well, I've felt better," Shepherd said, managing a smile.

"Nick says you did great."

"I don't know, I kind of blanked out. I think I just got lucky."

"Like hell," Tanner said. "I already told everybody over at the Tall Tree how you emptied your weapon at that asshole when he was walking me down."

"But I didn't stop him. He turned to shoot me, and you shot him. I remember hearing your gun."

Tanner paused before answering, glanced at Ruby, looked back at Shepherd. "That's right. You didn't kill him. You hit him, and I punched his ticket, and in our respective reports to our bosses, that'll be clear. But to the good folks of Orick, girlfriend, you're Annie-fucking-Oakley. Remember, I'm just a harmless writer."

"Very few people still buy that," Ruby said.

"Not sure anyone does," Shepherd smiled.

"Can't believe I ever did," Ruby added.

Tanner looked at both of them and shook his head. "Drink your beer," he said.

Ruby sat on the edge of Shepherd's bed, her hand resting on the blanket shaped over her leg. "Does it hurt?"

"Not yet." She took a swig. "With the pain meds, I'm probably not supposed to have this." She took another swig.

"So the surgery went well?" Ruby asked.

"The surgeon said real well. Said they'll be some rehab I gotta do, some months of it, but eventually I'll have eighty percent usage, maybe more. They reconnected bone, blood vessels, nerves…it's amazing what they can do. They gave me a local. I was awake for all of it."

"So you said."

"Made my mouth so dry."

"So you also said."

"Sorry. I think the meds are making me a little loopy."

"I'm really glad you're okay, Shep," Ruby said. She grabbed a tissue from a box next to the bed and blew her nose. "Excuse me a second."

She stood and hurried out of the room. Tanner watched her leave, then turned to Shepherd.

"She's gonna miss you when you're gone. So's everyone, for that matter."

Shepherd squirmed, trying to get comfortable with her arm hanging overhead. "Well, actually I've been thinking about that. I'm not so sure about the transfer anymore."

"Really."

"Yeah. I mean, I've put in a lot of time here, and it's an important area to protect. There's a lot of things going on, somebody new coming in, there'd be a long learning curve. All kinds of things could happen they wouldn't know how to deal with."

"True."

"And giving tours at the Statue of Liberty, I mean, I've been thinking that could get pretty boring after a while."

"Would for me."

"Right. And here…" She stopped.

Tanner leaned in and kissed her on the forehead. "For what it's worth to you, I think it'd be great if you stayed, Shep. I think you're perfect for this job."

Chapter Fifty-One

Hollywood, California

Goldstein had worked in this town long enough to know a break when he smelled one. And this, at long fucking last, smelled precisely like a break.

Like most breaks, it was out of the blue. A sudden turnabout, a month after the bear debacle ended. He'd spent most of that time in a spate of unrelenting ass-kissing, pitching *Motorcycle Murder* to the majors, then the first-tier indies. No bites there, so he'd dropped to the second and third tier, finally sinking to the direct-to-video hacks. Everywhere he went it was unapologetically, unequivocally, and even vehemently rejected. He had to face the truth. *Motorcycle Murder* was toast. It wasn't an easy call, telling the treatment writer he wasn't going to be able to pay her, but thankfully she was non-union and couldn't raise much of a stink.

The brutal run of rejection triggered another bout of depression, further fueled by booze, coke, and occasional unsatisfying blow jobs that burned up his remaining dregs of rhino horn. And while Goldstein had escaped physically unscathed from the incident at Doctor Wu's, there was no going back there. Doubly frustrating, because his brief foray as a vendor of exotic animal parts had been reasonably successful, up until the ill-advised partnership with Calhoun. He'd made a decent dollar selling all that Chinese shit into the Hollywood crowd, but now even that revenue stream—truthfully, more of a creek, but still—had dried up.

All of which tossed him into the same murky pit that had motivated his first suicide attempt. He was strongly considering a second try when he had his epiphany. It came as he lay nearly comatose on the bathroom floor, too drunk to roll away from the vomit that had missed the toilet. The Muse, barefoot and naked, whispered softly in his ear, stroked his cheek, calmed his soul. *Money Bear,* she said. You've lived it. Write it.

Money Bear. Of course! Practically wrote itself. An action-packed tale of evil poachers, insidious Asian traders in illegal animals and parts thereof, clueless cops, and the heroic documentary producer who single-handedly brings down the bad guys. With a requisite amount of fucking and violence, of course, so you get that R rating.

Three keyboard pounding, chemically fueled days and nights later he had the story treatment in hand. The act breaks were solid, the hero's arc pure money, the villain juicy enough to attract an A-lister. After clicking the Print icon, he'd gone to the kitchen, hunted out a bottle of cab and a wineglass, and repaired to the living room to enjoy the red and channel surf.

And then came the break, in the form of a vibrating cell phone. He didn't recognize the number and almost didn't pick up.

"Goldstein."

"Mister Goldstein, I'm so glad I was able to reach you? Your agent was unresponsive, so I took the liberty of contacting you directly?"

The voice on the phone came off like a real flamer, nearly every sentence ending on an upnote. "Who are you?"

"My name is Nick Christopher? I'm a—"

"How did you get this number?"

"Um, well, I'm resourceful?"

"And I'm hanging up."

"Please, wait. Wait. I represent a small consortium of investors, and we're all huge fans, sir. *The Mutiny Cruise,* well, I've seen it more times than I can count."

Goldstein paused. Probably bullshit, but what the hell. That flick made a lot of money, and probably should have at least been nominated for Best Picture, no matter what that bitch at *Variety* had said. "Go on."

"As I say, we're a group of investors, and while we've never invested in film before, we've done quite well in other arenas? Now we'd like to give film a try. Moreover, it's our understanding that you've been shopping a new project?"

Goldstein almost knee-jerked his way into what would have been certain rejection by bringing up *Motorcycle Murder*. Fortunately, he caught himself in time. "Y'know, between you and me I've got something much better than what I've had out on the market, something no one has seen yet."

"Oh?"

"Yeah, this one's maybe the best I've ever come up with, so I haven't shown it around quite yet. Been waiting for exactly the right fit."

"Well. That sounds very interesting, of course. What can you tell me about it?"

"I'm sorry, what was your name again?"

"Nick Christopher."

"And you're with…"

"Well, until we've talked further, I'm afraid I can't reveal the names within our group? But if it helps, this is Silicon Valley money we're talking about? And as I said, we're all huge fans."

"And this consortium of yours has never invested in films before?"

"No sir, this would be our initial foray? But we've done our homework, Mister Goldstein. We're prepared to invest a minimum of one-hundred and fifty million dollars in the production budget. That puts us in the league of summer blockbusters, and in fact matches the budgets for several of your biggest hits."

The guy's tone hardened when he started talking dollars. Maybe that's a good sign, Goldstein thought. He could feel a dose of adrenaline fire into his belly, his pulse quicken. "Yes, that's roughly the amount, although of course things have gone up. Including my fee," he added.

"That's understandable, and not to worry. We have a sizeable contingency fund as well. And of course we've also budgeted for promotion and advertising. So if I may be so bold, sir, I propose you and I meet? Say, Nobu at eight tomorrow night?"

249

Goldstein felt a stirring in his pants. Hell, who needs rhino horn when there's a deal spreading like a Vegas showgirl, all juicy and ready to rock? "Tomorrow night. Well, let's see." He waited fifteen seconds, then said, "Tell you what, Mr. Christopher. I'll cancel a couple things, and I'll give you an hour tomorrow night. But no promises, you understand."

"Of course."

"I have to know you're the right fit. This is a passion project of mine. I haven't discussed it with anyone."

"Understood."

"All right. See you tomorrow at eight."

* * *

"Wow," Nick Christopher said, leaning back in his chair. "That's an amazing story. I had no idea that kind of thing went on."

Behind him was a floor-to-ceiling window. From across the table, Goldstein had a great view of the restaurant floodlights dancing along the crests of the Malibu waves.

"Oh yeah," Goldstein said. He tipped another oyster to his lips and slurped it down. "Lot of research went into this." He was having a great time. Nick Christopher was as prim and proper as his voice, suited up like a lawyer yet clearly a neophyte when it came to Hollywood dealing. He was also a fussy little fudge-packer with a man-bun who, it seemed to Goldstein, might have a little crush going. Something to work with.

"Oh, I can tell. And Mister Goldstein—"

"Please. H.H. We're friends now."

Christ, the guy actually blushed. "H.H. I have to say, the *Money Bear* story, it's just so mind-boggling? And the reason these animal...I don't know, parts, organs, whatever, the reason they're so valuable is...I mean, do they truly have medicinal value?"

Goldstein's ears perked. "You asking do they work?"

"Well, yes."

Hmm. Interesting. Goldstein leaned forward. "Can you keep a secret?"

CHAPTER FIFTY-ONE

Christopher scooted his chair forward and bent close. "Of course."

"A while back I was having a little trouble, you know, getting it up for action, know what I mean?"

Christopher looked a bit flustered. "Oh, um, sure."

"So, I get clued in to this doctor down in Koreatown, and I score something called—fuck, I don't remember what they call it, but it's powdered rhino horn."

"Really? You mean, like from a real rhinoceros?"

"I shit you not. And let me tell you, it works." Goldstein sat back, took a healthy swig from his highball glass, and rattled the ice around.

"Would you like another?" Christopher asked.

"Only if you join me."

"Well then." Christopher half-stood out of his chair, signaled to the waiter like a Rose Parade queen, then pointed to each of the drinks.

"I like your style," Goldstein said. He stabbed a forkful of fried calamari, dipped it deeply into the sauce, and filled his mouth.

Christopher smiled, but looked a little pensive, like he wanted to say something but couldn't quite spit it out. They each ate in silence for a few minutes until the waiter arrived with the drinks. Goldstein watched as Christopher took a long, bracing swallow.

"You have something on your mind," Goldstein said.

"I do. You're quite perceptive. But I'm afraid it's entirely, I don't know, inappropriate?" Christopher set his drink down, then drummed his fingers on the table.

"You thinking twice about the deal?"

"Oh, no, not at all, that's not it," Christopher said quickly. "Rather...well, I'm sorry, but that rhino horn. You mean it? It really works?"

Goldstein smiled. This kept getting better. "Did for me."

"Huh." Christopher looked down at this drink. "I was wondering. Is that something you could, I don't know…"

Goldstein leaned forward and lowered his voice. "Nick. It's okay to ask. You want some?"

Christopher paused a long time before answering, then looked side to side and cleared his throat. "Um, I do. And to be clear, this has nothing to do with investing in your film, Mister…H.H. This is purely personal." He smiled shyly. "Frankly, a little embarrassing? Probably had too many of these," he said, and took another gulp from his glass.

Goldstein kept his own excitement hidden. He let silence build the moment, then began the process of reeling in his catch. "Tell you what, Nick. I've got a deal for you. I know where you can get as much rhino horn as you want. But I can't go there, I'm too recognizable, you understand." Christopher nodded reflexively, and Goldstein continued. "Here's the deal. When you go, you get some for yourself, and you pick some up for me too. Fair enough?" He stopped there. Waited. Like a guy holding pocket aces.

Christopher had both hands on his glass, spinning it in circles on the table, eyes down. I've got you, Goldstein thought. You're gonna do this. Think about it, rationalize it, and then…

Christopher looked up. "Fair enough, Mister Goldstein. You tell me where to go for this rhino horn, I'll get some for you as well. And as far as *Money Bear* goes," he stuck his hand out over the table. Goldstein reached across and shook it. "Here's to a prosperous deal for us all."

"My friend, you will not regret this," Goldstein said.

Christopher smiled and finished his drink. "H.H., I'm sure I won't."

Chapter Fifty-Two

Koreatown, Los Angeles, California

"We don't know that there'll be any resistance," Tanner said. "I imagine it depends on what he's got in the apartment, how much, who else is there, so forth. But there's always a chance, and right now we've got at least two murders connected in some way to this smuggling operation. Maybe more."

He turned away from the oversized wall monitor, which showed a split-screen Google Earth shot of Wu's Koreatown apartment, and a driver's license photo of Wu. Tanner faced the task force scattered around the cramped briefing room in Fish and Wildlife's L.A. headquarters. The majority of the group—eight in all—were LAPD. Four of those were SWAT, three were uniforms, one was a plainclothes on loan from Santa Monica, a Korean named Ki-Nam Kwon. RAIC Steve Moore was there to provide operational oversight on behalf of Fish and Wildlife, along with another Fish and Wildlife agent who would document the raid on video.

"Our target is the resident of apartment one-oh-six, ground level," Tanner continued. "Name is Li Wei Wu, goes by Doctor Wu, although no listing for him in the AMA. City records show the whole building is owned by a Chinese corporation, but my contact says that each time he visited the good doctor it was in one-oh-six, so that's what we're going with.

"The sequencing is this: Officer Kwon pushes his shopping cart up Romaine and starts rooting around in some trash cans." He looked at Kwon.

"Anything you find, you keep."

"Bonus," Kwon said.

"Kwon will let you all know if anything goes wrong with my entrance, in case I can't. When he's in position, I roll up. I've already made contact as a buyer, Wu's expecting me. I'm going in wired, and you'll all have ears. Once I'm inside, the squad cars seal off the street, SWAT moves into position.

"If I can make the bust myself, I will. No need to go crazy. If that happens, I give the all clear, Fish and Wildlife takes over and LAPD goes home with valuable parting gifts.

"If it goes south and I can't make the bust, I'll say, 'This can't be happening.' That's go-time for SWAT."

"How many doors?" one of the SWAT guys asked.

"It's an apartment, so only the one," Tanner answered. "Ground floor corner, so windows on three sides. Front side one, alley side two, back side one plus a small bathroom window.

Other questions."

One of the LAPD officers spoke up. "Any chance this guy Wu is involved with 18th Street or MS-13?" The two Hispanic gangs had pretty much divided Koreatown between them, and the support of either of those two gangs virtually guaranteed violence.

"We have no evidence of that," Tanner said.

"Those guys tend to turn up whenever there's money," the officer said. There were nods around the room.

"It's our best guess that this is a Chinese operation, with Wu being the go-to guy on the mainland for both incoming and outgoing trade," Tanner said. "The Chinese don't usually let others in."

A SWAT guy spoke up. "They may not have had a choice."

Tanner nodded. "Okay. Your turf, you know better than me. If I give the word, come in fast and hard. Like I said, I'm not expecting anything. These animal traffickers typically fold up and take their medicine. The penalties aren't stiff enough to warrant a shootout."

"If it's a gang thing, us being there is enough," said the SWAT guy.

"Understood. Of course, we'll try to do this without a shot being fired,"

Tanner said. He paused. "Unless of course we get lucky, and you get to shoot everybody."

A few laughs.

"Just be sure to miss the good-looking gay dude in the suit."

* * *

The man who opened the door was slightly smaller than the Chrysler building. Bulging arms, thick neck, shaved head, slathered in tattoos like boxcar graffiti. Reflective shades of a chain-gang boss.

Tanner looked up and smiled. "Wow, look at you. I'm here to see Doctor Wu. I'm Nick Christopher."

The man nodded and shut the door. Tanner stepped back a bit, tapped his foot, fixed his hair. An overhead security camera was in plain sight. He looked directly at it, gave a little wave. The door opened.

"If you're armed, tell me now and turn it over," the big man said with a hint of Spanish in his voice. "If you tell me no, and I decide to search you and find you're armed, I'll break your back."

"*No tengo un arma, hombre grande,*" Tanner lilted. "But of course you can search me if you must." He held his arms high and spun.

"Stop that," the man said, glancing around the neighborhood. "Get in." He moved aside as Tanner entered, and checked the street, left and right. Nothing but some trash-picker pushing a battered shopping cart. He shut the door.

Tanner was led into the dimly lit main room. "This is Doctor Wu," the big man said.

On the floor, legs crossed behind a low table, sat what looked like a UCLA pre-med student. He gestured for Tanner to sit.

"Doctor Wu. I'm so happy to meet you." Tanner sat, then extended his hand, which the young Asian ignored. Instead, Wu fixed his eyes on Tanner's. The stare was emotionless and unnerving. The silence was long and heavy.

"Do I have a booger or something?" Tanner asked.

That got the doctor to blink. "What?"

"You're staring like I have a booger hanging out of my nose or something."

"No. You don't."

"Well, that's a relief."

Wu lifted his tea to his lips. "So. You're here for *Xi Jiao*."

"Is that the rhino horn powder?"

"Yes."

"Then yes, that's correct."

"I don't recall how you found me," Wu said.

Sure you don't, Tanner thought. "Well, as I mentioned to you on the phone, I'm in the film business? There was a source in Hollywood for this kind of thing for a short time, which is how I found out about it. But suddenly he's not selling anymore, and he wouldn't let on where he got it from? So, I had to do a bit of detective work. In the end, it was a nice Chinese lady, I think a make-up artist, maybe wardrobe? Anyway, she pointed me your way."

"Interesting." Wu took a sip, then gestured to the steaming cup in front of Tanner. "Please."

"Is it herbal?"

Wu smiled. "Most definitely."

"Well then, bottoms up, I say," Tanner said, and sipped. He set it down quickly, waved his hand over his mouth. "Ooh, hot, hot!"

"You know her name?" Wu asked.

"Who?"

"This Chinese lady, from make-up or wardrobe. You know her name?"

Tanner squinted in thought. "With my memory? It's like a sieve, I'm sorry to say. Was it Patti? I think so. Patti something."

Wu nodded. A long, uncomfortable pause followed.

"Perhaps you wonder why I say your request for *Xi Jiao* is interesting," Wu said.

"Um, I don't know. Why?"

"Because I look at your eyes. Your skin tone. Your general build. And you know what I see?"

Tanner smiled coyly. "Doctor Wu, are you hitting on me?"

Didn't faze the little man. "I see a wealth of testosterone."

CHAPTER FIFTY-TWO

It took Tanner a beat or two to respond. "Really? Which means what, exactly?"

"It means I'm surprised you're here for something to help you achieve an erection. I wouldn't think that would be a problem for you."

Tanner laughed. "Well, you're sweet to say that. But unfortunately, there it is. Look, it's not something I'm proud of. I suppose it could be, I don't know, emotional? In my head, or something?"

"Perhaps." Wu paused. "Or maybe you don't have this problem at all."

Wu's eyes flicked to the side, and Tanner felt movement behind him. He started to rise, but a huge hand dropped on his shoulder and held him down.

"Now, wait a second," he said. "What's this all about?"

"I'm going to ask you to remove your shirt, please."

"I beg your pardon?"

"Remove your shirt. Or I can ask my associate to remove it for you, but he tends to be a bit heavy-handed."

Tanner held up a hand. "Oh, for Chrissakes. You think what, I'm concealing some kind of recording device? I feel like I should be insulted." He looked at Wu, then back at Hernandez. Neither said a word. "Okay, okay. You want a little strip show, a strip show you shall have." He turned and looked up at Hernandez. "Please?" Hernandez removed his hand, and Tanner slipped out of his suit jacket. He laid it carefully on the table. He loosened his tie, pulled the loop over his head.

Then he picked up the coat and tie, turned to Hernandez and said, "Can you hold these for me please?" Reflexively the big man took the garments, at which point Tanner upended the table and rolled to the side, hooked his left leg behind the big man's knee and swept him forward to the ground.

"This can't be happening!" Tanner yelled, and a heartbeat later the door exploded.

"Freeze, freeze, freeze!" SWAT officers exploded through the front door two by two, laser sights cutting through the dimness in the room. A woman screamed from the kitchen. Hernandez scrambled off the floor, and Tanner lunged at him. "Stay down!" He grabbed at a leg, but the big man kicked loose, grazing Tanner's head with what felt like a jackhammer, and launched at one of the SWAT members.

"Shit!" Tanner rolled again, covering up as a volley of bullets slammed into Hernandez. At the same time, he spotted Wu crawling for the hallway and tried to yell over the blasts. "That's Wu! I need him alive!"

He scrambled to his feet, hurdled the table, and went after Wu, along with two SWAT officers. Wu ran for the hallway bathroom, and the three pulled him to the floor before he could even slide the tiny, frosted window open.

Chapter Fifty-Three

Century City, California

I t was deal-signing day for Goldstein.

Nick Christopher had invited him to visit the home office of his investor group, a pricey address near the top of one of the Century Plaza towers, on the aptly named Avenue of the Stars.

The elevator doors unveiled the 26th floor like curtains on opening night, revealing deeply tinted glass walls surrounding sleek furnishings of chrome and leather. The ambient lighting was soft and seemed to emanate, rather than glow. It may have been ten in the morning, but inside it was the pre-sunset "magic hour," with pools of added illumination from fashionable desktop and floor lamps. As his heels clicked on the white stone floor that led to the gleaming reception desk, Goldstein took it all in.

The sights: To the west, the Pacific Ocean sparkled with surreal clarity. North, an endless army of automobiles trudged sullenly up the Sepulveda Pass, captives on the commuters' daily Trail of Tears. To the east, Beverly Hills, Hollywood, and the compressed, jagged skyscape of downtown L.A.

The sounds: a busy kind of quiet, softly clacking keyboards, the hum of voices on headsets. Phones that chirped. Soft flamenco guitar from overhead speakers.

The smell: money. Lots and lots of money.

Goldstein congratulated himself for his wardrobe choice. Conservative, charcoal, nothing loud, nothing that screamed Hollywood. Givenchy suit, wool and mohair, no tie of course. At a couple grand, not opulent, but not from hunger. Serious, not showy. Sent the message, *I'll be careful with your money*.

The receptionist looked carved from onyx. Hair drawn back hard, cheekbones prominent, eyelashes impeccable. She allowed Goldstein to walk all the way to her desk before she looked up, enormous brown eyes free of expression. Girl's had some high-quality work, Goldstein thought.

"Good morning." More purr than voice.

"And good morning to you. H.H. Goldstein here to see Nick Christopher."

She nodded. "Please have a seat. Would you like water or a soft drink while you wait?"

He smiled. "I never drink water. You know what fish do in it?" Nothing. Those perfect lips didn't even twitch.

"I'll let Mister Christopher know you've arrived." She turned away from him, punched a few buttons on her keyboard.

Goldstein stood for a moment. Honey, that ass gets any tighter you could squeeze diamonds with it. He didn't say it, but he wanted to.

"Mister Christopher? Mister Goldstein is here. Thank you, sir." She looked up at him. "He'll be out in a moment. Please have a seat." This time she nodded towards a couple of couches in L-formation off to the side.

Times sure have changed, Goldstein thought. He plopped down on the couch and grabbed a Hollywood Reporter off a glass coffee table. Not so long ago that ice queen would have jumped up and waggled her tits for a chance to be in one of his films. The idea of him waiting in a fucking lobby? Unheard of. He'd have been met at his car and escorted directly to the meeting, past the star-struck receptionist and moon-eyed secretaries and guardians of the corner offices, ignoring them all, hail-fellow-well-met entrance into the conference room, handshakes around, seat at the head of the table.

Instead, here he was hunkered like Willy Loman on a cold call, rocking his butt cheeks on a sofa apparently stuffed with gravel, searching for a position that didn't irritate his hemorrhoids.

Ten minutes of that humiliation before Christopher showed up. Crisp white shirt, also no tie. Black suit, looked like a Tom Ford wool blend, so probably twice the price of Goldstein's.

Christopher walked to the couch with a dancer's bounce in his step, extending his hand. "Mister Goldstein, good to see you this morning."

Goldstein pushed himself up from the couch, took Christopher's hand. "You too. Nice suit, Nick."

"Thanks. Yours too." Almost sounded like he meant it.

"Let's walk back to the conference room." As they passed Miss Tight-Ass, Christopher said, "JoLee, I'm with Mister Goldstein for the duration."

"Yes, sir," she said. Goldstein looked at her. Yeah, you heard right. The duration. Maybe a little more respect next time, eh? Once again, he didn't say it, but he wanted to.

* * *

"You put out a nice spread," Goldstein said as he sprinkled capers over the lox and cream cheese he'd loaded onto an onion bagel. "Nate n' Al's?"

"Lenny's," Christopher said. "Took over the old Junior's."

"Yeah, that was a damn shame, losing Junior's," Goldstein said, and took a bite. He closed his eyes as he chewed and moaned slightly. "Mmm. Heaven."

Christopher looked at his watch. "One of my associates is due any minute, but if you like, we can get our first piece of business out of the way right now."

Keeping his voice casual, Goldstein said, "Whatever works," and brushed some stray poppy seeds from his lap.

"I met with Doctor Wu."

Goldstein looked up. "Great. How'd it go?"

"Very well," Christopher said. He glanced at the conference door, confirmed it was closed, and leaned forward. "I purchased the rhino horn."

Goldstein smiled. "Well good, I'm glad that worked out for you. Have you tried it?"

So funny. This guy Christopher had the build of a ballplayer, but he blushed like a little girl. Total creampuff. Goldstein was looking forward to the easiest film budget negotiation of his life.

"Let's just say that I'm not displeased with the results," Christopher said, and giggled.

"See? Told you the stuff was magic. And for your favorite movie producer...?"

"Yes, I have yours here." Christopher shot a quick look at the door again, then reached into a man-purse at his feet and pulled out a sandwich baggie bulging with powder. He handed it across the table.

"Holy shit," Goldstein said. He could barely contain his joy but played it off with a joke. "Hell, I could get all of Leisure Village hard with this much. You're too kind. Thanks, Nick."

"You're most welcome. I actually purchased a fairly large quantity. I have a number of friends who were interested as well."

I'll bet, Goldstein thought. Tell a bunch of fairies you've got an organic powder that'll put their cocks on instant high alert? They'd go as giddy as homecoming cheerleaders.

Which got him thinking. The bear bile had been a hit, but he'd been marketing to an older crowd, and the whole issue of supply had proven highly problematic. But here was a different market altogether. Mostly younger, although there were plenty of mature mincers out there still playing the field. Most important, it was a demographic with tons of disposable income and a fierce preoccupation with dicks.

"Pardon me asking, but are you charging your friends for the powder?"

Christopher seemed taken aback by the question. "Oh, goodness no. They're friends, after all."

"Uh-huh." Goldstein thought a moment. Whatever he'd make on this film, Uncle Sam was going to tax. Likely call in the back taxes he still owed as well. On the other hand, with a little creativity, a lot of that income could be untraceable, untaxable cash.

"Let me ask you a straight-up question, Nick. Is your group prepared to fund production of *Money Bear*? I mean, that's what we're doing here, right?"

"Yes, that's what we're going to discuss."

"Outstanding. And with that in mind, I've got a proposition for you."

Chapter Fifty-Four

Century City, California

"Mister Goldstein, your movie is never going to get made."
Literally the first thing this asshole said when he walked into the conference room. Big guy, could lose a few pounds, hair cut close to the scalp, cheap blue suit.

Goldstein didn't know what to say. He and Nick had just come to a neat little arrangement in terms of substituting some of the producer fee payments on *Money Bear* with baggies of *Xi Jiao*. Baggies that would easily convert to a great deal of cash at gay bars and parties throughout Hollywood. Not to mention a few road trips to Frisco.

So now who was this frumpy, Kansas-looking douchebag? And what was he talking about?

Christopher cleared things up, the musical lilt suddenly gone from his voice. "H.H., allow me to introduce Mister Steve Moore, U.S. Fish and Wildlife Services Resident Agent in Charge."

"Huh?" Goldstein felt his stomach flip.

"And I'm Special Agent Nick Tanner."

"Huh?" Goldstein said again. It seemed to be all he could say.

Tanner continued. "Your world has changed, sir. And now we're going to discuss how you adjust to that change and minimize the amount of time you spend in a Federal prison."

"Wait. What? You guys are cops?"

"Federal agents, sir. Fish and Wildlife Services."

Goldstein swallowed. "Are you saying I'm under arrest?"

"It may come to that, yes," Moore said, as he sat down. "Hey, bagels." He reached for a sesame seed bagel, used a plastic knife to smear on some cream cheese.

"If it did," he paused, took a big bite of the bagel, chewed a moment, and continued. "We'd read you your rights, you'd get a lawyer who'd tell you to shut up and take your chances on a trial. At the trial, we'd play the recordings of your discussion here with Nick about tax evasion and trafficking in illegal animal parts. We'd connect you to a piece of white trash named Cody Wheeler, who was apprehended poaching bears on Federal parkland. More significantly, we will connect you to Mickey Calhoun, the prime suspect in what's turned into a Macy's parade of dead bodies.

"Mister Wheeler will testify that he witnessed your hired man Calhoun strangle an Arcata resident named Harley Thompson. In addition, Calhoun is the prime suspect in the murder of two others, all while under your orders to procure bear gallbladders. Working directly for you. That could make you an accessory to murder on three counts, sir."

Goldstein's mind whirred. Was it possible Doctor Wu had let Wheeler go? How could that be?

"It may interest you to know that we currently have Mister Calhoun in custody. He's been very talkative," Tanner added.

Goldstein's vision narrowed, his body convulsed in violent shivers, his bowels roiled. They had Calhoun, and it sounded like the so-called tough guy had caved. He abruptly stood. "I have to go to the men's room," he said.

* * *

Fifteen minutes later, Goldstein was ready to land on his feet.

He sat back at the conference table, poured himself a glass of water, and took a long couple of swallows. He set down the glass and folded his arms on the tabletop.

"Here's what I'm thinking," he said. "The guy you want for the murders is Calhoun." He looked at Tanner. "And since you already know about Doctor Wu, you probably like him for wildlife trafficking. So, in return for immunity from prosecution, I give you everything I know about both of them, and believe me, I know a lot. How's that sound?"

Tanner smiled. "I like your style, H.H. Ready to turn on everyone to save your own hide."

Moore spoke up. "Let's back up, because you're missing some relevant data. First, we already picked up Wu, and confiscated his rather extensive pharmacy. Your offer to give us anything more on Wu is an empty one."

Goldstein listened without expression. Tanner said, "In the process of apprehending Doctor Wu, a thug named Ramon Hernandez got his switch turned off. Ever run into him?"

Goldstein shook his head. His skin went suddenly clammy and smelled like a molding rag.

"Big guy, tattoos everywhere, even on his shaved head?" Tanner saw Goldstein's eyes flicker. "He's MS-13. You heard of them?"

"They're a gang or something, right?"

"Salvadoran. International these days. Hernandez' presence in Wu's place would lead one to believe that MS-13 has moved into his TCM trade. Which is bad news for you."

"Why?"

"Because," Tanner said, "if we put the word out that *you* led us to Wu, where a new MS-13 business enterprise got busted *and* one of their soldiers was killed? I don't think you'd be looking at a bright and rosy future."

There was a long silence before Goldstein asked, "Why would you do that? Why would you tell them?"

"We don't have to. Depends on whether you can help us."

Goldstein blew out a breath. Okay. It was going to be a negotiation. He could work with that. "I'll bite. Help how?"

"I've lost contact with Cody Wheeler. Has he been in touch with you?"

Goldstein didn't hesitate. "I took Wheeler to Wu's."

Tanner and Moore both sat back in their chairs. "Go on," Moore said.

"He came to my house, accosted me with a gun. He wanted to be paid in full, even though the job had gone completely into the shitter. I didn't have the money to pay him, so he said he'd get his money from Wu. He forced me to take him there."

"How much money are we talking about?" Moore asked.

"Twenty grand."

Tanner sat forward. "Go on."

Goldstein nodded vigorously. "There was no reasoning with him, it was like reasoning with a rabid dog. And let me be clear, I didn't know anything about murders. Still don't."

Tanner and Moore said nothing. Goldstein took that as his cue to continue.

"So, we go there, and Wheeler tries to pass pig gallbladders off as bears'. Wu sees right through it, won't pay, so Wheeler pulls a fucking gun on *him*. Wants his money, wants full payment anyway. Wants his share and his partner's share, all of it. Wu tells him no. I see things are about to get real, so I take matters into my own hands and disarm Wheeler."

Moore's eyebrows hitched. "You disarmed him?"

"I did. I mean, I started the process, then the big Mexican finished it."

"Salvadoran."

"Huh?"

"The big guy," Tanner said. "Salvadoran."

"Whatever," Goldstein said.

"And then what happened?"

"I left."

"Just like that. You bring someone in who tries to con them, then pulls a gun, and they let you walk out of there?"

"Yes. On account of I helped disarm him. Doctor Wu is an intelligent man, he could see I was there under duress."

"Is that the last time you saw Wheeler?"

"Yes. I left, he was still there at Doctor Wu's."

"When they let you go," Moore asked, "they say anything, any kind of warning or threat?"

"Wu blackballed me. Said I wasn't to see him, speak of him, have anything to do with him."

"Yet you sent me there, no hesitation," Tanner said.

Goldstein shrugged. "I thought you were just some queer who couldn't get it up. It was worth a shot."

"But you knew they'd be suspicious."

"Okay, but see, look at it from my point of view. I had nothing to lose."

Tanner and Moore exchanged looks.

Goldstein kept talking. "Besides, you had that cover story we came up with, about the make-up girl."

Tanner smiled. "Right. No way he'd ever see through that."

"Hey, give yourself credit," Goldstein said. "You're a good actor. Had me going, and I've seen 'em all."

Moore said, "Did Wu say anything else to you, anything that might have hinted at what they were planning for Wheeler?"

"No." Goldstein thought a moment. "Maybe. Said he had some questions for him about Wu's man. Not the Mexican, another guy. Asian."

"There's another man missing?" Moore asked.

Goldstein shrugged. "I don't know anything about that. Guy's name was Hong, I know that much."

"Okay," Tanner said. "Hong." He looked at Moore. "Likely one of the guys we found up north." He turned back to Goldstein. "Anything else said before you left?"

"Last thing Wu said was he'd have eyes on me." He waved his fingers in air-quotes as he said it.

Moore looked at Tanner, who said, "Sounds like you don't take that seriously, H.H."

"Frankly? It came off like pretty cliché melodrama to me. This isn't the CIA we're talking about, it's a twenty-something little Chink in a shitty ghetto apartment."

Tanner shrugged. "Yeah, maybe you're right."

Moore stood and pulled a set of handcuffs from the pocket of his cheap suit jacket. "And now, Mister Goldstein, I'm about to read you your rights and advise you to call your attorney, as I'm about to formally place you under arrest."

"Ah, shit. For what? I told you everything I know."

"And we appreciate that. We'll work with the D.A. and charge you for everything; the trafficking, the accessory to murder, probably tax evasion just for good measure. Then you and your lawyer can propose the immunity agreement based on your testimony against Wu, Calhoun, and Wheeler if we can find him. Maybe you'll walk out free and clear, I don't know. Stand up, put your hands behind your back."

Goldstein stood, his shoulders slumped, his wrists crossed behind his back. "I'll be out on bail before you go home for dinner," he said. He turned to Tanner. "And listen. We need to talk about *Money Bear*. I mean, this whole set-up: the location, that receptionist, that four-thousand-dollar suit? Take it from a pro, pure magic."

Moore slapped the handcuffs into place, but it didn't slow down Goldstein's pitch. "I could bring you on as a technical advisor, hell, good-looking guy like you, maybe you could even read for a speaking role. Might have to lose the ponytail, though. At any rate, it wouldn't hurt to start thinking about where we could dig up funding."

Tanner looked at Moore. "I'm gonna be a star."

Chapter Fifty-Five

Somewhere near Albuquerque, New Mexico

Nearly three months later, and more than eleven hours after leaving Los Angeles, Tanner eyed the upcoming exit off eastbound I-40.

"I'm bushed," he said out loud. There was no response, so he took a quick glance in the rear-view mirror. Both his passengers were sound asleep in the back seat.

"Good timing," Tanner said, and pulled off the highway. He followed the nav system to an RV park just outside the Dancing Eagle Casino. To call it nondescript would have been magniloquence. It was a flat, gravel parking lot, with a squat management building and an 8-foot wooden fence the only landscaping features.

But it was a place to get some rest. Tanner checked in with the manager, a short, wispy-haired woman with chuckwalla skin and a cigarette welded to her lower lip. He steered the trailer into a spot along the eastern edge, facing away from the blowtorch that sat low in the western sky.

"All right, Raymundo, wake up. You're the first order of business," Tanner said.

Ray's head lifted. He yawned prodigiously, then untangled himself from his riding partner, who slept on, undisturbed.

Tanner left the engine running and the A/C on, knowing he'd be back in a few minutes. He clipped the leash on Ray Charles and the two headed out. It was like walking on a frying pan. Tanner guided the big cat outside the park's fence, and onto some equally featureless desert scrubland. At 5,000 feet elevation, the air was dry and thin, seemingly without substance or weight, little for the lungs to grab onto.

That critical chore done and policed, the two fell into the routine of turning the trailer into a home. With the hook-ups completed and the kitchen slide-out in place, Tanner went back to the Expedition, turned off the engine, and said, "Wake up, kiddo. We're stopping here for the night."

He went back to the trailer, pulled a cold beer out of the fridge. He'd settled behind the kitchen table when his phone buzzed. He checked the screen and picked up.

"Hey, Shep, long time."

"Hi, Nick."

"Got that finger pulling triggers yet?"

Shepherd's laugh was good to hear. "I guess I could if I had to. But that never happens up here."

Tanner chuckled. "I'm glad you called, it's good to hear from you. Saw you on the news a couple times. Big bust, congratulations."

"Yeah, that farm was so big the DEA came in. Had a nice bonfire, they figured around two million dollars up in smoke. And the shit those guys had there, the insecticides, fungicides, trash, all right there dumping into Devil's Creek. I'm glad we shot 'em."

"Me too. Y'know, you looked good on TV. Had that alpha female thing going strong. Kinda hot."

"Ha! Listen, I called because I read all the news on the others, but how'd it end up with Wheeler. Did you find him?"

"Actually, he showed up last week. Dumped off Las Tunas Canyon above Malibu. Had his hands and his feet removed. Ligatures on the forearms and shins, looked like tourniquets had been used to stem the blood flow."

"Ugh. To keep him alive?"

"That's the guess."

"Holy shit."

"Hey, no tears here." Tanner sat back. Through the window, he could see the Sandia Mountains on the horizon, surging abruptly from the tabletop desert plain.

"Well, I also called to see how *you're* doing," Shepherd said.

"Me? I'm both fine and dandy," Tanner said.

"You work it out with your daughter?"

At that moment Kiera came in through the trailer door, bed hair sticking up, eyes still puffy from sleep. She went to the refrigerator and pulled out a bottle of water.

"Yeah," Tanner said, "bang me over the head with a two-by-four and I usually see the light."

"You're going to let her move on with that program?"

Tanner sighed and smiled at Kiera. "As a matter of fact, she's with me right now. We're headed towards a meet in Amarillo. Stopping for the night near Albuquerque."

"Well, listen to you," Shepherd said.

"Hey, it's her passion. If we don't follow our passion, what the hell do we follow?"

Shepherd laughed. "You're a lot smarter than you look, Nick."

"That's not a high bar. Hey, I miss all you nut-jobs. How is everyone?"

"Oh, we're slammed lately. Another Bigfoot craze."

"A sighting?"

"Yeah, two weeks ago this guy from Trinidad got a pretty clear hit on one of his cameras."

It was Tanner's turn to laugh. "From Trinidad? Guy calls himself Toad?"

"Joel Friedland is the guy's name."

"That's him! He was my neighbor up there, he's the one that had Calhoun on camera."

"Oh, yeah? He's become quite the celebrity. Got one of the clearest shots I've ever seen, I'm about ready to become a believer myself. The place is swarming with press, Bigfoot fans, myth busters, we got 'em all. Every campsite in or near the Park is booked. Amy's in heaven, the Tall Tree is packed. This keeps up, we may have to hire another seasonal ranger or two."

"Hey, that's great." He smiled. "And you're still there."

* * *

Shepherd swiveled her chair so she could look out the window. Across the parking lot, she could see the flow of cars along the 101 Highway, and beyond that, acres and acres of the tallest trees on the planet.

She smiled. "Yep. Still here."

Chapter Fifty-Six

Orick, California

TEN DAYS EARLIER...

A hard rain pounded the corrugated metal roof of the Tall Tree Tavern in Orick. Inside, Frank Mazzeo knocked back a final shot of Jack, turned the shot glass over on the bar, and wiped his mouth. He checked the clock over the bar glass. Three A.M.

Amy threw the deadbolt on the front door, came back to the bar and leaned on her elbows. She looked pointedly at the upended shot glass. "I just wiped that. Now it's gonna have a ring."

Frank sighed, lifted the shot glass and wiped its circular footprint away with his sleeve. She took the glass from him and set it in the sink.

"That was too close, Frank."

"I know. Guy moved the camera, wasn't where it used to be."

"Way too clear."

"Yeah."

Amy moved to the register, rang up a No Sale and fished in the open drawer. She grabbed some bills, knocked her hip against the drawer to slide it closed, and went back to Frank.

"It worked out," she said. "So, no worries. You got the walk right, posture's good. Next time be more careful, that's all. Here." She handed him the sheaf of bills. "I appreciate you waiting the week for this. Here's two-fifty."

Frank shook his wooly head. "Too much, Amy."

"What I always paid Davey."

"He was better at it than me."

"He did it for years. Next time you know better."

Frank nodded and pocketed the bills. He stood, worked his massive arms into his jacket, and pulled on a stocking cap. "When you want the next one?"

"We gotta give it a bit. I'll let you know. You ain't told nobody, right?"

Frank shook his head.

"This kind of thing, only way it works is if you and I are the only ones. And the Mayor, of course."

"Beaver knows?"

"Sure. It was his idea in the first place, years ago, him and Louise. Figured it was the best way to bring some money to this town, everything else going to shit. They recruited Big Davey, swore him to secrecy. Louise, may she rest in peace, she made the suit, mostly from horse manes and tails."

"Damn. I never knew." Frank stretched his arms overhead and yawned. "I'm gonna head out, Amy."

"Thanks again, Frank. And listen. Davey'd be glad it was you."

Frank went to the door, turned the deadbolt, threw her a backhanded wave, and left.

Amy relocked the door and went back to the register. Punched in the code to run the day's total and printed it out. She slipped on a pair of reader glasses and took a look.

Very good day.

Time to hit the hay. She was due to open again in four hours, and the morning regulars would be waiting.

A Note from the Author

Thanks for joining Nick Tanner on this, one of many battles he'll fight in the war against wildlife traffickers.

By all estimates, international wildlife trafficking trails only drugs and arms in terms of illegal revenue generation and has escalated exponentially over the past decade. The perpetrators range from highly sophisticated underworld networks to family businesses to dirt-poor lone operators.

While some types of illegal wildlife trade are fairly well known to the American public—rhino horn and elephant tusk smuggling being perhaps the prime examples—countless other "lower profile" animals and/or parts thereof are exploited for trophies, medicinal use, clothing, collections, food, ornaments, and even (especially here in the U.S.) as exotic pets.

It's gotten to the point where U.S. National and State Parks have become, according to the USFWS, "...the last supermarkets for traffickers of illegal wildlife." That's no hyperbole; a budget request from the National Park Service a decade ago reported poaching had spurred the decline of "at least 29 wildlife species."

And that's only in the United States.

At the same time, Latin America's wildlife population has plummeted by 83% since the 1970s. In Africa, ten million elephants used to roam the plains and forests. Now, less than half-a-million survive. Of the world's eight species of bears, six are now listed as endangered, with black market poaching being the biggest threat.

Standing as our nation's first line of defense—and offense—against international wildlife trafficking are a mere two hundred USFWS Special Agents. These are elite, highly trained men and women who are also uber-masters of wilderness skills and survival. Many times, they work alone, in remote and isolated locations. They typically work in plainclothes, nearly always undercover.

While Nick Tanner is a fictitious character, he embodies the courage, dedication, and relentless determination of the real-life agents who fight the cancerous growth of wildlife trafficking. They are outnumbered, out-gunned, out-funded, under-manned and over-extended. They wake up to a Sisyphean battle every day, but they never give up.

In doing his part Tanner relies not only on his own abilities, but frequently consults and involves local residents in the fight. This is only fitting. As with any societal or environmental problem—and illegal wildlife trade is both—a true solution will come only with the concern and commitment of the citizenry.

Smokey the Bear famously said, "Only YOU can prevent forest fires." The exact same thing can be said of wildlife trafficking.

I hope you enjoy Nick Tanner's escapades as he wages war on this horrific underground industry. I also hope these stories raise awareness, spark outrage, and motivate your personal involvement.

We can't leave it all up to Nick.

Acknowledgements

I've been fortunate enough to pay the bills and raise a family as a writer, thanks in no small way to a pair of high school teachers, who, despite my utter insolence at the time, encouraged me to pursue a writing career. My eternal thanks to Kay Foster and Jim Vidakovich, both of whom went on to build hugely impressive entertainment careers of their own.

For the decades of friendship, encouragement, opportunities and advice, there is no way I can ever thank Jurgen Wolff enough.

Victoria Skurnick, my amazing agent at LGR Literary Agency, is a collaborative partner who pulls no punches in helping me get my work into fighting shape. I'm beyond fortunate to have her on my side.

My thanks to master writing coach Mark Malatesta. His guidance and expertise proved invaluable in launching this series. Find him at www.thebestsellingauthor.com.

Thanks to the Rough Writers of Cambria, who, along with beta reader extraordinaire (and a fine author herself) Mackenzie Kiera, offered valuable insights throughout the process.

I'd be remiss if I didn't give a few extra treats to my little blind tabby Stevie, the inspiration for Nick Tanner's unusual companion.

Finally, I'm grateful to all the writers who have defined the crime fiction genre, filled my bookshelves and Kindle, and inspired my efforts. Thanks, in no particular order, to James Lee Burke, Ross McDonald, John Sandford, Harlan Coben, James Scott Bell, Don Winslow, Barry Eisler, Jim Thompson, Lee Child, Stephen Hunter...okay, I can hear the band playing me off... Laura Lippman, Craig Johnson, Elmore Leonard, Carl Hiaasen...thanks to all of you, and many, many more.

About the Author

Kerry K. Cox was born in Hollywood, California. After four years at Oregon State University, he declared himself graduated and returned to Southern California, where he taught swimming, karate, and pre-school to finance a sputtering launch to what eventually became a lifelong writing career. Nowadays, when Kerry isn't writing, he volunteers with various wildlife, marine mammal, and feral cat/kitten rescue groups on California's Central Coast.

He lives by the ocean in Cambria, California, with his wife and too many critters.

CPSIA information can be obtained
at www.ICGtesting.com
Printed in the USA
BVHW081526230221
600663BV00001B/21